To my mother, Ann Mackenzie

PALE
HORSES

Also by Jassy Mackenzie

Random Violence
Stolen Lives
The Fallen

PALE HORSES

JASSY MACKENZIE

First published in the United Stated in 2013 by
Soho Press, Inc.
853 Broadway
New York, NY 10003

Library of Congress Cataloging-in-Publication Data

Mackenzie, Jassy.
Pale horses / Jassy Mackenzie.
p cm
HC ISBN 978-1-61695-221-1
PB ISBN 978-1-61695-364-5
eISBN 978-1-61695-224-2
1. De Jong, Jade (Fictitious character)—Fiction. 2. Women
private investigators—Fiction. 3. Murder—Investigation—
Fiction. 4. South Africa—Fiction. I. Title.
PR9369.4.M335P35 2013
823'.92—dc23 2012042205

Printed in the United States of America

10 9 8 7 6 5 4 3 2 1

PROLOGUE

Standing on the front step of his farmhouse, Koenraad Meintjies stared into the hazy distance, scanning the grey-brown vista of baked soil and sparse bushes that characterised this part of the Karoo Desert. Searching for any movement; listening for the slightest sound; looking for the reflection of light off glass or other telltale signs that somebody was already out there. Waiting for him, watching him.

From here, the dirt road that ran past his gate was barely visible. It snaked its way between the stunted thorn bushes and dry pans that lay to the east of his farm; a deeper channel of packed golden-brown dirt against the bleached landscape, defined only by its borders and the tyre tracks left by the occasional utility vehicles heading that way.

If Meintjies were to notice the faraway dust plume that signalled an approaching car, he would have ample time to get away. To climb into his battered Isuzu Bakkie and simply take off, sticking to the little-used farm tracks that only he knew well, where he could drive as fast as the Bakkie would travel, but where deeply eroded dongas and hard-to-see tyre-grabbing banks of sand would make speed impossible for the unwary traveller.

But flight was now an impossibility. As the events of the past week had shown him with dreadful, shocking clarity, he was as good as a prisoner here.

And after a childhood devoted to protecting his sisters, now, when it was most important, he had failed to keep them safe.

First Sonet, and now Zelda.

"In the end, all you have to show for yourself is failure," he muttered.

His words were swallowed up by the hissing of the wind that always picked up at this hour, as if the giant that had been stoking the furnace of the day was finally downing his tools and letting out a deep sigh.

The rusty windmill behind the house creaked into unwilling life, starting with a low groan and then escalating into higher-pitched cries as its blades moved faster. In the tuneless shrieks he fancied he heard his father's words; the grey-bearded man in full voice, towering over his breathless congregation as he approached the climax of one of the diatribes he called sermons.

"Mislukking!" the predikant would scream, slamming his fist against the pulpit to emphasise his words. "Failure! If you do not repent now, and prepare yourself for the Second Coming, everything you attempt will crumble into failure."

Even though his father had drawn most of his inspiration from the vivid imagery of the Book of Revelations, his god had been a true Old Testament figure. Vengeful and authoritarian. One who demanded the full payment of an eye for an eye.

Meintjies had turned his back on his father and everything he represented many years ago, and without guilt or regret. In any case, he knew repentance would not help him now.

The wind was swirling the stench of decay from the outbuildings at the back of the house. Fetid plants. Rotting livestock. He had no choice but to breathe it in, grimacing as he did so, unable to suppress a stab of fear.

In front of him was only emptiness, something he had learned long ago to live with.

Behind him was something far worse. Death and destruction. The final legacy of what he had started doing as a favour for his sister, but which had finished with him trapped inside this nightmare. How much time did he have left?

Was she even still alive?

Abruptly, Meintjies turned away from the darkening sky and strode back inside the old sandstone farmhouse. At the door, he stopped, bent down, and grasped the weathered wooden butt of the Purdey shotgun he'd propped against the wall.

The only thing he could be sure of was that they would be here before morning. Because what they had ordered him to do here, had now been done.

I

Magdalena Eckhardt loved nothing better than people watching. In fact, she prided herself on being an astute observer. Her book club friends had often commented that she could read them as well as if they were one of the Lisa Gardner novels that circulated within the group. Certainly, she had a keen eye for body language and a memory for detail. She was also blessed with a fertile imagination that allowed her to fill in the gaps, to her own satisfaction at least, where observation alone failed to give the full story.

Now, she was comfortably ensconced in the embrace of one of the sought-after armchairs at Chez Chic, the Sandton coffee shop with a legendary position on the corner of Nelson Mandela Square, just a few metres away from the massive bronze statue of Madiba himself. Sipping on her soy decaf latte, Magdalena was happily appraising her fellow patrons while she waited for her two-thirty appointment with the Botox specialist in the nearby Medical Mews.

One couple in particular had caught her attention today, if only for the fact that she couldn't quite work them out. They were definitely not stereotypical Sandton shoppers.

"Stereotypical!" she remembered one of the younger members of her book club exclaiming at their last get-together. *"That's such a cool word! Such a Magdalena word, don't you agree? Stereotypical . . . I love it!"*

The woman had arrived first, sat down and ordered water. But no matter how far Magdalena leaned sideways, she couldn't quite see her face. One thing was clear—although slim and young-looking, she was hopelessly underdressed for this smart establishment. Black jeans, tight-fitting black T-shirt, unstylish black running shoes and—horror of horrors—no handbag in evidence at all. She was also notable for her complete absence of accessories. No earrings, chains or rings were in sight and her brown hair was tied back in a simple ponytail.

The faintest of frowns creased Magdalena's artificially smooth skin.

She must be a Goth, she decided. Or those modern kids, what were they—the emos. Surely they were teenagers, though, which made it unlikely as this woman must be in her late twenties at least. If only she could see her face better. Was she wearing any makeup? Black eyeliner would offer a hint. Black lipstick would provide conclusive proof.

And then a man arrived. Out of breath and apologising for his lateness, he'd swung into the seat opposite her. Magdalena was almost sure, and if the irritating waiter hadn't chosen that minute to ask her if she wanted another latte, she would have been completely sure, that the man had started the conversation by introducing himself.

He, too, was rather casually dressed for this establishment. He wore a golf shirt—a good brand, mind—but he'd paired it with shorts. Shorts, in Sandton City! An abomination! Worse, his long, lean legs were unbecomingly pale. He had on expensive-looking leather moccasins, and a watch that looked like a premium brand, although it was so easy to be fooled by a good replica these days so perhaps it wasn't the genuine article.

Even so, there was definitely no shortage of money there. A lack of taste, decidedly, but not money. The man looked extremely agitated. He was fidgeting non-stop; his fingers either tugging at the tablecloth or raking through his unruly hair— *This is Sandton, you know. Would it have hurt you to put in a little gel?*—and from time to time darting down to the right hand pocket of his shorts and patting it as if to reassure himself his wallet and phone were still there.

Magdalena drained her latte, slid her gold card into the leather folder the waiter had brought, and continued to watch them closely.

Why were they here, she wondered. It couldn't be a business meeting. And they weren't old friends, not if introductions had been made.

And then it hit her.

Of course. This was a first date.

Why hadn't she realised this earlier? It explained everything. The man's nervousness; the fact that the woman, despite the quietly assured way she carried herself, wasn't dressed like a Sandton City regular. She obviously didn't live in the area, and must have made a special trip into Sandton for this very important reason.

She stared, rapt. How romantic! She, Magdalena Eckhardt, could quite possibly be watching the start of a relationship that would last. The spark that might grow into a bright and searing flame. That phrase sounded rather good, she thought. She'd have to memorise it and see if there would be an opportunity to use it at a future book club meeting.

The waiter returned the folder and she slipped her gold card back into her Ralph Lauren wallet.

She was going to speak to the couple as she walked past their table, she decided, and tell them why she thought they were here. She'd done this from time to time before, and could still remember the triumph that had washed warmly over her as the astounded faces of the patrons proved her correct.

"How did you know?" one woman, whom Magdalena had pegged as an Avon saleslady, had gasped.

"Intuition and observation," she'd replied, shrugging airily, as if anyone could do the same; as if what she had was not a special gift.

She climbed to her feet, balancing carefully on her Manolo Blahniks, which were gorgeously beautiful but with heels a fraction too high to allow for perfect comfort, temporarily denting the café's luxurious but utterly impractical Persian carpet. Then she scooped up her Prada bag and brushed a piece of fluff off her aquamarine linen jacket.

And then, perhaps alerted by her movement, the woman in the dark clothing looked round and for just one moment Magdalena met her gaze.

She felt the breath huff out of her open mouth and took an involuntary step back, balancing herself against the table with a perfectly manicured hand.

Her features were just as Magdalena had imagined them—attractive and strong and without a trace of makeup. But instead of the happy excitement she'd expected to see there, what hit her powerfully was the incredible tiredness in the woman's face—a hollow, exhausted look as if she were sick of life itself—and the cold, dead hardness in her narrowed green eyes.

Blinking rapidly, Magdalena looked away, flustered, the blood rushing to her face. The woman looked away, too, as if with that sideways glance she had allowed her mask to slip.

Abandoning her plans to approach the couple, Magdalena gathered herself together and hurried out of the café.

2

With an effort, Jade de Jong dragged her attention back to the man sitting opposite her. Theron, his name was. Victor Theron. A tall beanpole of a man in his late thirties, crackling with nervous energy. He could barely keep still long enough to get a coherent sentence out, and his hands fidgeted constantly, worrying at his watch strap and tugging at his hair. An outward expression of inner discomfiture, Jade wondered.

"I need your help," he said.

"I'm sorry," she said bluntly, glancing up again as the well-dressed woman who'd been watching them earlier caught her heel on the edge of the carpet and bumped her handbag against the counter in her haste to leave. "Mr. Theron, I only came to this meeting because I was passing through the area. As I told you when you called me just now, I'm not accepting any new cases at the moment."

A smartly uniformed waitress arrived. Jade asked for another mineral water.

"What can I get you, sir?" the waitress asked Theron.

"No. Nothing, thanks." He paused for a moment. "Actually, yes. I'll have a Coke."

Jade couldn't help wondering what the effect of the caffeine would be on a man who already looked wired to the hilt.

"Look, I—I don't think you understand my situation. How incredibly important this is, just how much trouble I'm in. Please, at least let me tell you." He was stammering now; in his haste to get the words out they tumbled over each other, spilling into the muted background buzz of the coffee shop.

"You did give me a brief rundown over the phone."

"I did. But you need to hear the whole thing to understand. There was . . . I don't know how to put this, even. For the last week I've been in a nightmare situation. What we did was a game. We took a calculated risk. I don't know what went wrong or why. Statistically it shouldn't have—that's the truth of it—but it did."

He pressed bony fingers against office-pale cheeks. Jade saw his hands were shaking.

She knew she shouldn't ask him but she did.

"Tell me, then. What happened?" she said.

"We went jumping last week. At night. From Sandton Views. You might know it—it's close to here. Sixty-eight storeys. It's the new and the tallest skyscraper in Sandton. The upper levels aren't finished yet."

"When you say jumping, what exactly do you mean?"

"Base jumping." He looked straight at her, blinking fast, and she noticed his eyes were an unusual light hazel flecked with green and gold. "It's not legal. Not a legitimate activity at all. But for thrill-seekers it's addictive. The adrenaline rush, you know?"

Jade nodded. She knew. Although parachuting from tall buildings was not her chosen hobby, she was all too familiar with the thrill of doing the forbidden, the dangerous.

Theron took a mouthful of his Coke and then told her more of his story, speaking in rapid bursts.

"I jumped first," he said. "I always do, when we go together." He blinked again and corrected himself. "I always did," he said.

"What happened then?"

"I don't know, Ms. de Jong. I just don't know."

"Please call me Jade."

He gulped down some more Coke and, as if being on first-name terms had given him encouragement, let loose a veritable flood of words. "Thinking it over now, I'm confused. If I hadn't been on such a damn adrenaline high, I might have been able to remember more clearly. I don't know what happened. Maybe she took a phone call, or her phone beeped, or something. Or maybe not. It was dark up there and I was focused on other things. At any rate, she turned away from the edge. Then she told me to go ahead and jump, and that she would follow me down."

"You jumped, then."

"I jumped."

"You didn't wait?"

He met her eyes again.

"It's a difficult thing to do, jumping. For me, anyway. Takes a lot of guts. Turning away . . . I don't know that I'd have been able to come back to the edge again. And I didn't know how she felt, or whether she was up to jumping that day. I remember thinking at the time that she probably wasn't going to do it. Besides, I wanted to go first, so that if there were any problems with the landing, I could get them out of the way. Make it safer for her."

"Had she ever backed out before?"

"No."

Jade took a long breath. "I guess there's always a first time."

"I suppose so. Whenever I'm up there, standing on the edge, I wonder if I'll be able to go through with it."

"So what happened to her, then?"

"She fell."

Jade frowned. "What do you mean?"

"I mean just that. I don't know what happened. One minute I was standing on the lawn down below, packing up my chute, and the next minute . . ." He closed his eyes and grimaced before continuing at a slower pace and in a quieter tone. "She was falling. I heard her before I saw her. Heard the chute flapping—a partly opened parachute makes a horrible sound.

"I ran, Jade. I sprinted over to where she was going to hit the ground, to try and break her fall, but I was too late. I didn't know what on earth had happened, but I knew from the moment I heard her hit the ground that there was no way she could have survived."

Jade studied his eyes. Watched him blink rapidly. He wasn't quite blinking back tears, but emotion was there—so strong she could sense it, and she wondered what the nature of his relationship with Sonet had been.

A tragic accident. A partly opened parachute and a dead woman who had either lost her nerve and flubbed the jump or else simply been unlucky.

"I need to know what really happened up there." Theron insisted.

Jade frowned. What had really happened up there after he had jumped was more than likely a secret that Sonet had taken to her grave.

"Please," he repeated. "Trust me, money is not an issue. I've got a chequebook with me. You name the amount, I'll pay."

"I don't need the money right now."

Theron gave an attempt at a laugh, strangled as it emerged. "We all need money. We live in Johannesburg, the city built on gold. We're sitting in Sandton, within the richest square mile in Africa. Cash oils the wheels, you know. My view is you can never have too much of it."

Jade did not argue the point. She knew Theron would not understand; could not understand; that there were instances where the money was not worth it. Not when earning it forced you to sell your soul, as her most recent assignment had done.

She could have said no to Robbie, the gangster who'd asked her to help him out with the killing. But if she had, she would have made a dangerous enemy out of a man who had recently helped her to escape from jail, and save a friend's life in the process.

Choices like that were never simple. But this one was. She *could* choose to walk away from Theron and his problems.

"There are plenty of other investigators who can help you. I'll give you a couple of names of people I trust," she told him.

"I was referred to you by Wouter Wessels from Software Technologies. He's a client of mine. He said you'd done work for him a while back and you were great. He said I must insist on using you. Anybody else would be a compromise."

Jade sipped her water and thought back to that case. She liked Wouter Wessels, and she would be sorry to disappoint him.

"What I don't understand is why you need a P.I. The police will have to investigate. Death by misadventure—there will be an enquiry."

"That parachute should never have malfunctioned." Now Theron looked her straight in the eye. "Jade, I packed the chute for her before she jumped. I packed it, and it malfunctioned, and she fell to her death. I'm more than just a witness in this case. I'm going to be a suspect at best, and at worst I'm going to be charged with culpable homicide."

"But when the investigation . . ."

"No, wait. Please listen. I work in a business where my reputation is extremely important. My clients trust me. Being accused of this could ruin me. That's why I'm asking you, as a favour, to just take a look at where it happened. It's a five-minute walk from here. We can go there right now."

3

Victor Theron was a fast walker. His long legs ate up the ground in gargantuan strides, and Jade might have found it difficult to keep up with him had it not been for the crowds of shoppers that thronged the Sandton City Mall, their presence curbing his impatient pace and continually forcing him to sidestep.

Hurrying along beside him, Jade was regretting having agreed to look at the site where the accident occurred. Already, she was starting to feel as if she was involved.

Now that he was on the move and able to expend his seemingly boundless energy, Theron seemed more relaxed.

"You mentioned you were nearby when I called. Are you a Sandton local?"

"No," she replied. Crossing the polished floor of the atrium and moving past the succession of sumptuously decorated shop fronts featuring gold and bling and brand names all screaming for attention, Jade had to admit there wasn't much here for her. "I was visiting a friend in Sandton Clinic this afternoon, though, so I was in the area."

"Oh." Seeing a small gap ahead, Theron thrust his shoulders forward and made up some distance. "Your friend okay?" he asked, glancing back in her direction.

"He was a victim of a stabbing a couple of months ago. He almost died and there have been complications since then. But he's turned the corner now. Doctors are confident he's going to make a good recovery."

"That's Jo'burg for you," Theron muttered. "Does he work in the same industry as you?"

"No. He's an environmentalist."

"Did they manage to arrest the attacker?"

"Not as far as I know," Jade said carefully. After all, it wouldn't do to confess to Theron that she and Robbie had been responsible for the perpetrator's disappearance into a shallow, unmarked grave.

"Too bad when that happens, isn't it?"

"It is indeed," Jade said, uncomfortably conscious of the irony of Theron's remarks.

"That's why I like this place." Theron made a sweeping gesture with his arm that seemed to take in the entirety of the mall. "Security's top-notch here."

"You live here?"

"Not quite. I have an apartment in the Da Vinci Towers. I can shop, gym, eat, socialise, in fact, do everything I need to do under one roof without having to go outside." Theron sounded as if he thought this was a good thing. If nothing else, it explained his pallid colour.

"I enjoy Sandton City," he continued. "Do you know, the original development was a massive gamble. This area was way beyond the city limits of the day. This mall and the office tower were built out in the middle of nowhere, surrounded by rural properties and veld and trees."

"I didn't know that," Jade said.

"The founders had foresight. Vision. Although it wasn't an easy road. I read in a history of Sandton that the father and son team who started it came from humble beginnings. The father was originally a baker until he started developing property in Yeoville. He was more of a gentleman developer. His son, Michael Rapp, was the real entrepreneur. When Michael wanted to finance the hundreds of millions it would take to build Sandton City mall and tower, his father went apeshit. Said he'd destroy the company with borrowings on that scale. But Michael got his way and their concept took off, and today Sandton City is the new CBD of Johannesburg. Of Africa, even. I admire that tenacity. Rapp's gamble. Or should I say, the calculated risk. I do it every day in my job."

"Which is?" Jade was curious now.

The corridor they were on, lined by smaller but even more exclusive boutiques, led to the main entrance of the Sandton Sun Hotel. They stepped from tiles onto plush carpeting and Theron led her confidently towards the bank of lifts on the far side of the imposing lobby.

"Taking a shortcut through the hotel is the quickest way to get there," he assured her, pressing the button to summon the lift. "We're going down to the street level exit. Sandton Views is literally a block away."

In the lift, Jade was interested to see that his nervous habits returned. He twisted his fingers together, tapping a foot on the floor, glancing frequently up at the display as the lift descended.

"I'm a trader," he told her, moving forward to stand in front of the doors as the lift reached its destination. "I trade in derivatives. Futures and options. I used to work for one of the bigger banks but I left about fifteen years ago. Since then, I've been operating on my own. I trade for myself and I handle investments for a few selected clients."

"I don't know much about futures," Jade admitted.

"Most people don't. They're very complex financial structures, based on the forward trading of commodities, and their origins are just about as old as civilisation itself."

"Is that so?"

"Going back in time there's evidence of futures being traded in olives in Greece, tulips in Holland, rice in Japan. All sorts of things. Futures as we know them today began about a hundred and fifty years ago with grain trading in Chicago. To avoid being caught out by a lack of demand for their produce when it was harvested, farmers started to sell their crops for forward delivery. This concept led to the development of futures."

"Sounds complicated," Jade said, just as the lift came to a halt.

The uniformed doorman stood aside and they stepped out of the comfortably air-conditioned hotel and into the blustery winter afternoon. They hurried down the uneven pavement, and Theron raised his voice so that Jade could hear him above the constant roar of passing traffic.

"High risks, high rewards. There's way more opportunity to make big money than via conventional trading, but because futures are so highly leveraged, if the market moves against you, you have to pay in a fortune to maintain your positions. One bad trade can bankrupt an individual and take a company under. It can basically destroy you."

He fell silent, as if his own words had reminded him of the situation in which he found himself.

They turned the corner and there, straight ahead of them, was Sandton Views.

The building was a monster.

Set on a paved plinth, wide marble stairs leading up to an imposing lobby, the skyscraper itself was smooth-sided and brilliant and endlessly tall. Behind the plinth, Jade could see the large square of mown lawn where Victor must have landed safely and Sonet plummeted to her death. Shading her eyes as she stared up, Jade had the impression its design narrowed towards its apex, further exaggerating the impression of height. Its glass-clad sides telescoped away from her, the exterior reflecting the deep blue of the clear winter sky.

It was dizzyingly high. Jade's stomach flipped as she imagined standing on the very edge of that concrete rim with no railing or banister to hold onto. Just the idea of leaning out and looking directly down into the empty space yawning below made her palms sweat.

Jade wondered how well sound would carry downwards.

Had Sonet screamed or cried out during her fatal descent? Perhaps there had been no time; perhaps the speed of the descent had hammered the air from her lungs and rendered her voiceless. Or perhaps her cries had been snatched away by the speed of her fall. While Victor had clearly stated that he'd heard the noise of the parachute, he hadn't mentioned hearing Sonet's voice before she hit the ground.

Nevertheless, staring up again at the mirrored glass, Jade was sure of one fact: if she'd been the one who'd fallen, she certainly would have screamed.

4

The man sitting next to Ntombi Khumalo smelled sour.

She had a keen nose, which meant she caught a whiff of it from time to time, overwhelming the fake pine scent of the air freshener and the fainter but far more expensive smell of leather. It was the acrid stink of days-old sweat. The odour of a man who had been travelling too long without showering or changing. Beneath his immaculate jacket, she guessed that his grey collared shirt had been soaked in perspiration more than once. Wet, dried, and wet again.

Ntombi didn't want to think about why. She gripped the steering wheel more firmly and tried to ignore the way her stomach felt; tight and sick with fear.

"Is the heater on too high for you?" she asked. She'd rather not have spoken to him at all, but she'd been told to make sure he was comfortable at all times.

He turned to face her. Black skin, deeply tinted glasses, and an expression darker than both. He didn't answer; just looked at her for a couple of long, cold seconds, as if he were memorising her face for future reference, before giving a small headshake.

Now Ntombi felt sweat spring up under her own armpits. God, she hated doing this. Hated it, and all the more so because now she had no choice.

She inched carefully over the final speed bump on the way out of the airport car park— the one that had little steel blades in it and shredded your tyres. Right now they were inside the slits in the raised metal, but she still drove over carefully, in case the blades were accidentally activated, bringing their journey to a disastrous stop with their tyre-shredding sharpness.

But the blades remained out of harm's way, which Ntombi thought was wrong, because they were designed to stop criminals, and they had just let one pass.

She was familiar with the route they would be taking. She'd studied it yesterday, using a map book she had since closed and put away in the driver's seat's side pocket. The car she was driving was equipped with a GPS, but Ntombi knew that it was not to be used for trips such as this, trips where no record could exist. And so the GPS on the dashboard was turned off, its screen blank, an unseeing eye.

On the highway, she took the route to Pretoria. They wouldn't be going all the way there, they'd switch to the N1 highway and turn off at Randburg.

Her passenger shifted in his seat. He wasn't wearing a seatbelt, and as he took a document out of his inside jacket pocket, she glimpsed an empty leather holster buckled to his belt.

Ntombi's stomach clenched still further.

She could imagine her employer reassuring him with the words, "She'll be cool. You can trust her one hundred per cent."

Or perhaps he had laughed and said, "Don't worry—I own her." It was a phrase she'd heard him use more than once recently. Certainly he had used it the first time she had chauffeured this dark-skinned man, which had been a week ago now. She hadn't actually expected to see him again, or at least certainly not so soon.

The man was a killer. That was all she knew; all she needed to know. Her mouth went dry when she realised the implications of this—what it meant for her and her son, affectionately known as Small Khumalo.

She should refuse to do this. But she knew she couldn't. Not with Small Khumalo now in her sole care. The energetic and gifted young boy was already showing himself to be both an academic whizz and a force to be reckoned with on the soccer field. Thinking of him simultaneously filled her heart with love and with dread.

Small Khumalo had effectively made her a prisoner.

Don't think of him—not now, she told herself. He was safely at school. A good school—Redhill, in Morningside. A school she could never have afforded to send him had it not been for her current job.

"Can you really drive?" her prospective employer had asked, his tone one of amusement, when he had first interviewed her. "You come from a small rural community. Not many people from those parts of South Africa have an education, never mind a driver's license."

"The school I attended in Bronkhorstspruit was a rural school, but a good one. I passed my Matric with a distinction in House-crafts," she had told him, raising her chin to display a confidence she did not feel. "My husband owned a car for a while. He taught me how to drive, and in that very car I obtained my license."

"Well, I need a housekeeper who can cook, because I'm too busy to make my own meals. Your main job will be to keep my place in order and the fridge well stocked with food. As far as driving goes . . ." At this, he'd looked thoughtful. "It's certainly something I could make use of in the future. But tell me, why did you decide to leave your community and come to work in Johannesburg?"

Don't think of that fateful interview now. Think of food instead. Her employer's fridge was currently full, but she needed to cook for herself and her son. What should she make for dinner tonight?

Driving along the R21, keeping just within the speed limit, Ntombi forced her thoughts to her greatest passion in life apart from her son—her cookery. The kitchen in her furnished apartment was small, but it was well-equipped, with multiple electronic gadgets and tools, expensive pots and pans, a whole cupboard full of recipe books, and her greatest joy—a state-of-the-art Kenwood food processor.

She'd make bobotie, she decided. A traditional Cape Malay dish, perfect for a winter evening, with spiced mince and raisins topped with an egg custard and oven-baked for an hour to bring it to sizzling golden-brown perfection. This would be accompanied by saffron rice and a simple but tasty salad. Sliced avocado—there were some beautiful ones in the kitchen that had ripened to perfection—with wild rocket, chopped cucumber and crumbled Danish feta.

She could already visualise arranging the ingredients in a shallow bowl, creating a pyramid with the avocado and chunks of cucumber. A good dressing—a balsamic reduction would work perfectly—with perhaps a few homemade croutons to top it off.

Ntombi's fierce grip on the steering wheel started to relax as she planned her menu. But when she realised cars in front of her were slowing, the two lanes narrowing into one, and she saw the orange cones that signalled a police roadblock they tightened again.

Her heart started to pound fast and hard.

Her undesirable companion put the piece of paper back into his jacket pocket and fastened it, concealing the holster, before doing up his seatbelt and leaning back in his seat, eyes closed.

Let her get through this. It was bound to be a routine stop, with the police checking for valid driver's licenses and registration. Surely they hadn't had a tip-off about the man she'd picked up at the airport barely fifteen minutes ago?

Stop it, Ntombi told herself. You can do this. The only thing that will give you away is your own fear.

An officer waved her over and she pulled into the emergency lane, the tyres bumping gently over an uneven patch in the tarmac. She buzzed the window down.

The black policeman bent down and peered into the vehicle's plush interior.

"License, please," he said, and although Ntombi could hear from his accent that he was Xhosa, he spoke to her in English.

She handed over the license card that stated she was Mrs. Thabiseng.

"You coming from the airport?" the cop asked. She got the distinct feeling that this was not just making conversation; that they were on the lookout for something.

"Yes," she told him, and to her immense relief her voice sounded steady. "I picked up my husband from international arrivals earlier this morning." She inclined her head to her left. "Please don't speak too loudly," she asked the cop, giving him one of her most vivacious smiles. "We might disturb his sleep. I think he enjoyed too many single malts in business class."

The cop grinned. He gave her back her license, walked around the front of the car, and peered in through the windscreen as he read the license disk.

"You can go," he said, waving her on.

Ntombi let out a long, shaky breath as she rejoined the highway.

Whatever or whoever the cops had been looking for, it was not a newly rich black couple on their way home from the airport. A wealthy husband and wife, such as they appeared to be, and no doubt as well-connected as they were well-dressed, put them instantly beyond suspicion.

Which was why her employer had ordered her to drive this client of his when he was in town.

Putting her foot down harder, Ntombi accelerated up to the speed limit, hoping that the dark-suited man wouldn't be spending too much time in Jo'burg afterwards; that in fact her next journey might be to take him back to the airport.

At any rate, she prayed so.

5

To Jade's surprise, Theron didn't walk straight up to the entrance of Sandton Views. Instead, he pointed across the street to what she saw was a rather odd-looking, tall, cylindrical bronze monument with carvings covering its surface.

"Before we go any further, I have to show you something. That's the 'Candle of Hope,'" he said. "I come here sometimes just to stand and look at it. I don't know if you know anything about it. Do you?"

Jade shook her head.

"It was commissioned by a developer called Dorrestein. He heads up The Legacy Group, which built Da Vinci Towers. He had it put up a couple of years back after his son was killed in an attempted hijacking. They call it a candle, but it's supposed to be modelled on a fig tree. The scenes on it are beautiful, if you look up close. So many important moments in South Africa's history."

"I never even knew it existed," Jade confessed.

"That tall glass wall behind it is covered with etchings of trees and inspirational sayings. And below the wall is a well of water. That's supposed to be where the tears of those who have suffered and lost are collected."

"That's amazing," Jade said, genuinely surprised. She'd driven through that intersection several times in the past couple of years and had never noticed the monument until now. "I'll have a closer look at it on the way back."

"You want to go into Sandton Views, while we're here?"

They turned away from the Candle of Hope and took in the far more imposing structure ahead of them. Sandton City's tallest building. For a few years at least, it would dominate the CBD's skyline.

"I can go in if you like," she found herself saying to Theron.

"Here." He took a white access card out of his wallet and handed it to her. "Security's tight, but this card'll get you through the turnstile. It'll also allow you to take the lift to the top floor. Make sure you hold the card against the magnetic sensor while you press the button. If you don't the lift won't go beyond the twenty-fourth floor. They won't let residents go up to the top floors because they're still under construction. From twenty-five up, the building is basically a shell."

"How did you get the card?"

"Sonet gave it to me," Theron said. "I don't know how she got hold of it. I suppose she found a way. I guess I'll have to give it back at some stage, but nobody's asked me for it yet."

Jade supposed that, for a base jumper, gaining illegal access to buildings was all part of the thrill.

"You don't want to come with me and show me where you went?"

He shook his head, "The card only admits one person. And, to be honest with you, I never want to go up there again. Not ever."

"I understand."

"Take the service lift. It's the one on the far left as you go in. You'll see our footprints at the top. And be careful. The flooring is uneven and parts of it are missing altogether. I put my feet exactly where Sonet trod, literally followed in her footsteps, and I suggest you do the same. Oh, and you'll need this."

He unclipped a small flashlight from the bunch of keys he carried on his belt.

"It's very dark up there," he said.

Inside the building, Jade's rubber-soled shoes squeaked softly as she walked across the shiny marble floor. A female guard was seated at the wooden reception desk near the turnstiles that looked distinctly temporary in the otherwise grand lobby. She glimpsed scaffolding set up behind a boarded-up area to the right of the entrance door, indicating that the builders' work here was not yet complete.

The place smelled brand new. Jade supposed it would for a while. Concrete had to harden, paint had to dry, adhesives had to set. The whole process could take weeks, and until they did their distinctive odours would continue to fill the air.

There was a turnstile for visitors and one for residents. Jade went confidently up to the residents' turnstile and held the card against the sensor. A green light flashed briefly and with a muted click the steel bar moved smoothly forward to allow her through.

On the wall ahead of her, Jade saw the signs for the companies that had already set up offices. These too were temporary looking, if a little smarter. The building had only a handful of tenants so far, all of them located on the first five floors. Two attorneys, a construction company, no less than three psychologists, a dentist, a private bank, a recruitment consultancy and a few other organisations whose names gave no clues to their functions.

She took out her notepad and scribbled down their details before heading towards the lifts, keeping close to the wall that sported an African-themed pattern of tiles in gold, ochre and brown.

Inside the nearest lift, Jade pressed the button for floors number three and four. She waited at three while the doors opened and closed again, just in case the security guard was watching where she went, and then got out at four. Here, she walked towards the furthermost lift. This was the service lift; its floor untiled and its sides swathed in heavy duty canvas.

With the help of her illegal access card, Jade pressed the button for the topmost level, number sixty-seven.

The floor pressed hard against her feet as the elevator shot upwards. When the doors opened, she stepped out into almost total darkness.

Raw concrete here. She breathed in its distinctive smell, and those others that spoke of construction work in progress. Dust, fresh plaster, drying glue.

Jade snapped the torch on and shone it around. Unsurprisingly, there were no carpets or wallpaper, no marble finishes, no round ceiling lights. Just rough flooring, gaping doorways, thick, white-insulated wires jutting like bony fingers from places where, one day, lights and plug points would be properly installed. Her shoes crunched over scraps of cardboard, loose pieces of concrete, discarded nails and lengths of unused rebar. She took each step carefully, peering down as she walked. After the warning Theron had given her, she didn't want to step into nothingness.

As she moved away from the lift, the shadows softened. Light could be glimpsed at intervals, through gaps in the walls that would one day be filled with doors leading into plush offices.

Just as Theron had told her, there were footprints in the thick dust, a multitude of them, mostly so old that the dust had just about obscured them again. It had been a long time since the team of construction workers had last been busy on this floor.

But some certainly looked more recent, and it was these that she followed. They took her on a winding route that led away from the main areas of traffic and through a couple of sections where the floor dropped terrifyingly away, leaving only a couple of rickety planks to bridge the darkened gaps below. The tracks ended—and not before Jade was ready—outside a closed steel door.

Jade gave it a push and found, much to her relief, that it was locked. After the accident, the caretaker must have come up to secure access to the roof. The rather scuffed-looking prints she could see presumably belonged to him, and the trainer-patterned prints must belong to Theron, who must have indeed placed his feet squarely on Sonet's footsteps, covering her tracks with his own.

This didn't explain the other set of prints. Somebody else had walked along this route recently, and in shoes with larger and heavier-looking soles.

She doubted that the police had been here yet. There was no sign of large-scale disturbance and the handle of the solid door, although coated with a week's worth of dust, bore no evidence of the silver-grey powder the detectives used to dust for prints.

And why would the police have come up here in any case, when their concern was with what lay below? The crumpled body of the woman and the malfunctioning parachute that had caused her death.

Either way, somebody else had been here, and she wanted to find out who.

6

Theron was waiting for Jade when she walked out of the building, following behind a pair of pinstripe-suited men who were arguing about a legal case.

She'd expected him to be pacing and fidgeting, or perhaps standing by the Candle of Hope and reading through the inspirational sayings, but instead he was peering down at the screen of a small gadget he held in his right hand. All his attention was focused on this and he barely glanced up when she reached him.

"Hang on," he muttered. He pressed a few keys and waited, frowning down at the brightly lit screen.

A little while later he nodded and let out a deep breath.

"Online trading," he told her. "I have positions in the S&P 500 futures market in the States. They've just opened and trading has gone crazy. They're extremely volatile right now. I've taken short positions as there's a lack of consumer confidence over there at the moment."

"And that makes a difference?"

"Oh, yes. Markets are, to a large extent, affected by investor sentiment. With a short position, if the indexes fall, I profit. And hugely, with every point they go down. But if they strengthen, I'm in trouble."

He pocketed the gadget, and now, his concerns with work temporarily resolved, she saw his worry about his current personal circumstances return. "So, did you see anything at the top of the building? Anything you could pick up on?"

"Who else went up there, Victor?"

"Nobody. Not that I know of. I spoke to the superintendent

the day after it happened, to explain what we'd been doing. He said he'd sent the caretaker up to lock the access door, but that he didn't think anybody else would be doing work up there until the police had had a look. But the police haven't been there yet."

He looked at her directly and Jade saw silent appeal in his eyes.

She didn't want to take on the case. There were so many compelling reasons not to. For a start, she was exhausted, as much mentally as physically. The job she'd had to do in exchange for the favour she had received from Robbie had been tough and brutal.

A killing.

It was ironic that, so soon after finding out that her mother had worked as a paid killer, Jade had found herself once again in a similar situation. Willing herself to damp down the adrenaline that surged through her, suppressing all her fears of what might go wrong, refusing to think about the person into whose chest and head she had accurately fired two bullets with a borrowed gun, the weapon unlicensed and untraceable.

Which brought her to yet another, more practical reason why she should refuse this case. Her own gun, a Glock 19, was still in the hands of the police. It had been confiscated at a roadblock a few months ago, after the police had refused to accept a photocopy of her gun license as valid documentation. She knew she'd have to cut through a forest of red tape to get it back. For the time being, she had no weapon of her own. No way to defend herself if a case turned bad.

No way of taking the law into her own hands, either, which was probably a good thing, given her history and now, perhaps, her genes.

She wanted to turn her back on the business now, before it was too late.

Although she couldn't help wondering if it was already too late.

The money she'd received for helping Robbie with the contract killing was still sitting in her bank account untouched. A massive sum, unwanted and unappreciated, as toxic as a tumour.

If she took on Theron's case, she wouldn't have to touch this blood money. She would have some time to decide what to do with it, even if it meant signing the whole damn amount over to Friends of the Cat or another worthy charity.

Jade sighed. "I'll investigate your case for a week," she told Theron. "Seven days from now, we can reassess. I don't know if I can help you, but I'll try."

His face softened and she saw a smile doing its best to crack through the tension.

"Thank you, Jade," he said.

7

Superintendent David Patel had started going to the gym four days a week—all right, then, three days on really bad weeks when the case load gobbled up every spare minute and the Organised Crime department's resources were spread thinner than Flora Light on a dieting man's rice cakes.

The gym he'd chosen was a privately owned setup, not one of the big names. He wouldn't get any points from Virgin Active on his Vitality card for taking the short walk—round the corner from Johannesburg Central police station, down two blocks and then a left turn—that took him into an area of the city centre even more dilapidated than he was accustomed to seeing. It was easier to count the panes of glass that remained whole in the crumbling tenements than it was to count the broken ones.

The gym was in the basement of one of the buildings, and David had absolutely no idea who lived in the flats above. One thing he was pretty sure of was that if the shabby looking tenants were paying rent, it wasn't to the building's legitimate owner.

He was ninety five per cent certain that the six-story apartment block was another of Jo'burg's "hijacked" buildings, abandoned by owners who were daunted by the prospect of carrying out massive repairs, not to mention evicting the squatters who had taken up residence in the meantime and who were contributing still further towards the building's decay.

In due course, David assumed, it had simply been taken over by the Nigerian "landlord," Obji, who was doubtless managing to extract some form of rent from the occupants and had also installed the almost-new gym equipment—although how exactly he'd got his hands on it was something David didn't want to know.

He contented himself with the fact that membership was cheap, even if the gym's atmosphere was somewhat lacking. The space must have originally been part of a car park. Two small sections within it had been partitioned off, one for men and the other for ladies, with a toilet, shower and a few lockers inside each.

When he'd first seen it, David's overriding thought had been how amused Jade would be by this setup. "It's like a dominatrix's whipping room," he could imagine her saying, green eyes sparkling, "Bend over, you naughty boy, and drop your trousers!"

He'd smiled at the idea, but his lightheartedness had swiftly dissolved as he'd realised that this was a comment Jade was unlikely to utter in his presence. In fact, they hadn't spoken for months. Not since David had moved back in with Naisha, his wife, after she'd told him she was pregnant. And that was partly the reason he'd started looking for a gym to attend in the first place. Since he'd felt he'd lost control over every other aspect of his life, he decided he was damn well going to try and get a grip on his own fitness and get rid of his inappropriately named love handles.

The gym equipment had to rely on two plug points, and one of those sometimes tripped the lights. There were three sockets installed, but as the surprisingly well-spoken owner had explained gently to David when he'd shown him round, "The third one causes fires, I'm afraid."

That hadn't inconvenienced David so far; he was often the only one there. In any case, he preferred to use the free weights and the weighted machines. He was damn well going to get back into tip-top shape, even if doing so killed him—and sometimes when he was struggling alone and unsupported, bench-pressing dumbbells that were too heavy, he feared it actually might.

Tonight, as usual, he was the only customer. Obji was nowhere to be seen when he'd walked in and headed down the raw concrete stairs. David changed quickly, not bothering to use a locker but instead leaving his clothes in a neat pile on one of the plastic chairs, and made his way into the gym. One treadmill was switched in and the other working plug point was powering a large ghetto blaster which was belting out rap music.

He did a half-hour run on the treadmill, in the process becoming better acquainted with Soulja Boy's latest hits than he'd ever wanted to be, before stepping off, towelling his face dry, and turning down the volume on the irritating machine. Pressing the heel of his left hand against the right side of his chest, he massaged the area where a reddened, shiny scar bore witness to the bullet he'd taken earlier that year.

The pectoral muscle had been damaged, and his shoulder blade, which had been shattered during the bullet's exit, was now held together by a series of metal pins and plates. After every gym session, the entire right side of his upper body felt raw and bruised.

With the music thankfully muted, faint voices of people outside were now audible. Heading over to the free weights area, he arranged the heavy discs to his satisfaction, adding another two kilograms more than he'd lifted the last time. He lowered himself down onto the bench, feeling his back pop as he manoeuvred himself into position.

Cardio was all very well and good. But these days it was only when he was struggling with the weights, heart pounding and muscles quivering, that David managed to get some distance from the personal circumstances that were weighing him down, heavier than any dumbbell could ever be.

He shifted his position on the bench, hoping to alleviate the nagging ache in his back, courtesy of a bad night's sleep in an awkward position.

Oh, wait. Make that more than sixty consecutive nights of uncomfortable and interrupted rest.

When David moved back in with Naisha, from whom he had previously been separated, one of the first sacrifices he'd had to make was giving up his extra-long double bed—the only one he'd been able to find that comfortably accommodated his six-foot-five frame.

Gently but firmly, Naisha had insisted that in the small master bedroom of the compact Pretoria townhouse where she and Kevin now lived, a long bed would mean that the built-in cupboards opposite could not be easily accessed.

"I don't want to have to squeeze past the cupboards every morning," she'd explained to David in a tone that had brooked no argument. "The doors won't be able to open all the way if we have your bed in here. Besides, the room is too small for it. It will look messy and cluttered."

"Oh, come on, Naisha, my bed's only six inches longer than this one. Can six inches possibly make that much of a goddamn difference?"

As he spoke, looking at his wife's rounded stomach under the maternity blouse she wore, David had wanted to let out a mirthless guffaw at his own words. Thanks to the one regrettable night where he'd slept with his wife during their separation and she had fallen pregnant, his affair with Jade was now history. Here he was, living with Naisha again, their marriage officially back on.

So yes, he supposed, in that case, his own six inches and what he'd chosen to do with it had made all the difference in the world.

Rather than having his feet jut out into the cold—Naisha couldn't bear a warm bedroom at this stage of her pregnancy and insisted that the air-conditioning be turned up full blast—David now slept in an awkward curl that, by the morning, left him feeling as if he'd been welded into position.

Pushing weights would help with his sore back, though, he was sure of it. He'd do twenty reps, then rest, then another twenty.

Hefting the bar into the air for the first set of repetitions, David gasped at its weight. His muscles screamed with the effort and the blood soon began to pound in his ears. He realised he could actually feel the pressure building behind his eyes. The breath was forced out of his lungs in an involuntary huff.

"Come on, do it," he grunted.

His world narrowed down to the metal bar above him, held by his own tightly clenched brown fingers. And above that the concrete roof and flickering strip light that left garish purple stripes on his vision when he blinked.

One. Two. Three.

He'd made it way too heavy this time. Start light was what he'd been told to do by his physiotherapist after the injury. He knew he should do that: start light and go heavier. Why, then, did he always end up ignoring his own advice?

Four . . . don't drop it . . . Five.

Above the noise of his own staggering breath, David thought he could hear soft footsteps coming down the stairs. He was going to be sharing his gym session . . . or perhaps it was Obji, the owner, checking up on who was using the facilities.

Six . . . Seven . . . Eight. He had to stop now. His arms were quivering. He was going to end up dropping the weighted bar onto his chest. Crushing his ribs. People had died that way. No one was supposed to do free weights without a spotter. He knew this, but still he broke the rules.

Nine . . . Ten. Whoever had arrived, it wasn't Obji. He could hear the sound of the treadmill starting up again. The humming of the mechanism sound grew higher and louder as the speed built up. Whoever this person was, they were running as if the devil himself was in pursuit.

Or were they?

Because, listen as he might, David couldn't hear anyone actually running.

Eleven . . .

And then he almost dropped the weights as, with an explosive crackle, the ghetto blaster burst back into life. At full volume this time. Gangster rap louder than he'd ever wanted to hear it. The sound bounced off the walls and reverberated in his head.

Ignore it. Just ignore it, okay? He blinked stinging drops of sweat out of his eyes.

Twelve . . .

Thirteen . . .

And then the strip light above him suddenly went out.

His first thought was that this new arrival, whoever they were and for whatever demented reason, had also plugged in the rowing machine and tripped the power. But he swiftly realised that was impossible, because the music was still playing and he could still hear the frantic whine of the treadmill's machinery being pushed to the edge of its limits.

So, he or she had deliberately turned off the lights.

And here he was, effectively trapped by sixty kilograms of solid steel, his shaking arms rapidly reaching the stage where they could lift no longer. But a gym injury was now the last thing on his mind.

With no one at the front desk, he realised that anybody could have entered the gym. He'd left his wallet in his trouser pocket, with all his cards and six hundred rand cash inside. As well as his brand new iPhone, and his car keys inside his good leather jacket, the one he treasured, the one which Jade had given him back in the days when they had been lovers. Why hadn't he put his stuff in the locker?

Because he'd planned on having a short session. Because there was never anyone else in the gym. Well, he'd pay for his naivety, he was sure. He'd been robbed.

With an effort that wrenched every fibre of his body, David sat up and dropped the bar to his right. It fell with a crash onto the floor, sending sparks flying. He gulped in fast, deep breaths, feeling suddenly as if there was nowhere near enough oxygen in the room to meet his needs.

He stood up on wobbly legs, flexing his sore fingers, almost crying out at the sharp bolt of pain that lanced through his right side. He really had pushed himself too far this time, and he knew he was going to pay for it, probably in more ways than one.

David made his way over to the light switch by the stairs. He held his left hand out front of him, groping like a blind man to avoid crashing into anything, but even so, his shin connected with the edge of the rowing machine, causing him to swear as much from disgust as from the impact itself.

He snapped the light switch on and after a two-second pause, the strip lights flickered back into life.

David narrowed his eyes against the sudden brightness and checked there was nobody still in the room. Then he turned and strode more quickly towards the locker room, stopping on the way to turn off the damn ghetto blaster and to punch the STOP button on the treadmill before it burned its motor out.

It was then he noticed that nothing else had been plugged in and socket number three was still empty.

He shouldered his way into the change room, already formulating in his mind an angry request to the Nigerian for a security door.

He stopped in surprise when he saw that his clothes were there, seemingly in the same tidy pile that he'd left them, and his jacket hanging on the back of the chair.

"Well, bloody hell." The words burst from his lips.

Who had been in the gym, then, and why on earth had they done what they did? Had he been a victim of a practical joke? Or was it somehow possible that the new arrival had not even noticed David in the corner, and had simply turned the lights off to conserve electricity when he or she had left?

That explanation made even less sense when he considered that the music and equipment had been left on.

It was only when David picked up his clothes, intending to put them inside the locker before getting back to his gym session, that he noticed the slim white envelope that had been placed underneath them.

It was addressed, in laser-printed letters, to Superintendent D. Patel—Organised Crime.

David shivered in a way that had nothing to do with the cooling sweat on his body. He couldn't stop himself from glancing apprehensively over his shoulder, but there was nobody behind him, nor any sounds outside.

Suppressing the questions that were flooding his mind—*What the hell? Who knows I come here? What is this, a death threat? Which sensitive cases am I handling right now?*—he tore it open. Forensics be damned, because whoever had done this had surely been careful enough to leave no prints or DNA behind.

Inside he found a single piece of A4 paper containing a single typed sentence. He read it through twice before refolding it and putting it back in its envelope.

Two minutes later, dressed in his work clothes, David Patel left the Nigerian's gym and headed back towards Johannesburg Central police station at a run.

8

It was after ten P.M. when David opened the door of the small Pretoria townhouse and walked inside, breathing in the combined scents of mutton curry and disapproval.

"You said you'd be home by eight," Naisha called accusingly from the lounge. "I wanted to discuss Kevin's extramural activities with you, if you remember."

"I'm sorry. Work was . . ."

"Yes, I know. Your dinner's in the microwave." Her voice sounded flat and toneless, and only David could recognise the anger seething underneath the words. "I'm tired now. I'll decide on the activities myself and fill in the form tomorrow morning."

He thought of going into the lounge and kissing her on the cheek, offering another apology. Then he decided against it, doubting that the gesture would do anything to thaw her frosty demeanour. He caught a glimpse of her as he passed by the door. Hands laced over her swollen belly; stockinged feet up on the padded stool; eyes fixed on the television. Kevin's bedroom door was closed, which hopefully meant his son was sound asleep and unaware of the friction his timetable had unwittingly caused.

David twisted the dial on the microwave and waited for the ping. He carefully removed the plate and added a large dollop of mild chutney on the side. Where to eat—here or in the lounge? Neither appealed, but in the end the relative comfort of the lounge chairs won him over. He lowered himself into the sofa next to Naisha and stretched his legs out in front of him. For a while, the clinking of fork against china almost drowned out the muted babble of the television.

David hadn't expected to be hungry. He'd thought he'd never be rid of the cold nausea that had clenched at his stomach when he'd discovered that note. But now he found himself shovelling food into his mouth as if it had been a week since he'd last eaten.

His enthusiasm didn't last long. The curry was so highly spiced that he could only manage a few mouthfuls before he had to put his plate down, walk to the fridge and take out two cold beers. The first he downed where he stood, in a series of large gulps, before crushing the can and tossing it into the bin. The second he took back with him to the lounge before recommencing his attack on the food, this time more cautiously.

Naisha knew his stance on chillies. Half-Indian or not, he couldn't handle them. She usually humoured his needs, cooking mildly spiced dishes, but he had a nasty suspicion that this evening, every time she'd checked her watch and realised he wasn't yet home, she had lifted the lid of the pot and shaken in another teaspoon of chilli powder to punish him for his tardiness.

Now she was looking at him in a quizzical way that made him wonder if she'd heard the telltale pop of the first beer can opening, and if so whether she was going to comment on how fast he had drunk it.

"How was work?" he asked, hoping to sidetrack her. He hadn't expected much of a response, but to her surprise she muted the television's sound immediately.

"It's difficult at the moment," she said.

"Why?" David guided another fiery forkful into his mouth then clasped his hand around the cold beer can. Naisha worked for Home Affairs, and last year she had been promoted to the Pretoria head office. Her job was to stamp out corruption in the department, a task that David knew was the equivalent of trying to extinguish a bonfire with a water pistol.

"I've had to investigate my ex-colleague from the Commissioner Street office. You might remember her. Prana Govender. Until recently, we were close friends."

With a jolt, David realised he did remember Prana. She was a short-haired, cheerful woman a few years older than Naisha. He recalled her warm smile, her gold tooth, her air of capability. She had indeed been good friends with his wife. They'd attended the same flower-arranging classes, although that had stopped when Naisha had moved to Pretoria. And in the old days, he'd come home to the Turffontein house more than once to find them sitting on the couch and chatting over coffee. The sudden silence that had normally fallen when he'd walked in had made him wonder uneasily and self-consciously if they had been speaking about him.

"So she was investigated? Why?"

"Because somebody there has been accepting bribes. She deals with work and study permits, you remember? A number of those permits have recently been issued to people who didn't actually qualify for them or hadn't filled in the necessary paperwork, and would never have got them even if they had done."

"Surely not Prana? I know you never can tell, but still . . ." David chewed on another mouthful. This one was mostly rice, offering him some respite.

"The evidence points towards her, David. We suspended her from work for a week, pending the outcome of the investigation, but we couldn't find any concrete proof."

David nodded. He could sympathise with that.

"You sure she wasn't being set up by somebody else?"

"It's a possibility. The problem is that the only person in a position to do that is the department manager, and he's the one who reported the discrepancies in the first place. Prana has since handed in her resignation and left."

"But no matter who stayed or who went, those discrepancies would have been picked up by somebody else later on, wouldn't they?"

"Oh, yes. All the information is now double-checked."

"So if the manager knew that, and he needed someone to pin it on . . ." David reached for a paper napkin as by now his nose had started to run.

"We are looking into it." Now Naisha sounded annoyed, as if she didn't need David to tell her how to do her job. Or perhaps it was because he was using his napkin to blow his nose. He wasn't sure.

"Can't have been much fun for you, having to investigate your friend," he said, steering the topic back to safer ground.

"It was horrible, and it ended up getting really ugly. Our friendship is over. She and I were so close, David . . . she was like a sister to me. My very best friend. We exchanged so many confidences. We trusted each other all the way."

David crumpled his napkin and put his empty plate on the coffee table. "So sad when that happens."

There was silence for a while.

He wondered if he should tell her about the notes. They'd spoken more in the past few minutes than they had in the past month. Perhaps this would be a good opportunity to get her input on the matter.

"I've got a work problem that's troubling me as well," he began, rather hesitantly.

Naisha yawned. "You know I don't like discussing your work. If you'd wanted to speak about it, you should have come home earlier. I'm going to bed now. I'll see you in the morning."

She stood up with some effort, picked up David's half-finished plate and his empty beer can, and walked out.

9

Jade had been living in her rented cottage for more than eighteen months. She guessed that was long enough to classify it as "home." She was used to turning off the main road and juddering up the rutted dirt road and parking underneath the narrow steel carport that only offered any useful shade when the sun was directly overhead. She'd grown to enjoy sitting in the treed garden with flowerbeds that were now somewhat overgrown through neglect.

Jade had never quite grown to like the cottage's décor, the plague of frilly scatter cushions and the liberal use of pink. It just wasn't her style, although she'd never bothered to change it. She doubted that all the feminine frills and fluff would have been Sonet's style either. An intrepid base jumper would surely have preferred cleaner, sleeker, more neutral décor.

One of the few personal touches Jade had added to her living quarters was the framed photograph of her mother that she'd hung on the arch between her kitchen and living room—Elise de Jong's face full of love as she looked down at the tiny baby in her arms.

The quest to find out more about her mother might have been cut disappointingly short, but even so, whenever she looked at that photo she found it impossible to banish the ghosts of her own past. Memories swirled around her, as suffocating as smoke.

The feel of the Glock in her hands as she'd raised it, her arm steady, her aim true, to deliver the killing shot to the man who'd organised her father's death. The coldness in the pit of her stomach that she felt when she thought about what she had done. She had no remorse for anyone she'd gunned down—in each case she felt that the killings were justified. The dread she felt was for herself . . . for her soul and, more practically, for her future. What could the life of an assassin ever be except an existence based on constant fear, forever running and hiding, evading not only the authorities but also those seeking revenge or looking to cut off loose ends.

She sat down at her kitchen table, where no sooner had she opened her laptop and got out her cell phone than she was interrupted by a forlorn scratching at the wooden front door.

Getting up again, Jade let in Bonnie, the Jack Russell from the house down the road who'd become a regular visitor. Try as she might, Jade had never managed to spot her squeezing through the palisade that surrounded the cottage.

Jade bent down and scratched the dog's head, an action which prompted her stump of a tail to wiggle like crazy. Then she tossed a couple of dog biscuits into the plastic bowl that was now a permanent fixture on the floor next to the fridge.

Jade thought having a timeshared pet wasn't a bad arrangement. It was a whole lot better, in fact, than having a timeshared man. But she wasn't going to allow thoughts of David Patel to prevent her from focusing on the new job she'd taken on, albeit reluctantly.

Using Google and the phone directory, she found contact numbers for all twelve of the companies who had already moved into their new office space in Sandton Views, as well as the number for building management. The phone calls that followed would, she knew, be routine research, a process that had to be done, even if the chances of getting a successful result were slim.

If she ticked all the boxes and followed all the leads, there was surely a chance that somebody at one of these companies would have known Sonet personally and might be able to explain to Jade how she had been able to gain access to this otherwise secure building.

Before she'd had a chance to get started, however, her cell phone rang and she found herself speaking to Wouter Wessels, her ex-client who'd given her name to Victor Theron.

"Jade. How are you this morning?" Wessels always sounded upbeat and cheerful, as if everything was right with the world. He'd even sounded that way when he'd phoned her a year ago to ask if she could investigate his wife, who he suspected was having an affair and who had just requested a sizeable divorce settlement. "I hope you don't mind, but I passed your number on to a gentleman who handles some of my investments. Victor Theron, his name is. I told him if anyone could help him, it would be you."

"Thanks, Wessel. Actually, he's already been in touch with me."

"Good, good! Excellent. I know you'll sort him out. He's a good fellow, Theron. Trustworthy. No social skills, of course— all he can talk about is the markets. Pots of money, though, so mind you charge him your full rate." Wessels laughed heartily.

"I will do," Jade replied, trying to sound lighter than she actually felt.

"I owe him, you know. Years back . . . it was soon after 9/11, actually—my business got into some serious trouble and I needed to withdraw all my savings at short notice. I'd taken out a year's investment contract but when I phoned Victor he said he'd organise the funds for me within a month as a special favour. He sounded rather harassed and I felt bad asking for it."

"Go on," Jade said.

"It was only later that I found out he'd literally just heard that his wife had been shot dead during an attempted bank robbery."

"Really?"

Bonnie pushed her nose against Jade's leg and she leaned down and stroked the dog's ears absently, her attention entirely focused on what Wessels was saying.

"In spite of that, during what must have been the most traumatic time, he made a plan for me and thanks to his generosity I was able to save my business. I felt terrible when I realised that. So I owe him, Jade, I really do. Anyway, got to run now, I can see my secretary giving me wild semaphore signals so it must be something important. Chat soon, and thanks again."

Jade spent a few minutes digesting the information that Wessels had given her.

She'd instinctively thought Theron must have had a deeper motive for calling her in, and now she'd found it. He'd lost his wife in a botched bank robbery. Now he'd lost another woman he was close to. No wonder he was driven to learn the truth about what had happened, and by whatever means it took.

Jade wondered why Theron hadn't mentioned his wife's death. Perhaps he'd thought it was too personal. Or, seeing as he had few social skills, an observation she had also made, he simply hadn't tried—or thought—to tell her.

On the other hand, remembering how Theron had stopped and looked over at the Candle of Hope on the other side of the busy street, and told her the story about how it had been commissioned as an act of forgiveness by the property tycoon after the violent death of his son . . . Perhaps he had tried, Jade thought. Perhaps he had.

The first three phone calls Jade made led nowhere. The Sandton Views building management team was in a meeting. Brainstorming ways to boost the building's internal security systems, no doubt. She had no luck with the firm of attorneys she phoned next, nor with the recruitment consultancy. But on her fourth phone call, she struck gold.

"Good day. Williams Management. How can I help you?" The receptionist who answered the phone sounded well-spoken and well-trained.

"Hello. My name is Jade de Jong, and I've been hired to help investigate the death of the woman who fell from the roof of your building a few days ago while attempting to parachute down."

Jade paused, waiting for a response before she asked whether anybody in the company had known the woman.

Before she could even form the question, though, the receptionist spoke.

"Poor Sonet. It is such a tragedy. We are all devastated. How can I help you?"

Jade blinked. "Did you know her?"

"Well, of course. We all did. She worked here—didn't you know that?"

"No, I didn't."

"We've been waiting for the police, or somebody else, to come and ask some questions," the receptionist said.

Jade suspected that, for while at least, the staff at Williams Management were unlikely to receive a visit from the police. Which left room for somebody else to intervene—a position Jade was eager to fill.

"What time would it be convenient for me to come around?" she asked.

Williams Management was currently the only company occupy-
ing the fourth floor of Sandton Views. This time, instead of
using an illegally acquired access card, Jade signed in at the
security desk. After the guard on duty had called the offices of
Williams Management and given her a visitor's badge, he let her
through the turnstile.

The black receptionist she'd spoken to on the phone earlier
greeted her with a warm smile. She sat behind a curved white
console situated directly underneath a large green and gold
"WM" logo. The silver name plate on the console read "Lilian
Mkhize." Jade noticed that the artwork displayed on the walls
consisted of stunning framed photographs of farms: endless
golden vistas of ripening maize, smiling workers operating trac-
tors, women wearing patterned headscarves helping to offload
bags of seed under sunny, blue-white skies.

"Thank you so much for coming in. This has been such a
shock," Lilian said. She pressed a button on the switchboard and
spoke into the phone. "Mr. Engelbrecht?" she said. "The police
investigator is here. Would you like to come through and speak
to her?"

"I'm not actually a police investigator," Jade admitted. "I'm
working on behalf of a client. But if I come across any relevant
information I will pass it on to the police, of course."

Lilian put the phone down. Her fingernails sported the most
flawless French manicure Jade had ever seen, and her yellow
blouse was the exact colour of the maize fields in the portrait to
her right.

"I understand," she said softly.

Mr. Engelbrecht was lean in build and as immaculately turned out as his receptionist, wearing a dark suit and shoes that shone like mirrors. He exuded a brisk energy and when he shook Jade's hand, his grip was firm.

"Shall we talk in my office?" he said, once introductions had been made. "Hold all calls, Lilian. And would you get hold of the delegates on this list and remind them that the conference is starting an hour later than advertised?"

He tossed a cardboard file onto the reception console in what Jade thought was a rather dismissive way. She followed him across the thick carpet into a roomy corner office with a magnificent view of well-treed suburbia.

"Please, do take a seat." He indicated a plush leather office chair and walked around behind his glass desk before lowering himself into an even bigger seat. If Jade's chair was the "B" model in the luxury catalogue, Engelbrecht's was undoubtedly the "A."

"What does Williams Management do?" she asked him.

"Well, we're officially a charity," he told her, rocking back in his chair and lacing his manicured fingers together.

"A charity?" Jade realised she could hear the note of incredulity in her own voice. To be truthful, she hadn't tried very hard to conceal it.

"For tax and administration purposes, yes." Engelbrecht's pale blue eyes narrowed as he regarded her.

"In these premises?"

"Sandton Views offered us a three-year lease at an extremely favourable rate. They've been having difficulty finding tenants to occupy this building. The recession, you know. Companies are consolidating, downsizing, staying put, hanging on until things get better. We were looking to move a couple of months ago because our building was going to be demolished. So we came here. But that's not the issue this afternoon, is it?" he added, with some steeliness. "You're here to discuss Sonet Meintjies."

"What can you tell me about her?"

"What would you like to know? Bearing in mind, of course, that I may not be able to divulge certain information to you, because we do have confidentiality agreements in place for some of the work we do here."

"What kind of a person she was. What job she had. How long she worked here. Her background, if you know it."

"You seem to want a lot of rather general information," Engel-brecht observed. His shiny shoe was tapping on the carpet, making a soft, thudding sound. "Are you an investigator or a biographer? I was imagining that you would want to know more pertinent facts, for instance, what time she finished work on the day she died and how she obtained the keys to the locked access door she used to get onto the roof."

"And what time did she finish work that day?"

"She didn't actually come into the office at all."

"Do you know why?"

"No. She was supposed to be here. Her phone was turned off so we couldn't reach her."

"And how did she get hold of the keys?"

Now Engelbrecht smiled, although without warmth.

"I have no idea," he said.

There was a moment of protracted silence, punctuated by the soft ticking of a gold-framed clock on the wall.

"Well, now we've exhausted that avenue of questioning, would you be willing to help me with some biographical infor-mation?" Jade asked.

"I'll tell what I can."

"How long had Sonet been working here and what did she do?"

"She'd been with us for a little over two years. She usually worked in the office two days a week. On the other days she would travel, working on site in various locations, or attending meetings. Her job involved helping small, previously disadvan-taged communities to set up sustainable farming projects. Growing staple crops; mostly maize."

Engelbrecht glanced up and when Jade followed his gaze, she saw yet another of the large framed photographs she had noticed in reception. This one was of a group of women in brilliantly coloured traditional outfits tilling rows of small green plants. Soaring mountains provided a dramatic backdrop.

"That shot was taken in early summer last year, and the community you see there is the iThokoza farming co-operative, located north of the Magaliesberg. I think Sonet actually started up that particular venture."

Looking more closely at the photo, Jade saw that the printed legend "iThokoza, Rustenburg," was centred discreetly at the bottom of the print.

"Whereabouts did she usually work?"

"Rural communities, mostly in Gauteng, but occasionally further afield. She was actually starting to expand our operation to other provinces."

"I'm curious, how were the projects funded?"

"Government, big business, a few private individuals and charitable drives. That income breakdown is fairly standard for any NPO, which stands for non-profit organisation, if you didn't know."

Noting the slight frown that creased Jade's forehead, Engelbrecht smiled. "If you were expecting state secrets or internal conflict in the workplace, then I am afraid you are going to be disappointed. Sonet was a valued member of our team, and her work did an enormous amount of good. She will be missed."

"I understand," Jade said.

"I don't know much about her personal life, I'm afraid, but our receptionist might be able to assist you in that regard. I am an impatient person by nature and have never been one for water-cooler conversations. Lilian is a busy lady so if you could keep it as brief as possible, I would appreciate it."

With that, it was clear the conversation was over. Engelbrecht stood up and ushered Jade out of the office. The heavy door closed softly behind him as she padded back down the short, but thickly carpeted corridor towards reception.

When she saw Jade come back, Lilian straightened her small pile of papers and pushed them to one side.

"How can I help you? Mr. Engelbrecht said you might want to ask some further questions."

"Did you know Sonet well on a personal level?"

Lilian nibbled at her plum-coloured lower lip as she considered the question.

"As well as anybody, I suppose. She wasn't a secretive person, but at the same time, she didn't talk much about her private life. She was . . . reserved, I would say."

"Was she married? Engaged? Any love interest that you know of?" Jade couldn't help thinking of Victor Theron's lean, anxious face.

Now Lilian took so long to answer that Jade had time to read the captions on two of the other framed photographs. One was "Siyabonga Community, Doringplaas, Bronkhorstspruit," and the other was "Lehalala Community, Riverside Farm, Warmbaths."

"You know, I don't think so. She was very close to her brother and sister. I know she would sometimes speak to her brother Koenraad on her cell phone and she always sounded happy when she did. I know she got divorced last year, and it was clear that it was very acrimonious. If you want her husband's name and contact number I can give it to you. But as for having a relationship since then, I can't say."

Can't or won't? Jade wondered.

Lilian's fingers worried at the edge of the topmost invoice, which Jade saw was from a company called Global Seeds, for transportation of goods.

"Did you know she did base jumping?"

Lilian shook her head. "She never talked about it. But I wasn't surprised when I found out, though, because she did mention when she first joined us that she enjoyed parachuting."

"Did she ever mention Victor Theron, the man she jumped with?"

"I don't remember that name at all."

"Would it be possible for me to look inside her office?"

"You can if you like, but there's not much to see there. She only used a laptop, and she took it with her when she was out of the office."

Sure enough, when Lilian stood up, walked the short distance to the door in the corridor and unlocked it, Jade was confronted with a gleaming glass desk as free from paperwork as Mr. Engel-brecht's had been. Only two framed photographs interrupted its length. One was of a young woman with short dark hair that Jade thought must be Sonet herself, with her arms around a much taller man, and another longer-haired woman who could have been her sister and, from what Lilian had told her, probably was.

"That is her with her family," the receptionist confirmed.

The other picture was of an even younger Sonet, skinny and barefoot, standing outside a humble-looking house. Her hand was outstretched and touching the muzzle of a flea-bitten and equally skinny grey horse who, ears pricked, seemed to be hoping for a treat.

"She did not have a happy childhood, I think," Lilian said softly. "She said to me once, that because she went without so much, she was driven to do what she could for others."

"Do you know where she grew up?" Jade asked, but Lilian shook her head.

"Where does she live now?"

"I have an address for her in Killarney, but I don't think it is the most recent one. She moved a little while ago."

"Well, thank you for your time," Jade said. "You've been very helpful. Here's my business card. If you remember anything else, whether you think it is relevant or not, please call me."

As Jade left the building, she noticed two police detectives signing in with the guard. The official investigation into Sonet's death had now progressed as far as her workplace. Jade was glad about this, but even more glad she had managed to get there first.

II

It was 5:00 A.M. on a pitch black winter's morning and David Patel was already on his way to the gym.

He'd left Naisha still asleep, curled up on her right side with her back towards his side of the bed. He'd looked in on Kevin on his way out and found the boy sleeping in exactly the same position as his mother. He hadn't so much as moved when David had stroked his hair, and for an uneasy minute he'd been reminded of something that Captain Moloi, his friend in the homicide unit, had said about how the only memories he really had of his young daughter were of seeing her late at night and early in the morning, still fast asleep.

Successful Parenting 101. A course that any police officer working in Jo'burg Central would find difficult to pass.

Of course, David could have chosen to give gym a miss and have an early breakfast with his wife and child before driving straight through to the office. But he hadn't. What did that say about his family relationship, he wondered.

He could always blame his decision on the area's notoriously bad traffic jams. The M1 highway from Pretoria to Jo'burg was bumper-to-bumper during rush hour, and if you didn't want the fifty-kilometre trip to take well over two hours, you had to be on the road by 5:30 A.M. at the latest. The Pretoria–Sandton Gautrain link had helped to alleviate the traffic somewhat, but even so—better safe than sorry.

So, here he was, back in downtown Jo'burg. No one was up and about and, as usual, the Nigerian owner was nowhere to be seen. David himself had to turn on the overhead lights which, after emitting their familiar ticking and crackling sound, flickered into yellowish life.

He checked the changing room carefully as he walked in and then hung his ironed work trousers and collared shirt on one of the locker handles. Judging from the open locker doors and the fact the liquid soap was finished, he could see that others had come and gone since he'd last been there.

Yesterday's note was a practical joke, he told himself. Nothing more. If you suspected it was anything more, why would you be here? It's not as if you'd go out of your way to make yourself a target again, hoping that this time you'd manage to catch the perpetrator in the act.

Or is it?

He let out a short, mirthless laugh that sounded oddly loud in the otherwise empty gym.

Checking his watch, he saw he barely had time for a half-hour workout if he was going to be able to prepare for the seven thirty meeting that was due to officially start his day.

Twenty minutes later, he was lying down on the sweat infused leather bench, staring up at his straining arms and the still-too-heavy weighted bar his hands were struggling to keep a grip on. His pectorals burned with the effort; the right one felt as if it had been sprayed with acid. He was going to do this, dammit. He knew he could. Use it or lose it, and he was damned if he was going to lose it.

Sixteen . . . seventeen . . . And then he heard the unwelcome sound as the entrance door creaked open and, a moment later, slammed shut again. The light stayed on this time, but he heard soft footsteps coming down the stairs.

Do it.

But try as he might, his body would not allow him to push the weight forward and sit up. He was trapped underneath it, with his weaker right arm about to give way. With a flicker of real fear, David realised that identifying the stranger who'd walked in was the least of his problems. He couldn't hold this damn thing. His grip was slipping; his muscles failing under its weight. He was going to . . .

And then he almost shouted in astonishment as two slim-fingered hands grabbed the thick bar, which felt suddenly, bless-edly lighter. With a huge effort, he pushed it up and away and struggled into a sitting position.

Jade squatted down beside him. Her dark brown hair was tied back from her face, and her gaze could have cut through tungsten.

"Are you crazy? Rule number one: you never, ever do free weights alone. Where the hell is your spotter, David? Just what are you trying to prove?"

He stared at her, breathing hard, aware of the sweat running down his face.

"What are you doing here?" he asked her.

"I've come to ask you a favour." Jade looked around, taking in the well-used machines, the flickering overhead light, the black-ened plug point.

"No . . . I meant—how do you even know this place exists? And that I use it?"

"I have my sources," she said, with a flicker of a grin.

"And who would they be?" He was smiling now, for the first time in what felt like weeks.

"Classified, I'm afraid. But not even they can help me with the case I've taken on. So, I've come to you."

"What case is this?"

Jade didn't answer him, but glanced back at the cardio equipment.

"Do both those treadmills over there work?"

"They do, but the one on the left is stuck at a twenty-degree incline."

"You can take that one then, seeing as you're quite the gym addict these days. Come on. Let's run while we talk."

The treadmills stirred into life. David set his machine at a pace that kept him at slow jog. Jade was going much faster. She was running on the damn thing. But then, David told himself, her machine was not set at a savage incline.

"Okay, why do you need my help?" he asked, trying not to sound breathless. "I gather you're investigating a police case. Weren't you able to charm your way onto the team?"

He asked the question jokingly, since in most cases, if an investigator co-operated with the police, they were more than willing to share certain information. But her reply sounded serious.

"It's a death by misadventure-stroke-culpable homicide investigation, and it's going to be difficult working with the detectives on it."

"Why?"

"Because they're part of Captain Moloi's team."

David said nothing for a while; just focused on not falling off the fast-moving belt while he considered her words.

"And you hate each other's guts," he said eventually.

"Not at all. I think Moloi is a very diligent officer."

"Which, in translation, really means?"

"He's a narrow-minded old fart."

"Old fart? He's two years younger than me." Even to his own ears, David sounded aggrieved.

"You know what I mean. He lacks imagination. In any case, my personal opinion of him notwithstanding, he won't work with me."

Jade didn't even sound out of breath as she talked, David noted. Now unashamedly gasping for air, he stabbed at the SLOW button on the console, bleeding off the speed until he could drop back into a brisk walk.

"Moloi believes you should be in prison," David said.

"That's his opinion."

"And you know what? I can't argue with him there. His opinion is based on fact."

Now Jade was silent. She stared ahead, chin set determinedly, her ponytail bouncing as she ran. She was dressed for the gym, he noticed. Black close-fitting tracksuit pants, training shoes, a red gym top. Now that she'd removed the black sweatshirt she'd been wearing, he could see the way the stretchy red fabric hugged her breasts, their shape perfectly outlined against the . . .

"Dammit!" David missed a step on the treadmill, putting his foot down on the edge of the machine by mistake, which caused him to overbalance and nearly fall. He grabbed the support rail and managed to pull himself upright and stop the machine before the belt could sweep him ignominiously backwards and off.

Now Jade looked round in concern, stepping onto the sides of her own treadmill.

"You okay?"

"Yes, fine. Just mistimed a stride." His heart was racing, and not only from the near miss he'd just had. He could never work out why having a simple conversation with Jade gave him such a rush—a feeling of nervous delight, similar to what he remembered experiencing when he'd ridden roller coasters as a boy.

Of course, to explore the analogy further, David knew only too well that this particular rollercoaster was just as likely to fly off its rails and crash in a buckled heap of metal as it was to complete the ride safely.

They'd barely spoken since getting back from the ill-fated trip to the St. Lucia Wetland Park, where he'd broken the news to her that Naisha was pregnant. Now, ridiculous as it sounded, he didn't want to take any wrong steps in this conversation.

"I'll help you, if I can. But I'm not breaking any rules for you, Jade." he said.

"Great. Thank you." She speeded her machine up again. "Anything I find out that I think could be helpful to the investigation, I'll pass on to you and you can tell Moloi."

"You want to tell me what it's about now?"

"Everything you need to know is in that folder." Jade indicated with her thumb towards the yellow cardboard file lying on top of a pile of weights.

"I might not be able to give you all the details. Not if they are privileged."

"I know. I won't ask you to do that. In any case, I'm a few steps ahead of Moloi already. He needs to put some fireworks up his team's backsides. They only arrived at Sonet Meintjies's workplace today, a week after her death. Tell him to send them up to the building's top floor. There are footprints there that need examining, and someone needs to dust for fingerprints, too."

"But Jadey . . ."

"And they need to find out her current home address—she moved recently and her colleagues aren't sure where she went. If I find out first, I'll tell you."

"Jadey, the department is at a standstill right now. Moloi's three men short and the caseload is frankly overwhelming. I'm sure he'll get around to it soon."

"I'm sure he will. And I guess a case of death by misadventure-stroke-culpable homicide isn't exactly top of the list," Jade agreed.

"You want to do me a favour in return?" David found himself asking.

"Sure." She glanced at him before returning her attention to the humming treadmill. "What is it?"

"Last time I was here, somebody came in and switched the lights off, put the treadmill on full speed and turned up the music. I don't know who, because I was on the damn weights bench as usual. I gave them enough time to leave and after I'd turned the lights back on and checked my belongings, I found a note tucked into my clothes."

"That sounds spooky."

"Damn right it was."

"The note was addressed to you?"

"Yes."

"Handwritten?"

"No, printed."

"What did it say?"

"It said, 'Do you know you have a double?'"

"Cryptic." Jade slowed her machine and scratched her head, clearly giving it some thought. "It was just one person?" she asked.

"One set of footsteps came down the stairs."

"What did they sound like? You must have had some impression of them from the way they walked. Old, young? Heavy, light? Wearing trainers or not?"

"Definitely not heavy. Quiet, but purposeful. That's about as much as I can tell you."

"You have a double." Jade repeated, sounding thoughtful.

"That's funny. I always thought you were unique. If there was anyone who wouldn't have a double, I'd think that person would be you. If this is a taunt or a threat, is it meant for you personally, or could it be something to do with a case you're working on?"

David made a face. "No idea."

"It sounds personal in tone to me."

"You think?"

"Perhaps you should change gyms," Jade suggested wryly.

"I always thought this one was as private as you could get. Now it seems the world and his wife know where it is, and when I'm going to be there."

Jade laughed. "Seems that way. I'll give the note some thought. Let me know if you get any others."

"Believe me, you'll be the first to know," David said. And the only one, he thought. He wasn't going to burden his overworked team with this, and he certainly wouldn't be telling Naisha. Not after her abrupt refusal to communicate with him about his work issues.

"Well, that was fun," she said, bringing her treadmill to a halt. "Thanks for the workout. I'll be in touch soon, okay?"

She climbed off and walked up to David. For a moment he thought she was going to hug him and he felt his heart leap into his mouth as he imagined how she would feel in his arms, wondered whether he'd be able to stop himself from letting his hands clasp her body, pressing his lips against hers . . .

But Jade simply squeezed his hand briefly before letting go.

"Nice seeing you again," she said, before turning away and jogging up the stairs. A few seconds later he heard the front door slam behind her. And then she was gone.

12

Jade wasn't finding it at all difficult to understand why Marthinus van Schalkwyk, Sonet's ex-husband, was in fact an ex-. More confusing to her was why on earth the woman had married him in the first place.

Van Schalkwyk lived in one of the suburbs surrounding the small town of Bela-Bela. To get there, she had to take the N1 highway north, drive for well over an hour, and go through two tollgates. The route took her through miles and miles of flat, brownish farmland. At this stage of winter, nothing was growing and nothing was ploughed.

Once she had reached the town itself she turned off and followed the directions he'd very reluctantly given her. They led her down a zigzagging road and through narrow blocks of identical-looking small houses.

Van Schalkwyk's was notable for having an unkempt garden, an unwashed and ancient Mazda parked in the driveway, and a doorbell that didn't work, which forced Jade to hammer on the front door with her fist. After several minutes, it was finally opened by a dark-bearded giant of a man who glowered down at her as if she was selling something that he not only didn't want but actively disapproved of.

"You the P.I.?"

"Yes, I'm Jade de Jong." She held out her hand but he didn't shake it; he just turned and walked through the rather dusty hallway and into a cramped and surprisingly warm living room. He settled himself in an old leather armchair, his blue-jeaned backside fitting perfectly into the two deep dents in its seat.

He hadn't offered her a seat but Jade perched herself on a wooden chair surrounded by piles of magazines and newspapers, letters and pamphlets, some opened and some still in their envelopes. CDs as well as old-fashioned LPs littered the threadbare carpet. An old guitar was propped in a corner and Jade noticed two empty bottles of Captain Morgan rum half-covered by a discarded blanket.

Van Schalkwyk let out a long, frustrated-sounding sigh that fluttered the edges of the discarded papers lying near him in the stuffy room.

"What do you want to know?" he asked. "I'm sorry she's dead, of course, but I don't have much time. And to be honest, I don't really want to discuss this." She guessed he was naturally an Afrikaans speaker, because his English sounded thick and accented.

Jade sensed a smouldering anger inside this man—a deep resentment that left him unwilling to show her even the most basic politeness. Was this caused by his ex-wife, or something else? Who knew. She had a long list of questions to ask but, for the time being she put them aside and found herself asking something that was, in essence, a variation on the question uppermost in her mind at that stage—namely how on earth the two of them ended up married?

"What brought you and Sonet together?" Jade said.

Blindsided by a question he clearly wasn't expecting, Van Schalkwyk blinked rapidly before clearing his throat.

"Music," he said.

"Music? In what way?"

Van Schalkwyk's gaze slid towards his guitar and his hard expression softened slightly. "We met at a Steve Hofmeyr concert when I was twenty-one."

"How old was she?"

"Sixteen, but she told me she was older."

"Steve Hofmeyr—is he a favourite of yours?"

"Not really. But back then in the platteland, the countryside, you know, we didn't get much choice. In that little out-of-the-way dorpie where I grew up, the only other choice was the old juke box at the Kasteel—that was the local pub."

"So you two dated?"

"For a short time. She wasn't taking any precautions. She had no sense of responsibility even back then."

Jade thought it wiser not to ask why Van Schalkwyk hadn't been taking any precautions himself. Instead, she shifted her position on the uncomfortable chair and waited for him to carry on with the story.

"So the next thing I knew, she was pregnant and I had her crazy preacher father just about banging my front door down. Yelling about the Book of Revelations, and how sinners like me would be cast out into the darkness."

He rubbed his beard. "I soon found out that was nothing new for him. He did it all the time. Ran a church outside town that was more like a cult. Put the fear of God into people by ranting on about the Apocalypse. Once Sonet was pregnant, I had to listen to him for hours, Sunday after Sunday. He even did it at our wedding. Loosened the congregation's purse strings, I suppose. Not that it helped. They were forever getting evicted for not paying their rent."

While listening to Van Schalkwyk, Jade found herself glancing down at the piles of letters on the floor. A lot of them looked like bills, and she saw more than one final demand. Van Schalkwyk's sour comment about purse strings was no doubt prompted by this fact. Near the bills was a crimson pamphlet with yellow writing which she found difficult to read because it was facing the wrong way and clearly in Afrikaans. Something about the "Boere Krisis Kommando" was all she could make out.

"So she married you at sixteen?"

"She was seventeen by then. But yes, we got married. I often wonder if she got pregnant on purpose, just to get away from home. In any case it worked. We had a shotgun wedding; a month later she lost the baby. For a couple of years we tried again, but the same thing happened. Miscarried each time. So since having a family was obviously out of the question, she went to college. I paid for her to study. She qualified as a project manager or some such crap, and then went off to work. We hardly saw each other after that."

"Why? Did she work a long way from where you lived?"

"Her job—well, she had a few different ones over the years, but she mainly worked in Johannesburg. My farm was in Theunisvlei, the other side of Bronkhorstspruit, just after the second toll gate. Not dangerous or difficult to get to at night, and not too far from Jo'burg to drive either. But for Sonet it was too far. She made it too far in her own mind, which was ridiculous for someone who loved dangerous sports as much as she did. How can you jump off a skyscraper but be afraid to drive home in the dark? It was just an excuse not to come home. Anyway, she ended up staying in the city most weeks."

"So she was a thrill-seeker back when you were married?"

"Oh ja. She loved to parachute and to base jump. She'd spend all her—our—money doing jumps, travelling to crazy places, buying equipment. Sometimes she wouldn't come home on weekends because she was off with skydiving friends or finding another bridge to jump off."

Thrill-seeking behaviour. Now Jade wondered again exactly what Sonet Meintjies had been trying to escape from every time she climbed to another precarious summit before leaping off.

"And you are a farmer?"

"I was." He snapped out the words.

"Did you sell your farm?"

Her question was answered with an angry shake of the head. "There was a land claim. The Siyabonga tribe told the government the land was theirs. That their ancestors had lived on it and they had a right to it. Which was bullshit. The farm had been in my family for generations. Ever since the Boer War."

Jade fought back the impulse to point out that indigenous communities might well have been living there a thousand years before that. There was no point, she decided. In Van Schalkwyk's world, history had only started in 1880, when the first Anglo-Boer war had been fought.

His mention of the Siyabonga tribe was ringing a bell, though, but for the time being she couldn't think why.

"Their claim was successful," he continued. "I got thrown off my own damned land. It was handed over to a bunch of ignorant savages, including a few of my ex-workers."

"When was that?"

"Four, five years ago now. And what they did to it, you don't want to know. Within two years it went from being a successful commercial maize farm to being little better than a desert. Overgrown, full of weeds, bugger all done in the way of maintenance, and completely unproductive, of course. The only agricultural activity that was happening there was that they had cattle busy overgrazing the land. And every time they needed anything from bricks to light fittings to plumbing equipment to window glass they'd ransack the old farmhouse. They trashed it—it's just a shell now. Ignorant, useless savages," he spat out again.

"You must have been paid out fair compensation for it, surely?"

Van Schalkwyk looked down. "Farming's all I knew, but I wasn't going to go back to it. Didn't want to end up getting robbed of everything I'd built up, all over again. I used the payout to start up some other projects but nothing worked out." He spread his hands in a helpless gesture that spoke of business ventures on the rocks, successive failures eroding his capital away. Jade wondered whether he realised that the anger he was directing at the new occupants of his old farm was probably done so he wouldn't have to direct it at himself, for all the same reasons.

"In any case, Doringplaas was special. Nothing could replace that land," van Schalkwyk said. "It was part of our history. My great grandmother and grandfather were buried there, you know. I don't know what's happened to their graves. Probably sold their bloody headstones by now."

Doringplaas? Now Jade realised why the name of the tribal community had sounded familiar.

"I'm sure I saw a recent photo of your farm at Williams Management, the company where Sonet was working when she died."

And it hadn't looked like a desert, but more like a well-run, small-scale, commercial venture. Not that Jade was going to point that out to him.

Van Schalkwyk offered Jade a hard and cynical smile.

"Oh, yes. That was what put the lid on the coffin as far as our marriage was concerned. I couldn't believe it when Sonet told me she'd nominated Doringplaas for one of her charity projects. That she was actually going to help the thieves who'd stolen my property."

"But weren't you glad, at least for the sake of the land?"

"What do you mean?"

"That it's now being properly farmed again, well-maintained, and looked after as it deserves to be."

Van Schalkwyk gave a twisted, mirthless smile.

"Now what makes you think that?" he asked.

"I saw the photo in the Williams Management offices. It looked really good. I know it was taken in summer and that everything looks better when it's green and lush, but still."

Van Schalkwyk laughed. The sound was as joyless as his smile had been.

"Exactly. That all happened last year. I went to have a look. Sonet was there for a few weeks, together with some other advisers. White people, who knew what they were doing. Everything was done up, clean and neat. Rows of prefab houses for the residents, a storage barn, even a little mill that they put up on the banks of the river—the farm has a spruit running through it that flows all year round. That was for them to grind their own flour and mielie-meal."

White advisors. And wasn't that just great? Jade was beginning to find the pricks of Van Schalkwyk's constant racist remarks as painfully annoying as having to walk with a devil-thorn in her shoe.

At least she now knew the reason for the presence of the crimson "Boere Krisis Kommando" pamphlet lying at her feet. What she didn't know was whether Van Schalkwyk's rage at his ex-wife's actions might have been a force powerful enough to cause him to try and end her life.

"Well, at least everything turned out well in the end on your old farm. Now, I have one other question for you . . ."

But van Schalkwyk interrupted her, lifting a stubby finger in a "Wait a minute" gesture.

"Who said it ended well?"

"What do you mean? How could it not have?"

"The minute the whites stopped looking over their shoulders, those lazy savages stopped working. You really think they wanted to farm? To work so hard for nothing? They were told that the first year they would only produce enough to feed their own community. Only in the second year would they produce surplus to sell commercially. But they couldn't even be bothered to work that extra year and make some money."

Jade couldn't help it. She felt a cold sinking sensation in her stomach which she soon realised was disappointment.

"What happened?"

Van Schalkwyk shrugged his oversized shoulders. "Don't ask me. I went there a few months back and they were gone."

"Gone?"

"Moved out, lock, stock and barrel. The houses were ripped up; the mill was gone; their cattle were nowhere to be seen; there was not a person in sight. They'd abandoned their own bloody farm. Moved back to wherever they were living before, I suppose. And God knows what they did to the fields, but they're like a desert now. Trashed. They must have had goats on them or something, because that land was like bare rock. Not even a weed growing. So now you tell me, Mrs. Bleeding-heart Liberal, what was the point of all that money being spent when you're dealing with people like those?"

Jade must have let her consternation show because, watching her face, Van Schalkwyk smiled again. It was his first genuinely happy expression she'd seen since arriving at his door.

13

Jade left van Schalkwyk's untidy, airless home with a heavy heart. Walking to her car, she turned her face to the cool wind that was gusting outside, hoping it would blow away some of the disillusionment she felt.

On paper, at least, it had been a successful trip. She'd learnt a good deal about Sonet's background, as well as the names of Sonet's brother and sister. Van Schalkwyk hadn't known their addresses, but he had remembered the areas in which they lived. Or at least had been living the last time Sonet had spoken about them to him, which had been a couple of years ago.

Zelda Meintjies lived in Randburg, Johannesburg, and Koenraad on a farm somewhere in the Tankwa Karoo—one of the most remote areas of South Africa. Van Schalkwyk couldn't give her the name of the farm. He had, however, mentioned that there was a base-jumping location nearby which Sonet had visited a number of times.

That would mean a bridge, an antenna or a cliff, Jade guessed, since she certainly didn't know of any skyscrapers in the Tankwa Karoo.

She started her car and drove away, but found herself unable to shake off the lingering, bitter sense of disappointment. Perhaps she was just an idealist, but she still felt disproportionately upset about the fact that the Siyabonga community's story had not had a happy ending.

Why not, dammit? What had possessed them to rip up their houses and abandon their rightfully claimed territory?

She simply didn't share van Schalkwyk's ingrained racist

belief that the community had been too lazy, too unwilling to work on their land. It didn't make sense to her as an individual or as an investigator. People would never abandon a farm that they had first been awarded, and then been assisted with, simply because they were disinclined to work it.

For a moment, Jade had a vision of Van Schalkwyk and his right-wing buddies storming the area and, with threats of more violence to come, forcing the community to pack up before driving them elsewhere.

The crimson page of the Boere Krisis Kommando pamphlet tugged at her memory. Perhaps Sonet's ex-husband hadn't been telling her the truth. Or perhaps he hadn't been aware of the full picture, and instead of moving away, the tribe had simply relocated to another part of the farm.

She was still puzzling over the situation as she headed back onto the main road, ready for the long drive that would take her back to Jo'burg.

Had Van Schalkwyk's words not still been ringing in her ears, she might not have recognised the name on the sign at a minor junction, so faded it was nearly unreadable, just half an hour into her return journey.

Theunisvlei.

Somewhere in this valley, then, was where Doringplaas was located.

Twenty minutes later, Jade was easing her car over a stony, rutted dirt road. Loose gravel popped from under the tyres as she drove cautiously through a deep dip and then around a tight, left-hand bend.

She hadn't seen a soul since the tarmac had simply petered out a while back and the surface had turned to sand—no other drivers, no other farms, and, more puzzlingly, no pedestrians making their way along the rock-strewn roadside. Only the occasional thorn tree punctuated the route. Ahead of her, the mountains on the horizon were starting to look familiar; their craggy shapes taking on the distinctive outline she recalled seeing in the photograph at Williams Management.

And then the public road came to an end. Two steel gateposts marked the boundary between it and a two-track driveway with a central overgrowth of dry grass. A broken hinge on the left hand gatepost was all that remained of the gate that had once been there.

To the right of the gateway, on a weathered wooden signpost, Jade could just make out the lettering "Doringplaas."

"Well, it doesn't exactly look like a hub of agricultural activity, I have to admit," Jade said aloud. She decided it wouldn't be a good idea to try to drive her small sedan down the farm road as it looked too deeply eroded for anything other than a 4x4. Instead, she climbed out of her car and walked a few steps along the stony pathway.

Half-hidden behind a cluster of trees at the bottom of the hill, she could see a building.

The glare of the sun was blinding, and a cold wind was making the flesh on the back of her neck prickle with goosebumps. Turning back to the car, she took out a baseball cap. She pulled her hair out of its ponytail and ran her fingers through it, shaking it back over her shoulders to cover her neck. Then she put the baseball cap on, pulling it down low over her forehead.

Better.

Jade glanced back at her car one more time. The grey rented Fiat would be fine here for a half hour or so, she told herself. After all, this was not Johannesburg, but a remote rural setting. Besides, she hadn't seen anyone who looked in the least like a car thief since taking the Theunisvlei turnoff.

Trying to suppress her uneasiness about the fact that she actually hadn't seen anyone at all, Jade set off down the hill towards the building, her shoes skidding and scrunching over the uneven layer of stones on the track.

Ntombi pulled into the garage at two thirty and carefully parked the BMW in its allocated slot. Her nerves were shot and she felt like retching. Her mind had been bludgeoned by the enormity of what she had spent the day and most of the previous night doing.

How could she have become involved in all this?

She knew the man was a killer.

That had dawned on her last week, one of the first times she'd chauffeured him. That night she'd been ordered to drive him to Sandton Views and wait for him. She'd dropped him off at ten-thirty and, in response to his terse midnight phone call, had rushed back to the entrance to the skyscraper to collect him.

When he'd climbed into the passenger seat and barked at her to take him to the City Lodge near the airport, she'd noticed that he had a narrow, ragged scratch near his right eye.

Two days later, Ntombi had read about the woman who had fallen to her death from the roof of Sandton Views that same night. She'd been paralysed by panic and fear when she realised that the victim hadn't fallen at all, that she'd actually been pushed.

Ntombi knew with terrible certainty that her passenger had done it, and that she had unwittingly helped him. Since she dare not inform the police about her suspicions, she was now an accessory to murder.

She'd expected the worst when he'd come back to Jo'burg, but she hadn't known how very bad the worst could be.

Now she did.

Despite her most determined efforts to suppress them, images of the last 36 hours kept flooding back. Parking outside a large property in Randburg—a big house with an overgrown garden. Him getting out of the car, making a phone call—presumably to her employer—and then disappearing inside the house. Preparing herself for another lengthy wait, but a few minutes later seeing him come out carrying a body.

At that point Ntombi's heart had jumped into her mouth and for a horrified moment she'd considered flooring the accelerator and speeding off, leaving all of this behind. But she'd known she couldn't, and could never, simply because of her boy.

This dangerous man had walked round to the front of the car and the headlights had shone onto the image, lit up in stark bright white, until she'd dimmed them in response to his angry frown.

In his arms was the motionless body of a thin, long-limbed

woman wearing jeans and crimson top. Ntombi could see no sign of blood and her first thoughts were 'how had she died?'

Her long dark hair swung from her lolling head like a curtain in the breeze.

"Give me a hand here," he told her in his strongly accented English.

When the man saw the expression on Ntombi's face his own hardened into impatience, and then something worse.

"She's not dead." His words stabbed her like a blade. "And even if she was, you would still help me. It is what you are being paid to do."

She fumbled with the door handle, swung it open, and nearly fell out of the BMW in her haste to comply. Under his direction she opened the back door and climbed inside, pulling the woman into place as the dark-suited man pushed her in. Then she helped him buckle the seatbelt tightly around her, holding her upright, even though her head still swung forward.

And no, the woman was not dead. Her skin was warm, and upon hearing her soft breathing, Ntombi felt a surge of relief, even though she knew it was entirely unfounded.

"If the police stop us, she is our friend," the killer told her, in the hard voice she had heard him use before. "We are driving her home because she has had too much to drink. Her name is Tanya Fourie and she lives at number twenty-three Standard Drive in Blairgowrie."

He tossed a handbag onto the back seat. The brightly coloured leather bag would, Ntombi knew, contain the necessary ID.

"I . . . I'm sorry," she stammered as she climbed back into the driver's seat. "This was so unexpected . . . I had no idea what to think when I saw her."

She also had no idea what his response would be. She was hoping for reassurance, that he had forgiven her, that her shocked reaction wasn't going to count against her.

But none was forthcoming. He gave no sign he'd even heard her words; just slammed the car door and settled back into his seat.

Ntombi had fastened her own belt and pulled onto the road,

driving carefully, heading for the house where the sleeping woman was to be taken.

Listening to the silence of her passengers had filled her with a terrible coldness.

14

As Jade half-scrambled, half-slid down the last and steepest section of the old farm driveway, she was forced to finally acknowledge the truth which, deep down, she had known ever since she had first seen those two lonely metal gateposts.

Doringplaas was indeed abandoned.

The building she'd seen from the road was only a shell— an ancient one that probably predated the arrival of Van Schalkwyk's ancestors. Built of stone, with its crumbling walls reaching waist-height at their highest, it was a "kraal"— an enclosure where, at one time long ago, livestock would have been kept at night to keep them safe from predators.

Up on the far side of the hill she could now see the skeleton of the farmhouse; its roof all but stripped away, its windows gaping holes where the frames as well as the panes of glass had been removed. Nearby was an old barn that was in no better condition.

Apart from that, there really was nothing, as Van Schalkwyk had said. Nothing except the evidence of efforts discontinued and hope abandoned.

A large field that must once have been a neatly planned rectangle was now ragged-edged and flanked with spindly weeds that appeared to be struggling to grow. It looked impossibly barren, fissured, as if a miniature Armageddon had taken place, wiping all life from the soil.

Jade thought she could make out faint, squarish outlines in another flattened piece of ground where the worker's prefabricated houses had once been situated. And down by the river, which at this stage of winter looked shallow but still fast-flowing, she could see a concrete plinth that could indeed have been the foundation for a small mill.

Listening to the rush of water in the otherwise silent land, Jade felt incredibly small and impossibly sad. Van Schalkwyk had been right. After all, why would he have lied? She had been an optimistic fool to doubt him. Now, though, she couldn't help but feel as if her own personal hopes for South Africa's future had been crushed.

And then, from somewhere behind her, she heard a shout. A man's voice, calling out a friendly hello.

Jade spun round. At the top of the track she'd recently walked down stood a horse and rider. The wind tugged at the horse's mane and tail, which streamed out like a flag.

The man waved and shouted something that she didn't understand. Then he put the horse into a canter and came down the slope. Jade couldn't help noticing that the animal moved with a great deal more ease and grace over the slippery stones than she herself had done.

As he drew closer, he slowed the horse to a walk. Now she could see he was frowning under the wide brim of the Akubra hat he wore.

"Ag, nee wat," he said ruefully. "Jammer. Ek het gedink jy was die ander meisie."

Blinking, Jade did her best to translate from her own rather sketchy Afrikaans.

"You thought I was somebody else?" she asked.

"Yes." He switched to English, which was accented but otherwise good. "I thought you were the lady who comes here sometimes."

"Sonet Meintjies?"

He shrugged rather apologetically. "I don't remember her name. I saw her here a couple of times when I came past on training rides. We said hello, but then we just talked about horses. She told me she'd had horses on her farm, growing up, and she loved them. Arabians, like this one." He patted his chestnut's neck.

It must have been Sonet, Jade decided, remembering the photo she'd seen at Williams Management of the skinny young girl and the ribby, inquisitive horse.

"How long have you been riding here?" she asked.

"Not that long. I used to ride past on the road outside. Then, one day, quite recently, I saw the gate had gone, so I came in. I thought it couldn't be private property if the gate had disappeared. At least, I hoped so." He smiled again. "I do endurance riding, and my horse competes without shoes. This farm is very stony, so it's a great place to train and condition his hooves."

"He seems very sure-footed," Jade agreed.

"He is. And his feet are strong."

"They do look tough." Jade glanced down at the animal's hooves with what she hoped was a knowledgeable expression.

"It's like anything in nature," the rider continued. "If you support it artificially, you weaken it. Allow it to fight its own battles, and it becomes stronger."

"Yes, I do see that," Jade agreed again. She wondered why this conversation was sounding somehow familiar. Perhaps it was the fact that, at least once a week, she ran barefoot herself. After all, there was no point in allowing weakness of any kind if you could prevent it.

"What's your name?" she asked him.

"Loodts."

"Do you know where the people went?" she asked. "The ones who used to farm the land here?"

"Ag, they had a land claim years back and sold up. I don't remember exactly what his name was. Van Schaik? Van Schalkwyk?

"No. I don't mean the farmer. I mean the local community who took over the farm after the land claim."

Loodts gave her a rather embarrassed-looking grin. "Sorry, I misunderstood you," he said. I just thought . . . you were probably asking about Van Schalkwyk. But the local community—I don't know where they went. Now you mention it, I remember the other lady also asked me something about them."

The horse snorted and swished its tail, brushing away flies

Jade couldn't see. Then it lowered its head and rubbed its nose against a foreleg. The rider loosened his reins to allow this and the horse stretched its neck even lower and began to nibble at the yellowed weeds.

"What did you tell the other lady when she asked?"

"Same as I've said to you. Oh, and I also told her we'd employed one of the guys for a while last year. One of the community who you asked about, I mean. Khumalo was his name, and he had a driver's licence so we used to use him on weekends, when our regular worker was off. He'd help out around the farm, sometimes take small deliveries into town, you know. Nice guy, I remember. Reliable."

"Why did he stop working for you?"

"He got sick, I think." Loodts looked away, as if, with the prevalence of AIDS in South Africa, he surely didn't need to say anything else.

"What happened to him?" Jade asked.

"It was very sudden. He started looking emaciated—we both commented on it one weekend, myself and my wife. He left work early saying he'd been vomiting blood and he needed to go to hospital and get his stomach right. But you could see he was terminally ill. Then he stopped coming. That was the last time we saw him."

The rider looked at Jade again and for a while neither of them said anything. The tearing sound the horse made as he ripped up mouthfuls of dry grass was all that broke the silence.

"He was a good guy," he said, as if he felt the need to supply a suitable obituary. Then he smiled. "I remember he used to ask to get paid in food."

"In food? I thought they were growing their own food in the community. That they were self-sufficient."

"This guy Khumalo, he wanted whatever we could give him. Anything from our pantry or freezer, and not always the stuff you'd expect those guys to ask for. We gave him meat, of course, but he also took vegetables, white flour, baking materials—hell, he even went home with a pack of tofu, soy sauce and rice noodles one time after we'd done a Japanese-themed dinner for the church. I remember he told us he had a wife who was trying to teach herself to be a chef."

Jade didn't ask if he knew what had happened to the wife.

She'd heard rumours of entire villages being wiped out by AIDS. Not in South Africa, though, in countries further north—Zambia, Malawi, the Democratic Republic of Congo—but she had no idea whether they were true or wild exaggerations. Very often it was the parents who died leaving their children behind. If an entire community had been wiped out here, which was unlikely, Jade was certain it couldn't have taken place in such a short time. That would take years, surely. And despite the stigma attached to the disease, wouldn't some people have sought help at the local hospital?

She looked again at the barren fields and then walked over to the closest edge. The rider followed her. The change in the quality of the terrain was obvious; a clear line where weeds and grasses ended and arid-looking soil began.

"Doesn't look like anything ever grew here," she observed. "Not that I'm a farmer, but this soil looks completely barren. You'd think there would be some sort of plant life taking root."

Loodts walked his horse out onto the field. The gelding dropped his head, sniffing the dry earth. Discovering nothing edible, he pawed the soil with an unshod hoof, raising a small cloud of dust.

"Ja, I can't say. If they were practicing slash and burn agriculture together with overgrazing, that could have degraded the environment quite quickly, although you'd see more evidence of erosion. So perhaps it was something different. Maybe they got the fertiliser balance wrong, or used too much herbicide or pesticide," the rider hazarded. He glanced over at the lush growth that hemmed the flowing stream. "The river banks look okay though, but of course the running water can wash pollutants and toxins downstream. Once they're on the field, they're in the soil, aren't they?"

"Do you use water from this river on your farm?"

"No. My farm, "Vyf Damme," over on the other side of that hill, is named for its water supply. We have five large dams on the property. Never had a problem, I must say, and I'd know pretty quickly if there was one."

He turned the horse around and rode back onto the grass. "Doing without those poisons is a way of life for me," he continued. "Natural, organic, unspoilt. That's what we try to do on our farm. We have the whole ecosystem working with no input from chemicals." He glanced down and checked his watch.

"I'll follow up on your theories," Jade said. And then, as an afterthought, "Have you ever heard of a group called the Boere Krisis Kommando?"

"That bunch of extremists? Yes, I've heard of them but I don't subscribe to their views. Anyway, I'd better get going now. Enjoy your day."

Giving her a friendly nod, he wheeled the horse around and cantered back up the steep slope.

Jade walked over to examine the outlines of the houses that had once been there. Nothing now remained of their walls and doors, or the floors that once surely must have been installed. It was as if the entire settlement had been picked up and removed from the earth.

The door to the old barn was gone, and so was its window glass. She walked around the inside, examining the walls, peering into the gloomy corners, but there was nothing to be seen. As she walked alongside the back wall, her foot brushed against something soft. She froze, looked down, but saw only the crumpled shape of a dirty sack. It looked as if it had been stuffed into a gap where the barn wall met the floor; perhaps to help keep out rain or rodents.

She eased it out of the hole. It was dusty and filthy, with congealed dirt caked into its folds. It was also empty, although when she shook it out—handling it carefully by the corners in case it had contained something toxic—she noticed a logo printed in black on the brownish canvas. She frowned, struggling to make it out in the dim light. Walking over to a brighter area of the barn, she could see it comprised three leaves in the distinctive shape of a trident, which she remembered seeing on the invoice in the Williams Management offices.

Not poison, then. Seeds.

She folded the sack up again and shoved it back into the gap between the bricks.

Outside, the sun seemed even more blinding. She blinked against its glare, looking away as she waited for her vision to adapt. She noticed a rocky outcrop in the shade of the twisted-looking thorn tree near the barn. The boulders had caught her attention not because of their smooth shape, but because of the streaks of rusty reddish-brown on their sides.

Curious, she walked over to take a closer look.

In this sheltered outcrop, she saw the only evidence that anything had ever lived here: a crimson liquid that had pooled on the flat surface of the rock and trickled down its sides. Dry now, it was faded on the top where it had been exposed to the sun's rays, but darker on the shadier sides. It looked suspiciously like blood.

Had someone lain here bleeding? Had an animal been sacrificed here, either to be eaten or to appease the spirits?

Jade took a photo of the rock using her cell phone. She needed it for the record because when the summer rains came this evidence would most likely be washed away for good.

She found no other traces of anything untoward in the remainder of her search around the dusty remains of the settlement.

Making her way back up the hill, Jade wondered what Sonet had been doing here on the land, after the tribe she'd worked so hard to help had vanished. Had she managed to find out where and why they had gone?

It was only when she was back in her car, which was warm from standing in the sun, that she realised something.

Taking off her baseball cap and tying her hair back into a ponytail, Jade suddenly remembered that Sonet had worn her hair short. Cropped to the nape of her neck like a boy's.

Down there on the lonely farm, Jade had been wearing her hair loose, blowing back over her shoulders in the chilly breeze.

There was no way that, from a distance, anyone could have

mistaken them for each other when the differences in their hair were so distinctive.

So who, then, had the horseman originally spoken to on that abandoned land?

15

Ntombi wrenched herself away from her thoughts and forced her attention back to her surroundings. The purr of the BMW's idling motor was so soft she barely noticed when she switched it off, especially with the constant flow of chatter from her son in the back seat. She had picked up Small Khumalo from school just a few minutes ago, the normality of this act seeming almost impossible after the long, dreadful hours she had spent with the hired killer.

Light spilled through the ventilation gaps in the garage's wall, giving her a glimpse of the street outside. Minibuses jostled for position at the taxi rank, most of them white or off-white in colour, many with dents in their bodywork, all with the compulsory yellow reflective strips along their sides.

Behind her, Small Khumalo undid his seatbelt and slid out of the car. She heard the miniature thunder of his feet as he raced away; she was just about to call him back when she realised he'd seen a school friend arriving home on the other side of the garage.

Ntombi got out of the car and stood on legs that were leaden with exhaustion. She glanced again at the taxis. Every single one, to her, represented an escape route. She could climb in and go . . . leave the evil behind . . . but go where? Where would be safe? Really safe?

She would have to sacrifice everything—her ID; her bank account; her cell phone; the money she'd so diligently saved. She knew from listening to her employer how people could be traced by these things, and he'd told her that he wouldn't hesitate to track her down if she tried to run. In fact, he was already tracing her. The phone she used had GPS activated at all times so he knew where she was. The car she drove had a tracker system in place. Even her bank account was controlled by him and was a savings account only, with a credit card but without the facility to make cash withdrawals. The cash she required for her everyday use was given to her by her employer, and every last cent had to be accounted for.

The only way she could obtain her freedom would be to give it all up. Climb into one of those taxis, paying for herself and Khumalo with the few hundred rands that was the most she ever had on her at any one time. And then disappear off the grid. But where would she go and how would she support her son? What sort of work would she be able to obtain with no identification and no references? Even being able to drive would be useless without a license.

Perhaps, with the cookery skills she had, a restaurant or fast-food outlet somewhere in a small town would hire her . . . but in small towns people talked and news travelled. And in the big city, although she was nobody, she would not even dare to stand at a traffic light begging for money in case she was recognised by one of the people who would doubtless be hunting for her.

She locked the car after taking her shopping bags out of the boot and hauled herself over to where Khumalo was having an animated conversation with his school friend, Bongani. The two boys raced out of the exit door, heading, Ntombi knew, for the private lift that led up to Bongani's apartment.

Bongani's mother was a stately woman with immaculately braided hair and expensive-looking clothes that were exquisitely cut to fit her generous frame. She turned from opening the boot of her gleaming black Toyota Prado.

"Hello, my sister." Portia Ndumo greeted Ntombi with a smile as sparkling as the large diamond pendant that rested in the cleft of her bosom. "Your Khumalo, how is he? My son tells me he is the class math champion."

Ntombi nodded weakly in reply. "He's well, thank you," she replied in a low voice.

"And you? How are you?"

She nodded again.

"Well, that is good. I myself have a problem right now, a worry in my mind that I do not know how to deal with. You see, my son . . ."

But Ntombi was not listening to the woman speak. She was staring at the grocery bags that she was unloading from the car and packing carefully into a wheeled carry bag for easier transportation up to her apartment.

Among the Thrupps delicatessen packets and Fournos bakery parcels, Ntombi saw the distinctive green and white bag; the package containing the brand of white maize-meal that was sold all round the country and was the staple food of the poorer people.

Before she could stop herself; before she could think better of it, she shouted, "No!" and grabbed the mealie-meal from the woman as she was transferring it to the carry bag.

Startled, Portia let go of the heavy package which also slipped from Ntombi's grasp and landed with a dull thud on the concrete floor. It split as it landed, and its contents spilled out in an ocean of white.

For a moment neither woman spoke. Ntombi stared down at the fallen bag, breathing hard, feeling tears prickle her eyes as she braced herself to incur Portia's wrath.

But when Portia spoke, her voice was surprisingly gentle, even if her words told Ntombi that she had misunderstood her futile gesture.

"Are you perhaps suffering from stress?" she asked. "Because you are behaving as if you are."

"I think so." Ntombi found herself blinking furiously. "I think I might be, yes."

"That is what I said to my husband the other day. I said: Khumalo's mother is too thin and her hands are shaking every time I see her. Is it post-traumatic stress, my sister? Have you been a victim of crime?"

Yes, Ntombi wanted to scream, but she shook her head.

"I was hijacked some years ago," Portia continued. "The

hijackers grabbed me at gunpoint and took me with them. They made me drive for half an hour before they let me out by the side of the highway. I was unharmed, but for a long time afterwards I found myself acting like you did. Outbursts of temper for no reason. The counsellor I visited said it is a common reaction to trauma. Are you sure you have not been traumatised, my dear?"

Now Portia looked more carefully at Ntombi, her expression quizzical and her brown eyes wide with concern.

"I have not," Ntombi whispered, but even she could hear the lie.

"Well, if you say so . . ." Having transferred most of the groceries to the carry bag, Portia picked up a plastic grocery bag, bent down, and carefully transferred the broken maize package, together with its remaining contents, inside. Another small stream of maize poured out as she did this. "Do you know, I was given a good piece of advice by a friend after that incident, advice that I wish I had taken."

"What is that advice?"

"My friend told me that, if you are hijacked and forced by the criminals to drive, you should make sure your seatbelt is as tight as possible and you should crash the car."

"Crash the car?" Ntombi echoed incredulously.

"Absolutely. Look for something solid to drive into and smash into it as hard as you can. Have you ever known a hijacker to wear a seatbelt? Mine did not!" Portia laughed. "If I'd done that they would have gone straight through the windscreen."

"But wouldn't you be killed as well?"

"A luxury car such as the ones we drive will protect its passengers with seatbelts in place. You may be injured, yes, of course. But injured is better than dead, or gang-raped, is it not, sister?"

Ntombi didn't want to think about that. Didn't want to remember how it had felt to drive the frightening man around; the one with death in his eyes.

"Here. Pass me another of those empty plastic bags and let me see how much of this I can clean up."

Ntombi knelt down next to Portia on the garage floor, which smelled faintly of rubber and engine oil. She scooped the gritty maize meal into her hands, even though the feel of it nauseated her, and poured the double handful into the rustling plastic bag.

"We were not always wealthy people," Portia told Ntombi. "I grew up eating this maize meal every night, and so did my husband. We made a promise that once a week, we would remember our roots. That our children would grow up knowing how to cook and eat a simple dish of maize meal, perhaps with some chicken and gravy or perhaps just with tomato and onion sauce. So once a month I buy a small bag of mielie meal, and every weekend we enjoy it together."

Ntombi began to cry, sobbing so violently she could hardly get the words out.

"One year ago, I made a promise, too. I promised that for twelve months, myself and my son would eat no maize meal; that every single dish I made for my family would be prepared by myself, from cookbooks and recipes. For breakfast, lunch and supper I would make food that could be served and eaten in a restaurant, because that was my dream. To leave the farming community where we lived and to find work in a town or a city as a chef."

"There, there. Don't cry so hard. Tell me what happened." She found herself in Portia's warm embrace, the two of them kneeling on the gritty maize as she held onto her and buried her wet face in the silky fabric of her blouse. Gently Portia rubbed Ntombi's back. She knew she shouldn't spill her story out; that telling it once had already landed her in the situation she was in now and that telling it again could only do more damage. But she had to share a part of it; she had to share her grief.

"For most of that year my husband worked weekdays and weekends. Sometimes he brought home food, sometimes money to buy the food. Occasionally he brought home utensils as well. Every morning and every afternoon I cooked on my small stove making breakfasts, lunches, dinners. Roasts and omelettes; cakes and breads; dishes from Italy and Asia and Argentina. There was always enough for two, sometimes for three, when my husband was home, but not always. He believed in me. He told me I had a talent; he used to joke that soon he would be able to retire when I opened my restaurant."

"Where is your husband now?" Portia's voice was soft.

Walking tiredly into the front room of the tiny prefab house . . . wiping his hand over his mouth then tossing a mielie cob into the kitchen bin . . . "The harvest's finished," he told her.

"He's gone," Ntombi sobbed. "He's gone."

She couldn't say "dead." It sounded too final. But she knew that Portia understood, because the other woman held her even more tightly as she sobbed and wailed her grief away.

16

While Jade was driving back down the seemingly endless minor road leading to the highway she noticed the signpost for a hospital on the right-hand side, about ten or twelve kilometres before the highway turnoff itself.

It was then she saw a lame man hauling himself along with the help of an old-fashioned wooden crutch. When he saw Jade indicating right, the grey-haired man leaned on his crutch and stuck out his thumb to ask for a lift.

Jade didn't have time to stop and help him. She knew that it was already going to be well after dark when she got home and, before it got too late, she wanted to try and locate Sonet's sister, Zelda, if she could find an address for her in Randburg.

Then, at the last minute, she couldn't do it. She just couldn't drive past, staring straight ahead, leaving him to make his slow and painful way to the hospital, his damaged leg twisting awkwardly with every step he took and the crutch chafing the worn armpit of his shabby woollen jumper.

She pulled over, having to brake so hard the Fiat almost skidded. The man limped over and climbed inside, manoeuvring his crutch into the cramped space with some difficulty.

"Dankie," he said. "Thank you." He stared at her for a moment and she saw that while one eye was bright and sharp, the pupil of the other was milky and unseeing. Then he looked down at his gnarled and work-worn hands. As she indicated to pull back onto the road, Jade was alerted by a sudden movement in her wing mirror. She looked round hurriedly and tensed as she saw that another man, in ragged jeans and a dark puffer jacket, had appeared out of nowhere and was running in the direction of her car. To her surprise and relief, he ran right past the vehicle without a second glance, and veered left off the road and down a stony path that was obviously a shortcut to somewhere.

Get a grip, Jade told herself. Stop being so damn jumpy. You're giving an old man with a limp a lift. This is not a potential ambush situation.

A few minutes later, Jade and her passenger were heading along a narrow road that criss-crossed its way over bridges spanning a deep, rocky gorge. Despite the badly potholed tarmac and the fact that the crash barriers, where they existed at all, were buckled and flimsy, the few other vehicles on the road— including a white Isuzu truck that had been tailgating her ever since she'd turned off the main road and which was followed by an ancient red minibus taxi—were all driving at high speed. With nowhere for her to pull over and a solid white line in the middle of the road, she had to keep her foot flat on the accelerator in order to prevent them from attempting seemingly suicidal overtaking manoeuvres.

Her overriding impression was that the hospital was in an odd location. Although she could make out a small informal settlement nestled in the hills to the left, there was no other development nearby. No town, no industrial centre, no hub of agricultural activity. Just endless miles of land subjected to the constant punishment of the westerly wind.

Who had built it here, she wondered. And why? Perhaps a lack of planning had played a part in its isolated location. Or maybe the hospital had been originally intended to form part of a node of development which, due to apathy on the part of the local authorities and/or the mysterious disappearance of the necessary funding, had never been completed.

Slowing down where the road petered out, she saw a group of patients clustered in the shelter of two shrunken-looking thorn trees close to the entrance of the modest, low-roofed building that was the hospital.

Two cars were parked in the lightly patterned shade of a third, bigger tree. Jade parked close by and waited for the old man to extract himself from the Fiat before locking it and making her way over to the entrance. Behind her, she heard the distinctive sound of a diesel engine as the Isuzu that had been behind her on the road pulled in and parked a few metres away. The driver, a white man, had his safari-suited elbow on the window frame and was talking into his cell phone, while his black passenger busied himself with watching the two women who had just got out of the taxi.

Jade walked towards the hospital entrance. She could tell that talking to a doctor today was going to be difficult. It was mid-afternoon and there were still about thirty people waiting to be seen. Some were coughing, gaunt, listless. A few of the women had brought their children along. One wide-hipped lady had four children in tow, the oldest of whom couldn't have been more than six years old. Presumably only one needed to see the doctor, but Jade supposed that all the others had had to come along simply because the woman had no people at home to look after them in her absence.

The older two were playing a noisy game, jumping and shouting, tugging at the trailing tree branches and kicking up dust. The youngest one was wrapped tightly against his mother's back in the woollen embrace of a large colourful shawl. He was fast asleep, while the other was dozing in her arms.

Wondering if perhaps one of these people had any knowledge about the disappearing community, Jade quietly asked each one if they had heard of a man called Khumalo or of the Siyabonga community. Due to the language barrier in this rural area, the exercise was not as easy as she had hoped, because many of the patients waiting understood only rudimentary English, and to her shame, Jade's knowledge of the local language was nonexistent. She ended up speaking the relevant words "Khumalo" and "Siyabonga" and watching for a reaction, but as she passed down the line, looking with some concern into face after tired face, there was none. No sign of recognition at the names nor, almost as importantly, any sign of fear. She was convinced that none of them were withholding information, and equally certain that nobody knew the Khumalo she was asking about.

■

Finally, she walked into the hospital itself.

In sharp contrast to the outside chill, inside the hospital it was warm. Noisy, too. Trolleys clattered across the uneven linoleum; the wind rattled a loose section of asbestos sheeting; and a chaos of voices emanated from behind flimsy partitions.

There was no sign of a receptionist, only a harassed-looking nursing sister hefting a laundry basket crammed with stained sheets. She directed Jade to a small office containing an old wooden desk and three plastic chairs. Rather than sit on one of the decidedly grubby looking chairs, Jade chose to stand. She waited, patiently at first and then less so. After a while she was ready to leave the room and go on a hunt for someone who could help her. All that stopped her from doing this was the thought of the patients outside, all of whom had been waiting far longer than her and for far more pressing reasons.

David, of course, would have passed the time by pacing back and forth relentlessly, a habit which she considered a complete waste of energy. Instead, she reviewed the case information she'd jotted down in her notebook, rewrote everything more neatly on a new page, and added a summary of the conversation she'd had with the rider earlier in the afternoon.

Jade de Jong—role model for time-efficient behaviour.

She had just started going through her voicemail and text messages, when a white-coated young woman passed by. She glanced into the room and, seeing Jade, she stopped and stuck her head through the doorway.

"Can I help?" she asked.

She wore a stethoscope round her neck and had blonde hair tied back in a ponytail. Jade guessed she was in her mid-twenties, although the dark circles under her eyes and the gauntness of her face made her look older. The badge above her breast pocket read "Dr. Harper."

"I came to find out about a patient who was treated here. A man called Khumalo."

A frown creased the doctor's brow. "Khumalo? Do you have any other details? We see so many people every day . . ."

"Not many, but I do know he was from the Siyabonga community in Doringplaas."

Was it Jade's imagination, or did her words elicit a flicker of a reaction from the doctor?

"Siyabonga? Yes, I think I remember that name. Do you know when he was treated?"

"It would have been around a couple of months ago."

"So, fairly recently, then." The doctor looked down at her watch, which hung bangle-like from her sinewy wrist. She seemed harassed; as if she wished she hadn't stopped to ask Jade what she needed.

"What do you want to know?"

Thinking fast, Jade offered: "I'm trying to contact his wife. I understand Khumalo was terminally ill. He did piece work for me every so often and I have some money for her for some late sales. I'd like to get it to her, if I can."

The doctor's expression softened slightly. "I understand. The problem is our patient information is confidential. I can't pass it on to you."

"But his records are here?"

As she spoke, Jade watched the doctor carefully. Sure enough, the mention of records made the doctor's eyes flick to the right.

"They should be, yes. Sister Baloyi deals with patient records but unfortunately she's off sick."

"Would you be able to pass on my details to Mrs. Khumalo if you do find her husband's records?"

The doctor sighed. "I could do that, assuming there is a contact number for her. Leave your number on the desk. I'm really not sure when I'll be able to get around to it though, because we're snowed under right now, and as I said, Sister Baloyi is ill. If you could leave your details, please, and write down what information you need," she repeated, indicating the barren surface of the desk.

Jade opened her notebook and made a show of rummaging in

her pockets for a pen. By the time she looked up again, the doctor had gone.

The woman was clearly overworked and if the relevant staff member was away, Jade didn't hold out very much hope of her getting back with any information; at least, not within a time period that would be useful to Jade.

She wrote out her name, cell phone number and the reason for her visit on the back of one of the sheets of paper on which she'd scribbled her original notes the first day she'd met Victor Theron. Then, after tearing it out and leaving it on the desk, she walked to the door and looked left and right, as if preparing to cross a busy road. In reality she was waiting for a moment when the corridor was empty.

She was wondering whether she could use the hospital's chaotic and understaffed situation to her advantage. It would be worth a try, she thought. And she knew the general location of the record office, because the doctor's gaze had moved in that direction when it was mentioned.

Jade tore another sheet from the notebook, this one blank. She folded it in half and left the room. Instead of heading for the exit, she turned right, holding the fake note between her thumb and forefinger as she made her way deeper into the clinic's warm and stuffy interior.

The clinic had a simple T-shaped layout. When Jade reached the junction, she paused to wait for a staff member approaching from the left. She didn't have to wait long. Within seconds a nurse appeared, carrying one wailing toddler on her hip and tugging a slightly older but equally noisy one along by the hand.

Jade took a step in her direction. "Doctor Harper asked me to leave this in the records office for Sister Baloyi," she said, holding the note up with an air of entitlement. "Could you tell me where it is?"

"Down there at the end of the passage," the nurse said. She looked as if she wanted to ask why Jade wanted to know, but the toddler she was leading made a bid for freedom, tugging her hand out of the nurse's grasp, and by the time she'd got hold of the child again, Jade had already walked down the passage and out of the nurse's sight.

The door that the sister had indicated was at the very end of the long corridor, and to Jade's surprise it led outside. A path tracked to a steel Zozo hut a few metres away. At some past stage it must have been paved, but it was now a medley of cracked tiles and sprouting grass. The door was open just a crack. And if Jade had had any doubts that she was at the right place, the word RECORDS painted on the door in bold white letters would have put them to rest.

Jade gently tapped the door twice. There was no response.

She glanced over her shoulder before she pushed the door open. Behind her, some distance away, she could see the now thankfully smaller group of patients clustered under the trees. Not one them was looking in her direction. She noticed, though, that her unexpected passenger was not among them, and found herself hoping that some form of triage system was in place and that he'd been seen early and not made to wait in line, leaning on his crutch, with his game leg propped in front of him.

Jade slipped inside and pushed the door closed behind her. She gripped the note tightly as if the piece of blank paper could somehow justify her presence in a room she had no right to be in, should she be discovered.

The hut smelled of musty paper and old cardboard. A large pile of folders—some new, most dog-eared, all with loose pages jutting out from them—sat next to an ancient computer atop an enormous desk. The computer was turned off; its screen blank and grey.

On the far wall was a bank of steel filing cabinets. Several of the drawers were partly open, allowing her to see rows and rows of yet more folders that had been crammed inside.

The records office was not in chaos, but it was in disorder. It spoke of too many patients and too little time; of filing hurriedly done by exhausted interns at the end of an arduous working day. None of the drawers were labelled, although the files did have labels glued to their top right-hand corners. She opened one of the top drawers at random and found surnames starting with B. How much further along would K be? Guessing three cabinets' worth, she headed for the fourth but stopped in her tracks when she heard a loud banging at the door.

Two thoughts collided in her mind. First, why would any of the doctors knock before entering? Second, the noise she heard was too loud to have been made by a human hand. But it could well have been made by a long wooden crutch.

The feeling of unease she'd had since turning down the road to the hospital grew suddenly bigger and darker.

"He's not who I thought he was . . ."

At that moment the door was shoved open roughly.

17

Brandishing the crutch like a weapon, the lame man blocked the doorway. For a moment there was silence filled only by the drumming of Jade's heart. To her immense relief, he lowered the crutch and nodded at her.

"You come," he said. "Come this way and see."

"See what?" Her voice sounded shaky. This could so easily have been a setup. Perhaps it still was.

"Outside," he insisted. "You come now."

"Where?"

The crippled man turned away without responding. He didn't head back into the hospital as she had expected. Instead, leaning heavily on his crutch, he made his slow way back across the uneven ground towards the group of patients that was now reduced to a small knot of people.

She noticed he had a small brown paper bag in his other hand. He'd obviously been to the dispensary.

Jade left the Zozo hut and closed the door behind her. Stuffing the blank note into her jeans pocket, she took a couple of brisk steps to catch up with the stranger.

"I look everywhere," he said. "Try to see you in there." Clamping his crutch impatiently under his shoulder, he jerked his thumb towards the hospital.

"Why did you want to find me?"

"I must show you this."

As they passed the group of waiting patients, Jade saw the woman with four children walking into the hospital, her noisy toddlers tagging behind her and the expression on her face one of unutterable relief that her turn had come.

To her surprise, the man made his way over to her car. The shade had moved since she'd gone inside the hospital and her car was now bathed in the glow of the setting sun.

Beyond it she saw an ancient-looking bakkie waiting to leave. The back was jam-packed with passengers, their combined weight so heavy that the exhaust pipe was almost trailing on the ground. When the driver saw the lame man, he hooted; the noise a tiny "parp," as small as the car itself.

Leaning on the bonnet of Jade's car he held up his crutch, telling the driver to wait. He shuffled around the passenger side and for one perplexed moment she thought he expected her to drive him somewhere; that whatever he wanted to show her was not on the hospital's premises.

Instead, he banged his crutch on the ground and aimed the end at something she couldn't see.

Her confusion deepening, Jade walked reluctantly round the car.

"Down there."

She followed his gaze; temporarily transfixed by the worn rubber tip of the crutch half-buried in the sandy soil. Refocusing, when she saw where he was pointing, she stared at the wheel of the car in consternation.

There was a two-inch gash in the tyre wall, a darkly gaping slit, just above ground level.

The rubber hadn't split all the way through. The canvas innards still held . . . for now. But without a doubt, the tyre would have burst once she was heading back along the narrow, potholed road that had brought her here.

She thought of the buckled crash barriers that were all that separated the worn strip of tarmac from the rocky gorges below and shuddered.

Her unexpected protector moved his crutch aside as she knelt down to examine the gash more closely.

It was definitely a cut, not a split. The edges were too exact;

she could see the ridge marks where a serrated knife had sawed its way through.

With the sun nearly gone, the wind was stronger now, and colder. It scudded over the bare ground, lifting swirls of dust.

The driver of the tiny bakkie hooted again. The noise wasn't any louder but it was definitely more prolonged. The old man turned away from Jade's car, his crutch scraping over the sandy soil.

"Wait!" Jade scrambled to her feet. Questions raced through her mind. Which one to ask first?

But he could not wait. As yet another hoot sounded, he shuffled over to the back of the bakkie where the hands of the other passengers reached out to help him on board. The truck sagged even lower once he was in. Then, with a belch of grey exhaust smoke, it pulled away, juddering over the hard ground.

"Thank you!" Jade called after him, hoping he could hear her. "Thank you for showing me!"

With the bakkie gone, she let out a deep breath.

And at some stage during this cloudless, chilly afternoon, somebody had cut into her tyre and somebody else—a child at play, perhaps—had seen them do it.

Jade looked down again at the ground. She hadn't expected to see any clues, but then noticed the distinctive, heavy tracked marks of solid work boots in the dust near her vehicle.

She remembered the Isuzu that had tailgated her down the narrow road.

A white man driving; a black man in the passenger seat. She'd thought at the time it was simply a farmer bringing an employee to the clinic. But why had she thought that? Because the truck had been driving behind her. It had come from the direction of the farmlands, not from the highway.

She hadn't given it a moment's consideration. Hadn't thought to note the number plate. In the parking space, the passenger had been looking away from her, and, since the driver's face had been largely obscured by a deep-peaked cap and dark glasses, she doubted whether she would recognise him if she saw him again.

Certainly, neither of them were anywhere to be seen now.

Had they already decided to sabotage her vehicle and known this would be a convenient spot to do so. Or was it the fact she'd taken the detour to the hospital that had prompted them to act?

Perhaps the men had guessed that there was only one reason for her to make the journey to this remote rural clinic—and that was to ask questions about the man from the Siybonga community who had died there.

Something for her to keep in mind. A sign that perhaps she was on the right track.

After checking the other wheels for any similar damage but finding none, Jade opened the boot and took out the jack, wheel spanner and spare tyre. In the last of the fading light, she managed to quickly change the tyre.

She would have liked to have gone back into the clinic. To have sat down in the waiting room and waited for the stressed Dr. Harper to materialise again, and to refuse to leave until she knew what had happened to Khumalo. But she was worried about leaving her car, and this time it would be without any kind eyes watching what was going on. Instead, watching her surroundings carefully, she did a three-point turn and headed for the highway and the relative safety of home.

18

Zelda Meintjies was listed in the phone book under an address in Randburg. She wasn't answering her landline, but Jade decided to drive there anyway. Climbing back into her car yet again, she arrived outside Zelda's wrought-iron gate at nine thirty. It was late for unexpected social calls, but she didn't want to wait until the following morning. Apart from the logistical problem the traffic-clogged roads would present, there was also the issue of her damaged tyre. The men who had done this must have been confident that Jade would not have survived the trip back home. But she had survived, and that meant that their job was not yet done.

The area she was driving through seemed to be in transition. A couple of blocks away from the main thoroughfare, Republic Road, the houses were an uneasy mix of old, established properties and recently developed office blocks and cluster homes. Older fence lines bristling with well-established trees and hedges alternated with brand new, face-brick walls topped with electrified wire. By the side of the road were piles of rubble, bricks and decimated shrubbery awaiting removal.

Zelda's house was one of the older properties and looked as if its time was nearly up. It must have been a few years since any work had been done on its exterior and the rusty palisade was almost obscured by a riot of leafy growth from the untrimmed hedge beyond.

She'd anticipated that she'd find the house in darkness, the owner asleep or simply out. But the wad of leaflets and envelopes jutting from the mailbox next to the gate suggested something very different.

The verge in front of the house was too steep to allow Jade to park so she drove round the corner until she found a place where her car was safe from the sparse but fast-moving traffic on the side street. She thought it should be secure enough there, as there were a few other cars parked nearby. Then she got out and jogged back, not wanting to linger.

Tugging the mail out of the box, she discovered it held a few day's worth of correspondence. None of it looked personal and the envelopes were all addressed to Zelda. There were flyers for plumbers, electricians, a pizza delivery service. Bills from Johannesburg Water, Eskom and Truworths, and a letter marked CONFIDENTIAL from Nedbank Credit Services.

It looked like the box hadn't been cleared since the previous Monday—the day after her sister, Sonet, had fallen to her death from the roof of Sandton Views.

A coincidence?

Jade doubted it. Looking up the driveway at the blank, dark windows of the house beyond, she shivered in a way that had nothing to do with the evening temperature.

Logic told her that the gate should be locked, but when she put her shoulder against it and pushed she was not altogether surprised when it slowly slid open, its runners protesting with a harsh metallic wail.

She walked up the driveway, her shoes crushing the dead leaves that were scattered over the uneven brickwork. Her heart was thudding hard, even though she was certain that nobody would be home in the house she was approaching.

No living person, at any rate.

The thought made her bite her lip with unease and she walked faster, bowing her shoulders into the wind as it gusted round the side of the house.

The place had a surprisingly Gothic feel to it. Perhaps it was the neglected garden with its overgrown privet and leggy conifers and Spanish moss. Perhaps it was the house itself, tall and narrow, its front aspect dominated by a black-painted wooden door flanked by two slit windows.

What kind of a person would choose to live here instead of

opting for the more conventional matchbox cluster homes that were readily available in this area? Jade was beginning to form a picture of the woman in her mind. Unconventional; bohemian; unafraid.

Jade took a deep breath and turned the front door handle. The door, at least, was locked, which gave her a small if unfounded twinge of relief. She hadn't wanted to be able to push it open and then have to walk inside and come face to face with what she feared would be there.

The paving continued around the house in a narrow buffer zone that separated its walls from the tangled overgrowth. She followed it, stepping carefully over loose bricks and tilting drain covers. The French doors connecting the sitting room with the garden were also locked. She cupped her hands and peered through the darkened panes but found that heavy curtains covered the entrance and all she could see was her own faint reflection.

She turned away, continuing her progress around the house, hoping to find a door or a window that would allow her to get inside. Even if the house was empty, Jade reasoned that it might still hold clues as to the current whereabouts of its occupant.

And then her heart stopped. Behind her, she heard a rattle in the lock of the French door she'd just tried. Then the door was flung open and a powerful torch beam was shone in her direction.

19

Jade flattened herself against the wall and froze, keeping her face turned away from the flashlight beam. Then as the beam swung further to the left, she took a chance and slowly looked round.

In the darkness, she couldn't make out who was holding the torch, but she knew it was a man when an anxious-sounding male voice called out. "Zelda?"

She didn't move. The beam wavered around the garden once more, lighting up dense pockets of foliage.

"Zelda, is that you?" the man called again, but softly, as if he'd realised that it might not have been Zelda trying the door and that by opening it he might just have done a very foolish thing.

Whoever he was, Jade decided he didn't look dangerous. And he seemed to be alone. She turned around and ran the few steps back to the open door and grabbed the torch from his unprotesting hand. As he gave a frightened, wordless shout, she bundled them both inside and slammed the door behind them.

Her arms bumped against soft flesh and when she shone the light on him, it revealed a pasty looking middle-aged man carrying some extra weight but no weapon. Bad for him, good for her. No holster was strapped to the straining waistline of his grey chinos, either.

No threat.

The man flung up a hand to shield his eyes from the glare, breathing erratically, and she lowered the torch.

"What the hell?" He was blustering now, trying to conceal his fear and the fact he'd just been physically bested. "What are you doing here?"

"I'm looking for Zelda Meintjies. Who are you?"

"I'm Ryan Harris. I'm a . . . a friend of Zelda's."

A friend who arrived at her house at half-past nine at night, carrying a Maglite?

"What are you doing here?" Jade demanded.

Harris drew himself up to his full height, which made him just a little taller than Jade.

"The question is, who are you, and what gives you the right to be prowling around in her garden?"

"My name's Jade de Jong. I'm a private investigator."

"What the hell are you investigating here?"

"I'm looking into the death of Zelda's sister, Sonet."

Even in the half-light, she saw the shock of her news register on his face.

"Sonet's dead?"

"Did you know her?"

"I never met her, no. But I knew about her, and I'm sure Zelda would have told me if anything had happened to her. Since I don't know who you are and you're on Zelda's property without her permission, I don't think I believe your story."

Jade sighed. "Could we have this discussion in a better light, perhaps?" She shone the torch across the walls—noticing the peeling and rather dingy paintwork—until she located a light switch.

"You're wasting your time," Harris said.

"Why?"

"Power's not working. I was here earlier on. That's why I came back with a torch."

"The power in the area's on." Jade had seen lights across the street when she arrived, and the nearest street light had been working too. That had been one of the reasons why this place had looked so forbidding; a house with darkened windows and no outside lights in an otherwise conventionally lit road. "Has the main fuse tripped?"

As Harris opened his mouth to answer, a loud banging from outside made them both jump. It was followed by a swishing, scraping sound that she realised she recognised: tree branches blowing against the steel patio awning. No need to panic. Not yet, at any rate.

"No. The power switch is up. It's in the kitchen. Here, if you'll give me back the torch, I'll show you."

Jade handed it over and they followed the bobbing beam across what looked like a games room. At any rate, there was a large snooker table in its centre, piled high with mountains of books and papers, and an ancient dartboard on the wall, its surface peppered with multitudes of holes. Next to it was a calendar from 2009 with the page still turned to September.

Jade stared at it in puzzlement as Harris pushed open the door that led to an open-plan kitchen and a dining area where yet more papers and magazines were strewn over every available surface. The fuse board was in a small cupboard on the wall and all the switches were indeed up.

"Did you trip the outside power meter?" Harris asked her.

Jade couldn't help but gape at him.

"What? Why on earth would I . . . ? Of course not."

Jade was beginning to wonder if she'd accidentally stumbled into a parallel universe. A missing woman, a dark and empty house containing more piles of books and paper than she'd ever seen in one place, and a strange man whose behaviour was rapidly altering her definition of paranoid. None of it was making any sense.

Harris gave her a disbelieving look.

"Let's find the outside board, then," Jade said, although she thought the exercise would be a waste of time. More probably the power had been disconnected due to non-payment.

Harris unlocked the front door from the inside and pocketed the key, which Jade saw was on a ring together with a remote control that was probably for the gate.

"This is a spare," he explained. "She gave it to me."

He didn't say why, and Jade didn't ask; just stumbled her way through the greenery and down the drive behind him.

"Was the gate working when you arrived?" she asked.

"No. The motor was on manual. It must be broken."

Jade found herself having to resist the urge to tell Harris she hadn't done it.

They went out through the gate and after a short foray along the overgrown verge, Harris located the grey metal door of the main circuit box. He handed the torch to Jade, squatted down and pulled the door open.

The mains switch was indeed down, but that wasn't all. Jade and Harris stared at the jutting ends of cable that curled out from underneath it, the colourful torn outer plastic insulation and the raw edges of the neatly cut copper wire.

The power hadn't just been turned off . . . it had been sabotaged.

Harris twisted round and looked up at her, a frown creasing his wide forehead.

"I don't believe this," he said. "This isn't what I thought . . ."

He didn't complete his thought out loud. Instead, he closed the door of the grey metal box and, putting a hand on top of it for support, heaved himself to his feet. Behind them, on the road, a car drove past going too fast for Jade's comfort. It didn't slow down at all when it saw them, making Jade acutely aware of their vulnerability to the late-night traffic.

"Let's go inside," Jade said. "I'm sure Zelda must have candles somewhere."

20

Ten minutes later, Jade and Harris were sitting side by side on the narrow sofa in Zelda's living room, which was just about the only piece of furniture not covered with abandoned manuscripts, magazine cuttings, used shorthand notepads and books.

Jade had discovered three candles in the bathroom—one squat and yellow, one pyramid-shaped and mauve, and one crimson, holly decorated one that looked as if it had come from the centrepiece of a Christmas table. These were now lined up in front of them, resting on an ancient hardcover dedicated to *Natural Livestock Keeping Practices* which, judging from the multiple wax stains on its jacket, was no stranger to this role. One of the candles was vanilla-scented and its sweet, fresh fragrance gradually freshened the room.

"I was worried about her," Harris said. After they'd seen the sabotaged supply cable he seemed to have warmed towards her, if only slightly. "Zelda didn't answer her cell phone when I called this evening. It was turned off."

"When's the last time you saw her?"

"A week ago. We attend meetings together."

Noticing Jade's enquiring look he elaborated.

"AA meetings, if you must know. Alcoholics Anonymous. She joined a year ago. I am her sponsor, actually."

"I understand," Jade said softly.

"That's why we have keys for each other's house. That's why I'm here now. We have a buddy system in place. If one of us doesn't attend the Wednesday meeting, the other will call, and if there's no answer, will come round and see if . . . if the other one is all right."

Now Jade could hear the edge of worry in his voice. Outside, the wind was still blowing strongly, blowing the tree branches back and forth, banging and scraping against the roof. It prevented her from hearing anything else and that made her uneasy.

"Have you ever had to do this before?"

"No. Never."

While searching for candles, Jade had done a quick check of the house. Although every room had been as messy as the next, there was no sign of forced entry, nor of a struggle. The double bed in the upstairs master bedroom was unmade, but in view of the general disorder everywhere else in the house, that didn't mean much.

One interesting fact was that the guest bedroom looked to have been recently used. There were skirts and blouses hanging in the cupboard and a couple of books by the bedside table. One was *Man on Wire*—the biographical account of tightrope walker Philippe Petit's high-wire walk between the Twin Towers.

Definitely the type of bedtime reading a thrill-seeker might enjoy.

Perhaps Sonet had moved in with her sister on a temporary basis after moving out of her old place.

Harris's revelation had changed Jade's impression of Zelda. She wasn't a free-spirited, bohemian soul, she was a woman battling some serious inner demons. And who had, so far, appeared to be winning.

If it hadn't been for the state of the electrics, Jade might have assumed that Sonet's death had pushed Zelda over the edge; that she'd relapsed and gone on a drinking binge, ending up in the slums of Hillbrow, in hospital, or worse.

The damage to the mains supply, though, told a very different story.

"Do you have ID on you?" Harris asked.

"Yes, I do."

"I'd like to see it."

"Sure. If I can see yours."

"Mine's in my car, which is parked round the back of the house. I'm not going to go outside again just to get it for you."

Jade took her driver's license out of her jacket pocket and handed it to him. She also gave him one of her business cards. It was white with black lettering and said simply "Jade de Jong" followed by her cell phone number and email address.

"It doesn't say anything here about your being a private investigator."

"Discretion is the better part of valour in that regard, I've found."

"Look, Ms. de Jong, if that's who you are, what happened to Sonet?"

"She was base-jumping from the new skyscraper, Sandton Views, when her parachute malfunctioned. At the time, it looked like an accident. I was hired by her jumping partner, a man called Victor Theron, to investigate. He doesn't think her death was accidental, but at the same time he knows he'll be the prime suspect if it wasn't."

Harris breathed out hard, his gaze fixed on the flickering candle flame.

"Mr. Harris, you didn't know about Sonet's death until I told you. I think Zelda would have, if she'd had the chance. But clearly, she didn't. Come with me. There's something else I want to check."

Jade got up from the sofa and walked back into the kitchen, Harris following at her heels. She pulled open the fridge door and wrinkled her nose at the unpleasant smell inside.

The contents of the fridge were modest. A half-full litre bottle of organic milk, now yellowed, separated and stinking. Some limp, leaking vegetables and an over-ripe cheese that looked to have come from a farmer's market as it had a handwritten price label. The near-empty freezer had defrosted completely, although its vegetarian contents—a bag of garlic rolls, soy burgers and tubs of gourmet soup were far less offensive finds than a supply of rotting meat would have been.

A week's worth of spoilage, give or take a day or so.

"Looking in the fridge isn't going to help bring her back," Harris snapped, just about elbowing her aside as he pushed the door closed. "I must ask you to leave now. I'm going to lock up here and go to the police station and report her missing."

"The power was cut off about a week ago," Jade said. "Round about the same time Sonet fell to her death. There was a week's worth of unopened mail in the box. All this points to the fact that Zelda's been gone for a while, Harris. And the longer a person is missing, the smaller the chances are of finding them. The first twenty-four hours is the most critical period of all. That's an industry statistic that all private investigators and the police are aware of, and that time is long gone."

Harris opened his mouth as if to retort, and then closed it again. His frown reappeared, the lines in his forehead deeper this time.

"Go to the police station, by all means. But before you do, tell me this. What publications did Zelda write for?"

Harris stared at her, surprised. "How did you . . . ?"

"I'm guessing she's a journalist," Jade continued. "Based on the evidence that my trained investigator's eyes have noticed here in her house."

"Yes." Harris cleared his throat. "Yes, she is. Freelance. She writes for a few of the leading newspapers and some magazines."

"Mainly about farming?"

"She'll tackle any topic, but she specialises in farming practices and land reform issues. She's very knowledgeable in that regard. She has a BSc degree in . . ." He stopped, clearly unwilling to say too much. However, Jade detected an element of pride in his tone. Glancing at him, she picked up a vulnerability in his expression. In the candlelight his features looked stronger, and she could see that in spite of the thirty-odd surplus kilos he carried, Harris was actually not a bad-looking man.

She wondered whether he had, in an ideal world, wanted the relationship with Zelda to progress further than the present buddy system which was in place.

Jade picked up one of the shorthand notebooks on the kitchen table and leafed through it. To her surprise, what she saw inside did not correspond with the general chaos of Zelda's home. Her handwriting was small and neat; the notations carefully ordered. In this aspect of her life, at least, it seemed that discipline took priority.

The date on the back of the notebook told her that Zelda had worked on this notebook in December last year, six months ago. Flipping through the book Jade realised the story was on land reform and the standard of farming before and after the changes of ownership. A thorny topic to tackle, and one that made Jade think again of Sonet's chosen vocation.

"What was Zelda working on when she disappeared?" Jade asked.

Now Harris's lips tightened. "I don't know," he said, although she was certain he did. "She usually worked on more than one story at a time."

"She must have a computer."

"She does. It's a MacBook Air."

"Where does she keep it?"

She takes it with her wherever she goes "

"That's a pity. The information on it might have been helpful," Jade said, disappointed but not altogether surprised.

"I warned her that she shouldn't carry it around because the risk of it being stolen is so high. She said she was paranoid about doing backups and that she emailed her work off to Gmail and DropBox and other sites every time she finished a page. She said the writing was what was important, and that the computer was insured." He spread his hands as if to say—I tried.

"Last time you saw her, did you pick up on anything that was troubling her?"

"She's an ex-alcoholic who comes from an abusive background," Harris shot back. "She has long-standing issues she sometimes struggles to cope with. It's not always for me to ask why, or what's wrong."

"Then I need to get in touch with her brother urgently."

"Why?"

"I also need a recent clear photo of Zelda and a general physical description," Jade said, ignoring his question. "There's a picture there on the mantelpiece but it's too small to be of any real use. Does she still have shoulder-length brown hair?"

"I think I'll give that information to the police."

"You could do both."

"Drive with me to the police station then. I'm not happy with you being here uninvited. I need to lock up; get her place as safe as possible."

Harris walked back to the kitchen door.

"We don't have time to do that." Jade said. "Besides, I don't know if I'll get another chance to come back here."

"What do you mean?"

"My tyre was slashed earlier today while I was out in Theunis-vlei, asking questions relating to a work project Sonet was involved in."

"Oh." A frown creased Harris's forehead.

"The cut tyre was a very efficient job. If somebody hadn't pointed it out to me before I'd left, it would have burst once I was back on the road and I most likely wouldn't be here talking to you now."

Harris worried at the dry skin under his left thumbnail with the thumb and forefinger of his right hand.

"I think both Zelda and Sonet got themselves on the wrong side of some ruthless people. That's why I want to get hold of their brother Koenraad. He might know more about this. I understand the three of them were very close."

"The brother's off the grid. I wouldn't know how to contact him." Harris's words were clipped and then he clamped his mouth shut as if to emphasise the point.

"I need to trace him."

"Well, I want to know where Zelda is. She's the one I'm worried about."

"I get that, I really do, but . . ."

Harris cut her off.

"I'm going to phone Randburg Guarding and ask them to come round and watch the property until it gets light. In view of what you've told me I think that's a sensible precaution to take."

Harris took his phone out of his pocket and speed-dialled a

number, walking over towards the French door while he waited for the call to connect.

Jade hurried back into the lounge. The majority of the note-books seemed to be discarded here; on, under and around the coffee table. Perhaps Zelda had stretched out on her couch, laptop on her knees, while she wrote up her stories. Given what Harris had said, Jade was certain that Zelda had kept multiple backups of her work online. At worst, though, there would surely be a wealth of information in these shorthand notebooks.

In the background she could hear Harris arguing with Rand-burg Guarding in an increasingly stressed tone. From the gist of the one-sided conversation, she gathered that Zelda was no longer a subscriber to their services.

Rummaging through the books, she discovered that Zelda had dated and labelled each one on the outside back cover. In addi-tion, she'd written brief notes about the contents.

Working as fast as she could she gathered the notebooks together and shuffled them onto the table in chronological order. There were one or two missing; a few gaps in the series. Those were probably buried in a pile in another room. What did stand out, though, was the fact that there seemed to be no books for the last couple of months at all.

"Right. Right, then. Good." Harris sounded as if he'd finally got his way with Randburg Guarding. "I'll wait for you here and sign the forms on her behalf. See you in ten minutes."

He paused, listening to the control room operator. Outside, the branches hit the roof again and inched their way off it, sound-ing like fingernails scraping down a giant blackboard.

And then came another noise. One that in the part of her mind that was forever watchful and paranoid, she had at some level been expecting and which prompted her hand to drop reflexively down to her right hip, reaching for a gun that was not there.

It was the splintering sound of the wooden front door being forced.

21

Harris heard the noise too and froze. He glanced at Jade, wide-eyed, the mild annoyance she'd seen in his face earlier on now transformed into naked fear.

"No . . . this can't be happening," he whimpered.

But it was. Jade had thought they would have had more time here without interruption; that whoever had opened the gate and vandalised the power supply had finished the job they had set out to do.

She'd been wrong. But her self-blame would be as much of a futile waste of time as Harris's denial.

They were unarmed, possibly outnumbered, and with only one torch between the two of them. Jade knew it would be impossible to stand their ground and suicidal to try and hide. Running was the only option.

She grabbed the notebooks, stuffed them into a green canvas Pick 'n' Pay shopping bag that was hanging from the arm of the sofa. She swung the bag over her shoulder, blew out the candles, and grasped Harris's wrist and pulled him towards the French doors.

Then, footsteps in the hallway; more than one person. Heavy shoes. No attempt at silence, which meant they had no idea that anyone was in the house. They would know soon enough, though, when they walked into the living room and picked up the scent of warmed vanilla and smouldering wick that still lingered there.

Outside, into the teeth of the strengthening wind. For the first time that evening, Jade was grateful for its noise—it would help them to escape unheard. She closed the French door quietly behind them.

Glancing towards the gate, her heart lurched when she saw a tall man wearing a bulky jacket standing there. He had his back to them and his hands in his pockets, head bowed against the worst of the wind. He was clearly watching for threats from the outside, not from within, but even so his presence ruled out that exit point.

Randburg Guarding would arrive soon, but not soon enough, and even if they did there was no guarantee their protection would be effective. That left only one option. They would have to climb over the wall into the next-door garden.

And then she heard shouts from inside the house. The recently used candles had been discovered.

"This way," Jade hissed at Harris, and sprinted along the paved walkway, following the route she'd taken earlier when he'd shone his torch outside.

Adrenaline was surging through her, making her hyper-aware of her surroundings. It was as if every sound was amplified ten-fold; everything she saw in the gloom was etched into sharp relief.

They ran past the house, past the verandah, past an ancient, half-filled and unfenced swimming pool surrounded by a border of ageing Slasto and down a sloping and unmown stretch of lawn. As she'd anticipated, the property was walled in on all sides. The eastern one had a row of electrified wire on top, and since it was obviously the neighbour's fence, it would still be working, unaffected by Zelda's sabotaged power supply.

Legs powering her forward as fast as they could go, with Harris not too far behind her, Jade sprinted down the grassy hill towards the southern wall, the bag with the notebooks banging against the small of her back.

This wall was made of precast concrete panels, and what it lacked in the way of electrified wires and spikes it made up for in sheer height. It was at least two metres high.

Harris stopped in front of it and stared up in dismay.

"I'm never going to be able to climb this," he muttered.

More raised voices and the wavering beam of a flashlight indicated they had no other choice. Their pursuers were now searching the garden and they were quickly running out of time.

"I'll give you a leg up," Jade said. She grabbed his left ankle, bent her knees. "Count of three, jump as high as you can. Ready? One . . . two . . ."

As she felt him jump she straightened up and boosted him, throwing all her strength into the movement. Harris grabbed the top of the wall, limbs scrambling, and Jade felt the panels give a little under his weight. His left leg smashed into her shoulder, throwing her off balance, and for a moment she felt him start slipping down again.

Then he got his knee over the top, gave one final thrash, and, with a brief cry, disappeared from sight. An audible thud signalled that he'd landed somewhere that was hard but thankfully debris-free.

Jade glanced back . . . and wished she hadn't.

Two figures had rounded the house and were standing at the corner, deciding where to look next. And then their torch beam found her, silhouetting her against the grey panels behind her. With a series of shouts both her pursuers sprinted down the slope towards her.

Jade flung herself at the wall, grabbing the top with cupped hands. The gritty edges bit into her palms as she fought her way up to the top, expecting at any moment to feel the rough grasp of hands pulling her back.

And then she was up. With moments to spare, she swung herself over and down, landing rather shakily on her feet, right next to Harris.

Two of the books had fallen out of the bag and onto the neatly swept paving below. She scooped them up and shoved them back inside.

They were standing in a trim-looking courtyard within a property that was far better maintained than the one they'd left behind. Better lit, too. A lantern shone above the closed kitchen door and a bright security light lit up the garden; it must have been activated by their presence. All around, dogs were barking, so if the residents were home they would be looking outside sooner rather than later.

Pushed into the soil of one of the two large pots of herbs by the kitchen door, Jade saw a small garden fork with a wooden handle and three sharp prongs. It wasn't much, but it would have to do. She pulled it out and turned back to face the wall. The concrete slabs grated together as the first man pulled himself up, boosted by the one below. His meaty fingers gripped the top just as hers had done. If she and Harris were unlucky, he'd get over before she could stop him, and then they'd be left to defend themselves, using only a miniature garden implement, against a criminal who was almost certainly armed.

As the man pulled himself up, Jade leaped as high as she could and, with all her strength, stabbed the fork downwards.

They met in mid-air. She had a split-second glimpse of his astonished face before the prongs buried themselves deeply into the back of his hand.

The man let out a howl of pain. He let go of the wall, ripping the fork out of her grasp as he did so, and fell heavily back down to the ground.

"Quick," Jade urged. She could hear the two of them conferring; an exchange that consisted mainly of expletives delivered in shouts and gasps.

Harris wasted no time. They ran. Across the tidy yard and up to a gate in the wire mesh fencing that separated the garden from the courtyard. It was fastened with a simple latch which would have taken only a moment to open had it not been for what stood beyond.

On the other side of the mesh, three pit bulls growled and yammered, their excited barking shattering the silence. Teeth flashed in hugely powerful jaws. The dogs flung themselves at the wire in gravity defying leaps, scrabbling up it with their paws in their efforts to get to Harris and Jade.

Jade loved dogs but she wasn't prepared to take her chances with these ones. She was sure that opening that gate would be the first step on a short journey to evisceration.

"Over the next fence!"

Nothing they could do but climb again; this time over the wall of the property to their left. Harris ran to the wall. It was just as high, but the climb was made much easier by the fact that there was an old kennel to stand on. Jade followed, pulling herself up onto the narrow slats. Every new property they ran through was an additional risk, and when she saw the brightly lit windows of the neighbouring home, all she could do was to pray that this resident was hard of hearing and had less lethal taste in pets.

The screech of a security whistle from inside the house told her that her first prayer had gone unanswered. But then they were through and rushing towards the front gate, whose design thankfully offered a foothold halfway up. A scramble over, a rattle of hinges, and Jade and Harris were stumbling towards the relative safety of the road.

Behind her, the renewed barking of the pit bulls told her that the men who'd been pursuing them were on the hunt once more, and closing in.

Then, from the crossroads ahead, the sound of a badly tuned engine.

"We need to hide." Jade realised she sounded breathless. There was a choice of cover, none of it ideal. Several metres to their right were a couple of parked cars and a large heap of discarded tiles. But their best option was a row of three black wheelie-bins on the other side of the road. Racing across the street, they reached its shelter and crouched down just as a pair of tungsten headlights pierced the darkness ahead of them. The shadows of the bins swung darkly over them as the vehicle approached fast.

Jade hugged the cold plastic that smelled of rotting food and dirty nappies. She could hear Harris's noisy breathing.

"This is probably Randburg Guarding," he whispered.

"I hope so. But I doubt it. The engine sounds wrong."

The car shot past and then braked hard outside Zelda's house. It sounded heavy and solid; the noise of the engine a diesel-type rattle rather than a finely tuned purr. Jade heard running feet and then muted male voices—she could pick up the sound but not the words.

Then the car's tyres scrunched, the lights swung round, and she heard the vehicle—and the footsteps—coming in their direction. Searching the area slowly and thoroughly, with the help of some very powerful headlights.

The silence with which they conducted the search and the lack of any audible walkie-talkie communication convinced Jade that her gut feeling was correct. This was not Randburg Guarding. There were the same three men they'd just encountered; the two who'd pursued them and the one who'd been waiting by Zelda's gate. And now there was no way that their hunters could miss them.

Harris's breathing was quieter now but still unsteady, as if he was trembling from head to toe. She could smell fresh fear and old cigarette smoke on him. She felt sorry for him; he was both mentally and physically unprepared for this, a man who had no knowledge or experience of such situations.

If it had been David crouched next to her, he would have known what to do. Before the hunters came too close, they would get up and start running as fast as possible. With a good head start they could make it round the corner, across the road, out of sight for just a few precious seconds, but that short time could make all the difference to the options available. They could double back, flag down a car and get out of the area. Or jump another wall and disappear. Or find better cover and call for backup.

Jade knew all this could have been communicated through just a few simple gestures.

Not with Harris, though. The most she could do was try to brief him, in an almost inaudible whisper, "When I say so, run with me."

He didn't respond, just stared at her as if she was mad.

And then a voice came from the last property they had run through. An elderly sounding, authoritative and altogether disapproving male voice, one whose owner might be an ex-headmaster who regularly wrote letters of complaint to his local paper and signed them: Angry, Randburg.

"What's going on out there? Who are you looking for?"

A moment of total silence ensued as the torch beams swung away from their hiding place and towards the speaker.

"What's going on?" he asked again, and now Jade heard uncertainty in his tone. "Who are you? I'm calling the security people."

And then she flinched as the twin thunderclaps of two gunshots split the air almost simultaneously. The unmistakeable sounds were followed by those of running feet, slamming car doors, screaming tyres, and a vehicle taking off into the night.

Jade jumped out from behind the cover, almost upending the wheelie bins in her haste. She was just fast enough to see the vehicle, a white Isuzu bakkie, disappearing around the corner. Gauteng number plates, last digit Y.

The brief vacuum of silence created by the gunshots gave way and the noise of the aftermath rushed in to fill it. The hysterical barking of dogs; the ones they'd come face to face with as well as others. More car sounds. Raised voices. Shouting from one of the houses nearby.

But no sound at all from Mr. Angry, Randburg.

She walked across the road towards the last gate they'd had to climb over. Walking not too slowly but not too fast. Wanting to know but not wanting to see.

The white-haired man, wearing dark pyjamas and a grey, flannel dressing-gown, was lying flat on his back just inside his property. Pale blue eyes stared sightlessly up at the night sky. The neat, crimson-rimmed hole in his forehead looked incongruously small compared to the pool of blood and other matter that glistened on the tarmac around him; the telltale evidence of a massive exit wound. The shoulders of his dressing gown were bloodstained too. A hollow-tipped bullet for sure, or something specially made up to cause maximum damage.

"Oh, my God, dear God, I don't believe this."

Harris had crossed the road and was standing a pace behind her, eyes wide, his hands raised to his mouth.

"Go back across the road, get behind the wheelie bins again, and call the police from there," Jade told him. It wasn't likely that the shooters would return but it wasn't impossible either. More importantly, though, the old man's sprawled body, staring eyes and bloodied head were the stuff of nightmares, and the longer Harris looked, the worse they would end up being.

A bunch of keys with a gate buzzer on the keyring lay a few inches from his outstretched right hand. Stretching through the gate as far as she could, Jade managed to grab it with her fingers before it ended up in the spreading pool of blood.

Behind her she could hear Harris's voice, several notes higher than usual, on the phone to the flying squad.

Then, with a squeal of tyres, another big vehicle barrelled down the road. This one was black with a bold red and gold logo on its side. Randburg Guarding had finally arrived.

22

Barely a quarter of an hour later, the street was swarming with people. Police, security, and residents looking frightened and shaken. Jade handed the keys and gate buzzer over to one of the dead man's neighbours; a plump, red-haired woman from one of the units in the cluster development to the left of his property.

"We should get the contact details for his family, shouldn't we?" the woman said, twisting her fingers together nervously.

That was the police's job, but Jade couldn't see any harm in assisting an overly helpful neighbour, so she followed the woman into the old man's house.

In the course of her nervous chatter, the lady told Jade that he lived alone, although Jade would have guessed it anyway after just one glance around the ordered, sterile-looking environment. Only one chair in the precisely arranged living room seemed to have been used in the last decade, and that was an ancient, leather-covered armchair positioned a comfortable, distance away from a surprisingly modern TV.

On the wall opposite the window was a series of framed photographs. A posed wedding portrait which might have been taken fifty years ago. A few other more recent looking family photographs. He must have had two daughters, since there were shots of two women in graduation gowns.

The deceased himself, in younger days, receiving an award from Old Mutual Insurance, and another of him, in military uniform, smiling proudly as he was presented with a trophy from the Wits Rifles Club.

The kitchen looked as if it had never been used. One clean

coffee cup on the draining board, and on the floor a china bowl, now empty, placed on a folded piece of newspaper. So, he had a pet—a cat, most likely, who was probably hiding somewhere. If the animal could not be found, perhaps she could ask the friendly neighbour to come back and look for it later.

"His daughters live in Australia now," the red-haired woman explained. She'd followed Jade into the kitchen. "He always used to complain they never visited. I wonder where he kept their phone numbers. This is just so terrible, isn't it?"

Jade walked back into the hallway and opened the top drawer of the highly polished wooden table where the telephone stood. Inside, as expected, she found a phone directory and a smaller, cardboard-covered index book.

"Try this," she suggested, and handed the book to the other woman.

"Oh, thank you." She paged through, frowning down at the neatly written entries. "Here's an overseas number. 61 is the code for Australia, isn't it? And I'm sure I remember him saying his eldest daughter was called Sonja." She closed the book. "Well, at least we can give this to the police. I suppose we'd better go now."

Jade glanced again at the framed photos on the living room wall.

"Just a minute," she said. "There's one more thing I'd like to do. Could you wait here?"

"Of course." But she sounded unsure.

"I won't be too long."

A flight of carpeted stairs led to the upper storey. Jade ran up, paused on the landing, glanced around. The door ahead of her stood ajar. She pushed it wide open and walked into the dead man's bedroom.

A double bed with a plain beige duvet cover and a couple of scatter cushions on one side only. In the corner of the room was another comfortable looking armchair that was the twin of the one in the living room, although less well used. Two windows on opposite walls, both with cream coloured curtains drawn. From the one on the left, she could hear the voices and walkie-talkies of the cops outside. Although the lamps in the room were turned off, enough ambient light filtered through from the security light outside the window and the spotlight on the landing to allow her to find her way around.

She hadn't seen a safe downstairs and there was no evidence of one in the bedroom either. Quietly, Jade opened drawers and cupboards, searching through piles of neatly folded clothes and linen that smelled faintly of mothballs, doing her best to look thoroughly while leaving everything relatively undisturbed.

She was about to lose hope when she found what she was looking for.

Wrapped carefully in chamois leather and hidden away in a suitcase at the bottom of the cupboard, under a shelf holding three pairs of well-polished shoes, was the very firearm that the man lying dead outside had been holding in the picture she'd seen on the wall.

It was a Colt .45. Although old, and obviously not used for a long time, the piece looked well cared for and in good condition. The grip gleamed and the barrel smelled faintly of oil. A showpiece item rather than an everyday weapon; but one that had clearly served its owner both faithfully and accurately.

Investigating further, Jade found a full magazine of ammunition in a sealed plastic bag, wrapped in another piece of chamois.

The gun must have had a holster at some stage, but now it was nowhere to be seen. Jade pushed the weapon deep into the waistband of her jeans and pulled her T-shirt out, which went some way towards disguising its shape.

The search had probably taken all of ten minutes, although it had felt like an hour, and she was sure by now the redheaded neighbour waiting downstairs was getting seriously uneasy, if not suspicious.

"Excuse me. Are you all right up there?"

The neighbour's tone was suspicious now.

"Give me another minute and I'll be right down."

Jade let out a deep breath. She walked over to the leather chair and sat down in it. She lowered her head onto her forearms. The padded arms felt cool under her skin. The dead man had spent his last night in this room, with its smell of mothballs and loneliness. She had no idea if he would approve of her stealing his weapon in the circumstances, but she knew the firearm represented her only chance.

What she needed to do was to make sense of what had happened earlier.

"Why did they shoot him?" she asked in a low voice.

A noise from the direction of the bed made her raise her head sharply. As if providing an answer to the question, a small grey cat wriggled out from underneath it, stretched rather stiffly, meowed once, stared at Jade as if daring her to question why he'd hidden there, and then sat down and began to wash his left paw.

Jade felt her tight expression dissolve into a smile.

"Well, hello there," she said. "You'd better come along with me, hadn't you?"

When she picked up the cat it began purring loudly. Making her way downstairs, Jade knew she now had no need to worry about the redheaded neighbour noticing the shape of the gun under her shirt. Or why she had been up there so long.

"He took a little while to come out from under the bed," she said when she reached the bottom of the stairs. "The shooting scared him, I think."

"Oh, thank goodness you realised he was hiding there!"

"It was the bowl." Jade pointed at the empty china plate on the floor next to the fridge.

"Well, isn't that a fine piece of detective work?" the woman said, words that almost made Jade smile.

When she and Harris finally left, Jade saw that the body had been removed. Harris, looking even paler than she remembered, was sitting on the grassy verge, well beyond the yellow barrier of crime scene tape that was still cordoning off the road.

The redheaded neighbour walked rather hesitantly up to the police to give the detective in charge the contact information for the dead man's family. Jade guessed that her hesitation was partly due to natural caution, but mostly due to the fact that she was now carrying the grey cat in her arms and she didn't want the animal to become frightened.

Jade had hoped to give the cat to Harris. He looked like a man who needed some company. But if the neighbour was a cat lover who could offer it a good home, who was she to argue? And from the way the woman was holding the cat, talking to the cat, reassuring him and stroking him under his chin, it was obvious it was going to work out well.

For a moment, Jade felt a pang of jealousy at this open display of love.

Her musings were interrupted by Harris, who said in a low voice, "The police want to interview us. That detective over there—he said I must wait for him, and that he would be ready soon. Oh. It looks as if he's ready now."

Jade took a couple of deep breaths. The gun felt hard and heavy—a large, awkward object which her shirt was doing a poor job of concealing. Any policeman would notice it in a flash. She always wore a jacket when she carried a gun, but seeing she still didn't have her own damn gun, she hadn't bothered with a jacket. All she was wearing over her shirt tonight was a fairly tight fitting jersey that, right now, was no help at all.

"I don't know what I'm going to tell him. How do I explain the fact you're here?" Harris said.

"Tell him the truth."

She watched the detective flip through the pages of his notebook to find a fresh sheet. Then he began walking in their direction.

Jade sat down on the grass next to Harris. Reaching into the waistband of her jeans, she wriggled the firearm free. She leaned over and stretched behind the wheelie bin as surreptitiously as she could, hearing the crinkle of plastic as she pushed the Colt underneath the bag with Zelda's notebooks, which she had left there when the shooting started. The hiding place was laughably inadequate, but it would have to do.

Harris stood up as the detective approached. She could sense his anxiety and suspected that her presence might have a lot to do with it. Still, he should count himself lucky. If she hadn't been there, Harris would have found himself alone in the house when the men had broken in, and things might have ended up a whole lot worse.

Tuning out their rather stilted conversation, Jade replayed the events of the previous half-hour in her mind.

The intruders pursuing them, then searching the street. Methodically, as if they'd had some training. Ex-army, perhaps. Another minute and they would have found the two of them hiding behind the bins.

And then the shooting. Two shots, almost simultaneous. A double tap, with one bullet passing directly through the fore-head of the elderly man. In dim light and in motion, that was either superb marksmanship or a very lucky shot.

Thinking it over carefully, Jade decided she was going to go with luck. There were very few people who could shoot so well.

In which case, she had the advantage, because in their haste to make a quick getaway, the men in the bakkie would have no idea they'd killed the elderly resident. In which case they would be back soon, looking for her. And this time she'd be ready for them.

Leaning back casually in order to nudge the bag covering the stolen gun even further out of sight while she waited for the policeman to question her, Jade thought her theory made perfect sense. The idea that she might be badly wrong never even crossed her mind.

23

By the time the police were finished with Jade it was nearly midnight. The detective who'd interviewed her thanked her for her time and, turning rather tiredly away, began packing the last of the traffic cones into the police van.

The area was quiet now. Empty of curious neighbours and onlookers. Empty too, Jade saw, of Harris. He'd left without saying goodbye or, more usefully, giving her his contact details. He had her business card, though. All she could do was hope that at some stage he got in touch.

She retrieved the shopping bag with the pistol and notebooks and walked back to where she'd parked her car. Carrying the stolen gun, she didn't feel particularly vulnerable on the lonely streets, but this changed when she reached the parking area and saw that all the other vehicles had gone.

There had been plenty of time and opportunity for somebody to tamper with the vehicle. Perhaps do something less obvious and more lethal than simply cutting a tyre.

Jade felt her heart speed up. Dammit, these thugs had already gained the advantage. Here she was, nervous about even climbing into her own car.

She breathed in and out slowly, trying to calm herself down. She checked the tyres, examined the bodywork and inspected the locks. She knelt down and pressed the tiny flashlight on her keyring and peered at the shadowy undercarriage, trying to assess whether it looked normal or whether there was something there that shouldn't be.

On that front, she didn't have a clue. Didn't know enough about cars to be sure.

"Oh, stop being such a coward," she told herself. "There's no way they would have stayed in the area. They'd have got out fast, planning to come back tomorrow."

She pressed the button to unlock the car and all four locks snapped up. She hated this feature of central locking.

The driver's door made its usual creaking sound when she pulled it open and climbed in. She closed the door, re-engaged the central locking, and stuck the key into the ignition.

Then, holding her breath and sitting absolutely still, she turned the key and fired the engine up. At that exact moment her phone rang. Its loud shrilling nearly made her heart stop.

The caller was David.

"You sound breathless," he observed when she answered. "Been running?"

"No." Jade clamped her mouth shut in an effort to control her breathing.

"I had a call a little while ago from the detectives at a homicide scene in Randburg. Said you were a witness to a shooting and that you'd mentioned my name during the interview. They wanted to know if you really were a private investigator."

She eased the car into first gear and moved off. No bangs. No bursts.

"Thanks for confirming my credentials," she said. "I hope the call didn't wake you."

What she really meant was: where are you?

"Of course not. I'm still at work. Only leaving now."

"I'm only leaving Randburg now. It's been a long night."

"Are you okay after the shooting?" David asked. Nice that he'd bothered to ask, even though his voice contained the same level of sympathy that an anti-bullfighting activist might show when enquiring about an injured matador.

"I wasn't really involved," Jade told him. "Innocent bystander. The shooters broke into an empty house while I was in the area."

David grunted something that Jade didn't catch, and for a few seconds there was silence on the line. Then: "Do you have a minute to speak to me?" he asked.

"Of course. Fire away."

"I meant in person," he continued, and she felt her palms dampen.

"I . . . yes, of course. Do you mean now?"

"If you have the time. I'll come to you. You say you're in Randburg. How about meeting up at the Baron on Main Road?"

"Sure. I . . ."

Unusually, Jade found herself at a loss for words. She didn't know what to say to David in response. She guessed he'd chosen The Baron because it was about the only place in the area likely to be open after midnight. It was a notorious pick-up joint, but jokes about that seemed inappropriate. And since he'd said he wanted to speak to her in person, he obviously wasn't going to offer any further information over the phone.

"I'll see you there then," she said, and hung up before the gaps between their words turned from uneasy to downright embarrassing.

24

Even after midnight, The Baron was busy. The music was still pumping and the air was clouded with cigarette smoke. The bar was packed with well-dressed patrons in their twenties and early thirties. Lots of cash being brandished about; lots of bling. Men with designer ties loosened and silk shirts unbuttoned a couple of holes. Gold chains, platinum watches, Blackberries and iPhones seemingly glued to their palms. Women with fabulous hair showing off gym-toned bodies in faded, hip-hugging jeans and bejewelled stilettos that shrieked "Bought in Sandton."

The restaurant area was quieter. A few people were lingering over coffees and waiting for their bills. There was no sign of David so Jade sat down at a corner table which had been recently vacated and not yet cleared. She pushed aside an empty whisky glass and a cup with the dregs of a cappuccino, and when the harassed-looking waiter arrived with a tray, she ordered a glass of Chardonnay for herself and a Black Label draught for David.

Her stolen gun was tucked inside the cubbyhole of her Fiat, which was parked between the gleaming bulk of a silver Toyota HiLux and a black Range Rover. From the road it would be invisible. Nobody had followed her here and she'd paid the car guard twenty rands to keep a special eye out for anyone who approached her vehicle. So, for now at least, she could relax and wait for David to arrive.

He walked in a few minutes later. Tall, dark-skinned, blue-eyed, and with a presence about him that turned the heads of several women at the bar in spite of the fact that he was about ten years older—and wearing clothes ten times cheaper—than the men who were chatting them up. If he'd been her partner, Jade would have felt proud to see him arrive. He wasn't, though, and that left her feeling lonely and frustrated. She'd gladly have swapped places with any of the girls at the bar. At least they had some chance of a future with their drinking partners.

David folded himself into the chair opposite Jade.

"Thanks for making the time," he said.

"No problem. As you know, I was on my way home." She pushed the beer over towards him and he clinked glasses with her before draining half the contents in a single gulp.

"What happened with the shooting?" he asked, and Jade felt suddenly hurt at the thought that perhaps this was why he'd asked to meet up with her, because he didn't believe what she'd told him and suspected that she had instigated it.

Doing her best to rise above these misgivings, Jade gave him a brief outline of her latest puzzling case.

David listened with his chin propped on his steepled fingers, interrupting her only to order them another round of drinks. Although he'd wanted to meet up so urgently, he didn't seem to be in any hurry to tell her what was bothering him.

"Wait a minute," he asked the waiter as he was preparing to leave. "Is your kitchen still open?"

"Yes, for another few minutes. I'll bring . . ."

"No, no, I don't need a menu. Can I have a cheeseburger and chips, please? I'm starving. All I've eaten today is a slice of stale carrot cake. It was Captain Thembi's birthday on Monday." He glanced at Jade. "Anything for you?"

"No, thanks. I've had supper." If you could call a banana and a large bag of chilli cashews eaten in the car while driving back to Jo'burg "supper."

"So you have a theory about why Zelda Meintjies's gone missing, then?" David asked when the waiter had gone.

"I'm sure it's got something to do with one of the pieces she's working on, and part of the reason I think so is that I couldn't find any of her most recent notebooks. Only the older ones."

"She could have bought a Dictaphone and stopped using them."

"That's a possibility, I suppose."

"Or she had them with her. In her car, perhaps. Which there was no sign of, by the way." And, in the mess of papers in the house, Jade hadn't noticed any documentation relating to a vehicle. She could only hope that Harris knew the car's make and model, or better still remembered the number plate, and had given this information to the police.

"And how is Zelda's disappearance linked to her sister's death? It can't be coincidence, but which happened first?"

"I don't know. All I can tell you is that both events happened at around the same time."

"So, do you think the men who fired the shots tonight are also responsible for pushing Sonet off the building after jimmying her parachute?"

"Well, there was another set of footprints on the top floor of Sandton Views. I still don't know who they belong to. But what puzzles me, though, is that if you wanted to kill someone there are far easier ways to do it."

"Plenty, yes. But not so many that would point a charge of culpable homicide directly at one person."

"True. It must have taken some planning to arrange that would-be accident though—and how did they know she was going to be jumping that particular night?"

"That's a good question."

A short but easy silence followed. Then the waiter appeared with David's burger and he started in on it immediately, eating at the same speed that a pack of wild dogs who'd just made a kill might have done.

"You reckon the guys who shot the old man also slashed your tyre?" he said, dunking a chip in tomato ketchup.

"I'm pretty sure. I recognised the truck they were driving, although I didn't get the license plates, unfortunately."

"Probably fake in any case. You're remarkably calm about this, Jade."

"I've thought it through. The shot was a lucky one. That means they're trigger-happy idiots, not professionals."

"They cut your tyre at the hospital and they turned up in Randburg just a few hours later. They're not going to stop, Jade. Are you sure they're not tracking your car?"

"Would you have bothered to put an expensive tracking device on a vehicle that you assumed was going to end up rolling over a steep cliff? Finding me now will mean starting from scratch."

"Well, how did they find you in the first place? What were they doing driving round a remote rural area waiting for you to pitch up at the farm and then go to the hospital?"

"Good point, David. I don't know why they were out there or if they were waiting for me, or for someone else. In any case, though, they've lost me now. But, if they're halfway competent, they'll have discovered where I live by tomorrow morning. If they're not it could take longer."

"And then?" He was frowning now.

"I'll know who they are."

"They're not playing games, Jade."

"Nor am I." Bravado, she knew, even with the dubious assistance of an old pistol.

David said nothing. Just took another swallow of beer. The frown hadn't left his face. The two deep lines in between his eyebrows looked as if they were about to become a permanent fixture.

"Those notes. Have you had any more of them?" she asked, changing the subject. She was sure he must have done, otherwise he wouldn't have wanted to meet up so urgently.

"I have. One. This evening, in fact."

"Same place?"

"Yes. At the gym, but this time it was taped to the door."

"And the message?"

"Different this time."

"Well?"

David didn't look like he actually wanted to tell her. He stared down at his empty plate and mumbled something inaudible.

"You don't *have* to tell me," Jade said.

"You might as well know. It said: So who's the proud father-to-be, then?"

Jade couldn't help it. The mention of David's pregnant wife triggered a surge of jealousy that made her want to get up, knocking her chair over and perhaps her half-full wineglass as well, and storm out of the restaurant. But that was only for an instant, before the seriousness of the situation hit home.

"They're involving your family now?"

"Yes."

And whoever was leaving the notes knew about his personal circumstances. This was all the more disturbing when Jade remembered that, as part of the Organised Crime division, David routinely dealt with drug dealers, arms smugglers and human traffickers. Ruthless, violent and powerful criminals who were more than capable of following through on their threats. And if they'd found out where he worked out, that meant they also knew where he lived.

With a nine-year-old boy and a heavily pregnant wife, David was at his most vulnerable, especially since Kevin had been abducted by kidnappers the previous year. Although the boy had been sedated for the duration of his capture, and was virtually unscarred by the event, David had been through the worst kind of hell, and Jade knew it was one of his deepest fears that something similar might happen again.

"Naisha and Kevin are leaving town tomorrow morning for the long weekend," David said as if reading her thoughts. "Naisha's uncle is over from London and they're all having a big family get-together in the Pilanesberg. When she asked me this morning if I really thought it was a good idea for her to go, I just about jumped with joy. I'm hoping now she didn't realise something was wrong."

"Let me know the next time you decide to go to the gym. Someone's obviously watching your movements. If you do, then I can keep an eye on the entrance."

"Thanks. I will." But he said it reluctantly, as if he didn't want to expose her to his dangers when she already had her own to deal with.

"Has anybody else in your team received similar notes?"

"I haven't heard anyone else mention it."

"And there's nobody you suspect? No case causing any particular problems?"

"Honestly, Jade, there's nothing, no one I can think of. And where there've been threats in the past they've contained specifics. You know the type. 'Drop the Rajnee case or your family will suffer'. Usually arrives in a grubby envelope, printed in all caps, with at least two spelling mistakes."

Jade smiled. "Well, let's think positively. Perhaps this is the disgruntled ex-partner of someone who you've already put in prison, and all they want to do is mess with your mind for a while."

"Let's hope so," David said, sounding unconvinced.

He insisted on paying the bill, and just before they left, he dug in his pocket and slid a small bunch of keys and a black remote control across the table.

"Take these and please use them," he said.

Jade stared down at them. "How? For what?"

"They're for my house in Turffontein. We tried to sell it a few months back, as you know, but the market's stagnant, so we've been renting it out. It's between tenants at the moment and I'd really appreciate it if you would stay there—for one or two nights at least."

Seeing the doubt in Jade's eyes and misconstruing the reason for it, he continued. "It's very secure. The gate and the garage are automated now and there are reinforced burglar bars on the windows. It's partly furnished—you'll be comfortable there."

"Thanks. Really." Jade took the keys. They were still warm from being in his pocket. Lucky keys. She and David hadn't touched at all.

And then, to her astonishment, he took her hand. Reached across the table and closed his long, slim fingers over hers. His grasp was as warm as the keys had been and his touch felt heartbreakingly familiar.

"Just be careful, Jadey, okay?"

Jade didn't reply. She didn't have the words. How could she tell him that she'd only now realised this meeting was not about him. This was about her. He was worried and doing his best to look after her.

David released her hand and got to his feet, and waited for her to do the same. Then he walked her to the Baron's open door and out into the half-empty car park.

25

David's Turffontein house was indeed tightly locked up—security gates closed and windows closely barred. It resembled a mini prison in a street that looked shabbier and more dilapidated than Jade remembered from the last time she'd been there.

As it was being rented out, Jade didn't expect to find any personal stuff of David's around, and there wasn't. The interior smelled of furniture polish and fresh paint. Turning on the hallway light, which was covered by what looked like a brand new lampshade, she made her way into the bedroom. The bed was stripped, but the black bin bag on top of the mattress contained bedding, clean and ironed. In lieu of a bedside table, a wooden chair stood beside the bed.

Before Jade went to sleep there was one final and important task she had to do.

She took the stolen gun and clipped a fresh magazine into place. Then she went outside into the chilly night, holding it muzzle-down, feeling the comfort of its grip in her hand, the shape simultaneously familiar and new.

The house and its tiny garden didn't provide many opportunities for target practice. She would have to make do with standing up against the wall and aiming it at the tool shed on the other side of the dry stretch of grass.

She took a steady breath. Sighted. Tightened her finger on the trigger and sent a silent apology to the residents in the surrounding houses for disturbing their sleep, even though she was sure that in this area gunshots were not an uncommon sound, and equally sure that nobody would be able to pinpoint exactly where it had come from.

She aimed for the centre of the second board from the left, about a foot below the corrugated iron roof. As she pulled the trigger she felt the sound blast her eardrums and the hard kick of the grip in her hand as the muzzle flash briefly flared and the used shell tumbled to the ground.

Jade picked it up and held her breath. Some dogs began to bark, but apart from that there was no response of any kind.

The gun worked, at least. Now to find out how accurate it was.

The bullet had left a perfect circle in the exact centre of the second plank, a foot from the top. From a distance it looked like a knot in the wood. She was sure David would easily be able to fix it with a tube of Pratley's putty, if he noticed it at all.

It had punched right through the half-inch board but the wood had slowed its speed, flattened and distorted it, and sent it tumbling down onto the shed's dusty floor. She put it in her pocket with the shell.

She had a weapon that not only worked but was also superbly accurate.

Double bonus.

Back inside, she locked the front door and then the bedroom door. In one of the built-in cupboards she found a small fan heater to help to dispel the empty chill of the room. Then Jade unpacked the sheets and duvet and made the bed, put her cell phone on the chair after setting the alarm for six, undressed quickly and eased herself between the cold sheets.

"That's enough for one day, I think," she said aloud.

Five hours of sleep was all she could have, and tomorrow would be another long day. She needed to trace Harris. He was a potential source of information and she was annoyed that he'd left while she was being interviewed. Whilst finding him would be a relatively easy job, it would take up time she didn't have.

She also needed to report back to Victor Theron. To inform her client about the latest developments in the investigation, and establish whether the police had been in touch with him, or made any progress regarding the circumstances surrounding Sonet's death.

But her biggest priority was going to be keeping ahead of the men who had slashed her tyre at the hospital and then turned up at Zelda's house a few hours later. Although logic told her she was safe and that they wouldn't think to look for her here, and that she needed her sleep, instinct disagreed.

Instinct told her to be wary of every noise. Better sleep-starved than dead.

Eventually, Jade's thoughts drifted to the man and the horse she'd met earlier in the day at the abandoned farm. The sheen of the Arab's coat, the smell of leather and sweat, the surefooted-ness as the pair had cantered away over the stony ground.

Jade slipped into sleep; her dreams punctuated by the rhyth-mic beat of horses' hooves.

The buzzing of the alarm tore Ntombi from a night of troubled rest. She fumbled for the OFF button, sat up and tugged her sweat-damp nightie away from her body. Her thoughts were racing so fast that the ticking of the old-fashioned clock next to the bed seemed sluggish by comparison. She switched on the light, banishing the oppressive darkness of the room.

She would never rely on an electric alarm clock. Not in a city where power cuts were so frequent. Besides, this clock had been a birthday present from her husband two years ago. Khumalo had thought it would be useful for her to help time her cooking, and it had been. Dish after dish had been cooked to perfection thanks to the clock that had stood on a trestle table in her hut, safely out of the way of the steaming pots on the hot plate and the baking trays slotted into the tiny oven.

Pushing the thoughts of her husband aside, Ntombi scrambled out of bed, calling to her son to get ready; that they needed to leave in forty-five minutes. His excited response told her that he'd woken up long before her, anticipating the fun of the day ahead. It was the last school day of term and his class was going on an outing to the Apartheid Museum and Gold Reef City.

"Take your school bag just in case you need it," she told him.

What did her boy need to take with him? Muzzily, she remembered Small Khumalo having given her a printed list of requirements for the day. Where had she put it? It had been the day when her employer's anonymous client had arrived, and everything since then had been eclipsed by the horror of what she'd had to participate in.

After a frantic search, tipping the contents of her handbag onto the duvet and then turning her bedroom practically upside down, she remembered she'd left it in the BMW's cubbyhole.

"Stupid, stupid woman," she chastised herself. She hurriedly tugged on a pair of blue jeans and a black woollen jersey. Wriggled her feet into her comfortable moccasins. She grabbed the keys and headed for the front door.

She was about to close it behind her when she heard the faint trilling of her cell phone in the bedroom.

Ntombi snatched the door open again and rushed back to the room. She grabbed the phone and retraced her steps, glancing down at the screen as she did so.

Her heart sank when she saw it was her employer on the line.

"Hello." she said softly, closing the front door behind her and pressing the button to call the lift.

"Plans have changed for today." She realised to her dismay that he sounded as hyped-up as Khumalo, which could only mean trouble. "You need to pick up our guest in half an hour. He'll be waiting outside the main entrance of the Sandton Sun hotel. It's going to be a very long day; in fact, you'll probably only get back tomorrow. Make sure the car has a full tank before you leave. Oh, and your dress code is to be smart-traditional, suitable for a road trip, and with shoes you can walk in."

But . . .

Ntombi never even uttered the word out loud. How could she? "I'll be there," she said in a low voice.

The lift arrived and she stepped inside. Ntombi pressed the button for the basement without even having to look and stared blankly at the closed doors as she descended the five floors.

Half an hour. She needed to get going right now. Going to the petrol station and filling up the car would take fifteen minutes, and getting to Sandton another five. That left her only ten minutes to pick out something suitable to wear.

It also meant Small Khumalo couldn't go on his school trip; the outing he'd been looking forward to for a fortnight.

The day would turn into another of those that her boy spent locked up alone in the apartment while Ntombi racked her brains for another excuse to explain his absence from school. Another handwritten note lying about him having a temperature that day; that the car had broken down; that he'd had an appointment with the bereavement counsellor—as much as she hated to use his father's death as an excuse, desperation had driven her to do so in the past two weeks.

The lift doors sucked open, exposing her to the oily tang of the basement air.

Leaden-footed, she trailed over to her car. She'd better go and fill it up right now and then come back, get changed and explain the situation to her son, who would be devastated. Then she would lock him in the apartment and leave.

Leave.

That was what she needed to do—leave. Get out. Run. More urgently than ever before, she needed to go.

She'd realised now her employer was never going to keep the promise he'd made. He'd assured her that he'd find out what had happened to her husband and her community. He'd guaranteed that he'd get in contact with the woman whose details she'd passed on to him.

He had broken his word. He was never going to help her to discover why her husband had died and why their community had been destroyed. All he was doing was using her to assist him with his own criminal activities.

And that was the problem. She was working for a criminal.

Where would they be able to hide and not be found? How could she protect her boy, now and in the future, with no money, no ID, no job, no surviving family or community, and no prospects? Her employer had told her he could buy connections and contacts in any city and any town he chose. And that he could, and would, pay people to find her and her boy no matter where they tried to hide.

Was he telling the truth? She wasn't sure, but she couldn't risk finding out the hard way.

Blinking tears away yet again, Ntombi faced up to the stark reality of her situation. She had to escape, but she had not the faintest idea how.

"My sister!" Ntombi spun round to see Portia's large and cheerful form approaching from the side of the garage where the lifts to the more expensive apartments, including Portia's own private lift, were located. She was swathed in a bright orange, green and black printed traditional dress that fitted the criteria of "smart but colourful" to a T.

"Is this not the most unbearable hour of the morning? What is the school thinking?" she laughed. "They are cruel, I think. Cruel to us, making us get up in the dark and the cold. I was hoping my husband could do the lift this morning, but he is in Polokwane today for the ANC conference. Where is my naughty son now?"

Portia's smile narrowed a fraction. "Bongani!" she yelled, her voice reverberating off the garage walls. "Come on. You wanted to leave early, and now you are playing around! Are you with Khumalo?"

"Khumalo isn't going," Ntombi said. Her voice sounded flat and dead.

Portia gaped at her, eyes wide, and clapped a hand over her open mouth.

"My sister, why not? What has happened? Is he ill? *Hai'khona*, he will be so disappointed, the small one!"

"I've just had a message from my employer. I have to start work early today. Now, in fact." It was all Ntombi dared to say.

"That is the only problem? You can't take him to school?"

Ntombi nodded, wiping a hand over her eyes.

"Then it is no problem at all. He can travel with me."

"But I'm working into the night. I might only be back sometime tomorrow."

"He can sleep over. They are good friends, those two. In fact, I was going to ask you when I last saw you—you are welcome to think about this, of course—but we are going down to the coast for a week tomorrow, to escape this horrible Johannesburg winter weather. Bongani was hoping to take his classmate Richard with him, but he is going overseas with his parents. So then he asked me if Khumalo could come along."

"To the sea?" Ntombi's eyes widened.

"To Umhlanga. The most beautiful beaches in the country, in my opinion."

"I would love him to go!"

"We will leave late tomorrow morning. Will you be back from work by then?"

"Probably not."

"Well, then, Khumalo must pack his bag now. They will not need much for the holiday. Some shorts, some T-shirts, a swimming costume. Nothing smart. Here, write your phone number down on this business card and take one of mine so we can stay in contact. Go now and call your son. Tell him to pack quickly and hurry down to our car. And when we get back from holiday," Portia's eyes flashed sparks, "you and I are going to make an appointment to see a labour lawyer. No, don't look so frightened, and don't try to argue with me. We are going to do it because I think your employer is abusing you."

Her unwanted passenger was standing just inside the foyer of the Sandton Sun when she pulled up—ten minutes late thanks to the discussion she'd had with Portia in the garage, and having to help Small Khumalo pack his bags, and the even more frustrating fact that the first petrol station she went to had been out of unleaded fuel. She was sweating under the long sleeves of the traditional outfit she now wore—a similar style to the one Portia had sported, although more muted, in rustic browns, creams and beiges, with intricate beadwork around the neckline.

He was dressed in a sharply cut black suit, red shirt and black tie. Dark Oakley shades covered his eyes. He looked every inch the wealthy businessman apart from his shoes, which although well polished were not dress shoes but tough-looking, steel-capped work boots.

He was speaking on his cell phone as she pulled up, tyres squealing briefly. He carried a briefcase in his other hand, which from the way he was handling it was almost empty, and a bulging black gym bag over his shoulder, which looked full and heavy and clanked when he hefted it onto the floor behind his seat.

"No, it's okay. She's here now," he said into the phone as he slammed the door. Ntombi realised with a sense of dread that he was speaking to her employer, who now knew she'd arrived late.

"Get onto the highway," he told her impatiently, before resuming his conversation. "We'll go straight there. It's ready, right?" He waited, listened. What was her employer telling him? Try as she might, Ntombi could hear nothing from the other side of the phone except a faint clacking.

"Yes, I can do that, but I want the money today. No EFT, that takes time. I want cash in my hands. Have it waiting for me when I get back to Sandton."

The clacking on the other end of the line suddenly assumed a higher pitch.

"I don't care. It's a risky job. I need it all up front." Another pause. "All right, then. Seventy per cent today; the other thirty via EFT to the Absa account tomorrow."

He waited again before speaking. "Your buyers are meeting you tomorrow night? I'll get the goods to you early tomorrow evening. Seven P.M. Yes, I can deal with the woman at the same time."

The woman?

Ntombi's heart nearly stopped as she remembered the unconscious female she'd been forced to transport the last time she'd chauffeured the man. She hadn't known what had happened to her, but she still suspected the worst. And who was she and how had she become involved? And in what? Trafficking? Drugs?

Ntombi didn't know. She didn't even know whether she felt relieved or terrified that the woman was obviously still alive.

Then he paused, listened, and glanced briefly over at Ntombi.

"Yes," he said coldly. "I can do that too."

26

Ntombi knew it was going to be a long drive when, at nine A.M., after three solid hours of driving, she was told to pull into the petrol station a few hundred metres ahead.

"We won't be stopping again till the afternoon," her passenger said. "Go and buy some food and drink."

As soon as the car came to a halt, he got out and strode off in the direction of the men's toilets.

How easy it would be, she thought, to simply leave him here and drive away. Leave him all alone at this newly refurbished Sasol garage, with its convenience shop and Wimpy restaurant and scattering of drivers. Just drive off, take the next exit, turn around and go back the way she had come. Head for home instead of going ever-further on the N2 in the direction of Kimberley and Bloemfontein, through endless golden-brown farmland that looked flat and surprisingly featureless, with little growing in the winter fields.

Of course, retribution would be swift and immediate. First her son, then herself. That was how it would be.

Abandoning the idea with something approaching relief, Ntombi undid her seatbelt, climbed stiffly out of the car and headed for the Wimpy. She ordered two burgers, two large portions of chips on the side, to go. Food for him, not for her. She wasn't remotely hungry. Quite the opposite. Her stomach was so tight she thought she'd bring up anything she tried to eat.

But she knew she couldn't keep going on nerves alone.

Turning back to the counter, she ordered a cheese and tomato sandwich for herself.

She knew what his food would be like. The burger roll mass-produced and lacking in substance, squishing as flat as tissue paper where the sauces moistened it, the meat over-salty and overcooked and hard.

She'd come up with her own recipe for a simple burger. Half a kilo of minced topside, finely chopped onion, one egg and a handful of breadcrumbs. Various spices—she'd spent a long time trying different combinations and puzzling over how to get the balance of flavour right. In the end, she'd added freshly chopped coriander and a dash of Worcestershire sauce and prayed it would have the effect she was aiming at.

She'd shaped the patties—not too flat, because thicker burgers were juicier and more tender—and fried them on the heavy ridged pan that Khumalo had bought from the second-hand shop. She was patient, waiting for the pan to sear black lines into the meat, flipping them only once. Brown outside, their middles were pink and tender and bursting with flavour.

"Cook with happiness." That was one of the pieces of advice she'd picked up after reading a magazine article on top South African chef Lucas Ndlovu. She'd cooked those burgers with pure happiness, and her son had laughed with delight as he'd eaten his, the juices running down his chin.

While she waited for her order, Ntombi followed the signs to the ladies' toilet. She found herself standing to one side to let an overweight white woman with a frizzy looking perm walk out. The big-bosomed, pink-cheeked female brushed past Ntombi as if she were invisible, without so much as an acknowledgment.

She squatted over the toilet with her colourful outfit bunched up in her clenched fingers, not wanting to let the material come into contact with the sticky floor, and then washed her hands with the harsh-smelling liquid soap. Walking back via the garage shop to purchase two big bottles of water and two cans of Coke, she collected her food and carried the already grease-stained bags outside to the car.

The same woman was leaving as Ntombi waited to cross over to where the BMW was parked. She was climbing into the passenger seat of a Ford bakkie, with a red-haired, solidly built man at the wheel. A farmer, she guessed, and the thought made her heart sore, because it was what her Khumalo had hoped to be one day.

She wondered what would have happened if she'd ended up working for that woman instead of her current employer. Would she even have bothered to listen to Ntombi's story, or believed it? She didn't think so. The woman looked like the type who thought black workers should not come to her with their problems.

At least her employer had listened carefully, and taken all the details she'd given him.

He hadn't acted on them, though. Hadn't troubled himself to help. Worse still, he now knew that thanks to what had happened, she and her son were all alone in the world, and that gave him power over her.

She should have said nothing. Just done her job like a good worker.

When the farmer's wife saw Ntombi walking over to the driver's side of a vehicle newer and far more expensive than her own, her face went sour, as if she'd bitten down on a rotten pecan. She turned and snapped at her husband and the Ford started up with a growl and grumbled its way out of the car park.

And then, above the noise of its unhappy engine, Ntombi heard another sound, one as unwelcome as it was unexpected. The high-pitched trilling of her cell phone.

She put down the bags of greasy takeaway food and rooted around frantically for the phone in her bag. The number was unfamiliar but the dialling code was not. It was from Bronk-horstspruit. Her heart doubled its speed.

She stabbed the answer button.

"Mrs. Khumalo?"

"Yes . . . speaking." Fear washed over her in waves. Who was calling? She could hear background noise, lots of it. The woman on the other side of the phone was raising her voice in order to be heard.

"It's Sister Baloyi here. I'm calling from the Theunisvlei clinic."

Ntombi's heart sank. The one place in the world she had never wanted to think about ever again. The place that had been unable to help her husband.

"What is it?" she said.

"We had a lady come in to the clinic looking for you on Tuesday. She said your husband did some work for her before he passed away, and that she owed him money. She would like you to have the money. I am calling to give you her details so that you can get in contact with her."

"Mrs. Loodts?" Ntombi asked, confused. She remembered the weekend work Khumalo had done at the nearby farm with the horses. The grocery bags he had brought back to her, filled with exotic ingredients. Bull's eyes and green glacé cherries; rocket and brinjals; glass noodles and pickled ginger.

"No. This lady is . . ." Sister Baloyi spoke slowly, as if she was reading it out. ". . . Jade de Jong."

"I don't know who she is," Ntombi confessed. "Perhaps she is trying to get hold of another Khumalo."

"Well, there's no other information on this piece of paper." The woman sounded kind but annoyed, as if she didn't have time to argue with widows who were questioning the prospect of extra money. "Wait, there is something here on the back. Some notes written down, and another name. Sonet Meintjies. Does that mean anything to you?"

Suddenly Ntombi couldn't breathe. The sun-drenched tarmac seemed to have sucked all the air away.

"Give me the number, please," she managed.

"Do you have a pen?"

There was one in her bag. But she didn't have the chance to look for it because at that moment the passenger door of the BMW opened and the man in the black-suit got out and turned to face her, his mirrored shades reflecting the sky behind her and turning the blue into bloodied gold.

"What's going on?" he snapped. "Who are you talking to?"

No time to think. "The hospital," she mouthed to him. Then, into the phone, "Yes, go ahead."

The sister gave her the number. It was easy to remember. 082, which was Vodacom, and then three digits in sequence. The last four she repeated to herself over and over again.

Thirty-eight, forty-two. Thirty-eight, forty-two.

"Thank you," she said hurriedly and disconnected. Her armpits were soaked with sweat, and the phone nearly slipped to the floor as she tried to place it in the palm of the man's outstretched hand without actually touching his skin.

"It was the hospital calling," she said, picking up the bags and putting them behind her seat before she climbed into the car.

"The hospital?" His tone was mocking, as if he was looking forward to catching her out in a lie.

Back in his own seat, his thick, strong fingers moved over the keys of her phone, checking the recent call list.

The evil emanating from him was palpable. She could have touched it; it was a force all of its own. She knew what would happen if he found out she was concealing information from him.

Think of your son . . .

"Which hospital? Why did they call you?"

Delving deep within herself, she found the strength to hide her fear and keep her voice calm.

"The clinic at Theunisvlei. They said there is an outstanding amount of money due for my husband Khumalo's medication," she told him. "The lady I spoke to said I owe them thirty-eight rands and forty-two cents, for some of the painkillers. That's what she told me. I'm sorry, but this lady didn't tell me her name."

The man grunted. He frowned again at the list of calls as if memorising it.

Then he dialled the number and had a brief conversation with the hospital receptionist.

"Next time you take the call in the car," he said, returning her phone. "You know the rules. Why didn't you this time?"

"I didn't think to," she said. "I was too surprised that they were calling about Khumalo at all."

The man said nothing. Just twisted round and transferred a bag of food to his lap.

"Get driving," he told her.

■

Jade had expected to be woken by the soft beeping of the alarm, but instead it was the buzzing of her phone. She was awake in an instant, sitting up in the dark room and reaching for it as it vibrated on the wooden chair. Blinking down at its glowing screen, she saw that it was four-thirty A.M. and the incoming call was from a cell phone number she did not recognise.

The caller was Harris and he sounded panicked.

"I'm looking for Jade de Jong."

"Speaking."

"Jade, this is Harris. You gave me your card when we were at Zelda's house yesterday evening. I'm sorry to call you at this hour, but I'm back at her place and there's a huge problem here."

"What's happened?" she asked. She leaned over and switched on the bedside light to banish the shadows.

"There's been a fire. Rather, there is a fire. Randburg Guarding called me half an hour ago and I've just got here. The place is an inferno, Jade." He stopped, coughed, continued. "The fire brigade has arrived but they're not going to be able to save the house. It's all gone. Gone."

He sounded on the verge of tears.

"Wait there," she said. "I'm coming."

Half an hour later, Jade parked again, a few streets away from Zelda's house, but this time on the opposite side of the suburb. This side was closer to the main streets of Cresta. There were one or two other vehicles still parked there. A couple of casually dressed student types were walking tiredly to their cars. Waitresses, Jade guessed, who'd just cashed up, the last stragglers in the bars having finally finished their drinks.

There was even a car guard sitting on the verge, wearing a battered-looking reflective vest, who got up when he saw her and waved her over to the side of the road.

As soon as she climbed out she could smell the smoke, and in the darkness the vivid glow of the conflagration was clearly visible through the border of trees.

Harris was standing next to the fire truck and literally wringing his hands. His face was ghostly. Only the ruddy glow of the flames gave it any colour.

"How did this happen?" he asked her. A pointless question, which she answered with one of her own.

"Weren't Randburg Guarding on duty?"

"They had a guard stationed at the gate. He saw nothing until the fire started."

Jade nodded resignedly. The property was large, inadequately secured, and there was no way one guard in one position could realistically provide anything except a placebo effect. The intruder, or intruders, could easily have climbed over the wall around the corner.

Smoke billowed out of blackened windows. The hissing of the high-pressure hoses was barely audible over the roaring of the flames. Even from as far away as the gate, the heat prickled Jade's face.

"They did a good job," she said, speaking almost to herself. Whatever secrets Zelda's house had hidden were now lost in the smouldering rubble. If there had been notes hidden somewhere they were gone now.

"Look, there was nothing you could have done to stop them," she told Harris.

"I've let her down," he muttered. "I couldn't keep her safe, and now her house is gone, too."

"Harris, you did all you could," she tried, but she could see that any attempt to console him would be futile. His grief insulated him from her words.

Other people had arrived at the scene. Residents from the surrounding properties stood in groups, watching the spectacle with concerned faces. Some wore dressing gowns, others had pulled on tracksuits. Men with rumpled hair and women with faces free from make up. Far too many people for her liking. There were townhouse complexes in the area housing hundreds of residents. In such a crowd it would be easy for their pursuers to hide and watch.

"You need to go home," Jade told Harris. "There's nothing you can do here now. Come back tomorrow when it's light. Then you can see if there's anything left to salvage."

He nodded but she wasn't sure he'd really heard her words.

"I don't think it's a good idea for you to be alone right now," Jade told him diplomatically. "You're welcome to come with me and have an early breakfast somewhere, but otherwise is there a friend you could call? Someone who'd be able to offer you company?"

"Yes, yes, there is," he said rather impatiently.

Her offer of breakfast rejected, somewhat to her relief, Jade wished him all the best and walked away. At least she had his phone number now. She'd be able to contact him in a couple of days and see if he was more willing to talk about Zelda.

Jade realised with a shiver that she was already thinking of the dark-haired woman in the past tense. The thugs who'd broken into her house had surely achieved now what they had set out to do. They'd disposed of her and now they had destroyed all evidence of what she'd been working on.

It was just starting to get light as she made her way back to her car with a heavy heart.

27

Jade had deliberately parked a fair distance from Zelda's burning house. And she'd taken precautions to ensure nobody had followed her. However, somebody must have been on the look-out because it wasn't long before she noticed a set of headlights behind her taking exactly the same course.

She turned left and chose the busiest route to the highway, a double-lane main road lined with jacaranda trees and high walls that shielded expensive houses from prying eyes. Safety lay in numbers, which in this case was traffic, she decided. She didn't want them taking the initiative before she was ready.

Although there was ample room for it to overtake, the car stayed at a steady distance behind hers. It wasn't the white truck. They'd obviously jettisoned that and were now using a luxury sedan, also white. She drove carefully, slowly and relaxed, not giving away that she knew they were following her. Inside, though, she felt a familiar clench of excitement and she eased the stolen gun from where she'd left it earlier, shoved out of sight down the side of the passenger seat, and stuck it into the belt of her jeans.

She decided she'd get on the highway and head back towards her house. She'd go a different way though. She'd take a short-cut through the large piece of land to the north which had recently been bought by a developer and re-zoned as a residential estate. Dirt roads had been created and notice boards had been put up, but the land itself was still vacant and construction had yet to start. It would be the ideal place to lead her tail into a trap, all the more so since the men had no idea she was armed, nor of her shooting capabilities.

There was only one more detail she needed to know—how many men were in the car behind her?

Three would be the best case, because then she'd be able to deal with all of them at once. Although if there were two she was sure they would be the same pair she'd seen at the hospital and not the other man, into whose hand she'd stabbed the prongs of the fork. He was definitely going to be on the injured list, and in any case she had the feeling that he was the most junior of the three.

By now it was light enough to dispense with headlights. If she did that, perhaps the driver behind would follow suit and then she would be able to see who was in the car.

As she took the slip road to the highway, Jade flicked her headlights off.

After a couple of seconds, the car behind her did the same.

As she followed the curve of the cloverleaf, she drove eastwards, heading directly into the rays of the rising sun. It shone through her windscreen, bright and clear.

Looking in her rear view mirror, she saw the driver's face bathed in the same perfect light.

Jade couldn't believe it.

She stared into the mirror, desperately hoping she was wrong; wrenching the wheel to the left at the last minute as her inattention sent her veering too close to the crash barrier.

Her judgement had been faulty and she knew her mistake could prove disastrous.

There was only one person in the car behind her and it was the man with the injured hand.

One of the main advantages of being a woman, Jade knew, was that most men had certain preconceptions about the fairer sex. They believed women were weaker, which was true to an extent. Although they didn't have the raw muscle power of men, the main problem was simply that they were unskilled at using their strength effectively. A fit, co-ordinated female could easily outrun and outfight the average man, bearing in mind that the average man was neither very fit nor brilliantly co-ordinated.

Women were equally capable with firearms, although in ideal circumstances they would shoot more accurately when using a gun of the right size. This usually meant they ended up choosing a more compact model, like Jade's preferred weapon, the Glock 19.

Apart from that, it was down to talent, competency, and the cold-blooded resolve to kill. In that regard, females could be just as callous. In particular, when she'd been on a bodyguarding assignment in New York, Jade had met some women who'd trained in the Israeli army whose lethal talents and lack of conscience had scared the living daylights out of every man in their team.

There had been many times when Jade's adversaries had underestimated her simply because she was a woman, and had lived to regret it later.

The men who'd broken into Zelda's house and shot the elderly neighbour, though, were hired professionals. They'd tried and failed to get rid of her twice already. There was only one possible reason that the team could have sent its weakest member after Jade.

And that was if they had had to split their forces because the other two were pursuing a quarry they considered even more important.

Driving at a steady speed in the slow lane, Jade grabbed her phone, holding it low so that the driver behind her would not see she was using it. She punched the redial button and waited, holding her breath, for the endless seconds it took the call to connect.

Answer, she prayed. Please answer.

She felt a flood of relief when she heard Harris's voice.

"Jade, I . . ."

"Harris, you're being followed. Drive straight to a police station."

"What are you . . . ?"

"There are two men driving behind you. Don't look and don't slow down. Don't let them know you've seen them. Just tell me where you are right now. This is extremely important."

"What?"

Resisting the urge to bang her head against the steering wheel, Jade repeated the question. "Where are you?"

"I'm on my way home. Vantage Road. I'm stopped at a traffic light."

"The car behind you. Give me its make, colour, and the number plate if you can."

Harris sounded confused. "But you're wrong. There's no car behind me."

And then the sound she'd dreaded. The explosive bang of a window smashing.

Harris shouted again, his voice high-pitched and panicked. Christ! Please, don't . . . No!"

Abruptly, the line went dead.

Jade shoved her phone into her pocket. Her hand felt hot and she unclenched her fingers with an effort. She had been so close to helping him. So close, but yet too late. If she'd only realised a minute earlier. If she'd only switched her lights off before the highway . . . if only the men hadn't chosen that moment to pull up next to Harris instead of staying behind him.

No use beating herself up over might-have-beens. There was nothing she could have done. The men would have got to him anyway, although it had probably been thanks to her phone call that they'd acted so suddenly. Realising, as professionals would do, that Harris was being warned about their presence.

Two thugs, in possession of at least one firearm, and they had him now. Worse, it wouldn't be long before one of them phoned the man who was following her and told him that the game was up.

Changing her plans, Jade took the next exit off the highway and increased her speed, driving fast along the main road towards Sandton City.

28

What the hell was the girl doing, Graeme wondered, as he swerved across two lanes of traffic to follow her, eliciting angry blasts of hooters from taxis and commuters in more comfortable vehicles. She'd suddenly turned off the highway, taking him completely by surprise. Now she was racing along in the direction of Sandton City as if she'd suddenly realised she was about to miss the start of the winter sale.

Either that, or . . .

His suspicions coincided with the ringing of his cell phone. He answered the call, grimacing with pain as his injured right hand was forced to take over the job of steering. The visit to the emergency ward in Sandton Clinic involving eight stitches and a shot of antibiotics, had cost him two grand and the doctor had said he'd been very lucky that it hadn't fractured a bone.

He should be more careful next time when gardening at night, the doctor had warned. Most accidents happen in the home.

"Yes?" he said, snapping the phone open.

It was Lance, his "boss" and the one who'd personally hired him. They went back a long way. They had both worked as bouncers ten years ago. Rough stuff, like this job. Bring it on. He was used to it. In fact, quite enjoyed it.

"We've got the guy."

"I'm following the girl, but she's running."

"He was on the phone when we got him. Might have been speaking to her. She could have heard something. I'll find out."

Graeme listened to the meaty thud of a well-aimed punch. "Who were you on the phone to? Well, who? Tell us!"

He heard ragged breathing and then a response, high-pitched and terrified. He was reminded yet again of the teens he'd dragged out of nightclubs. The fear in their eyes. The way they'd puked their guts out on the sidewalks, as pain finally sounded the alarm in their alcohol-dulled systems.

"Ja. I think it was probably her on the phone," Lance said, speaking rapidly, his voice stressed. "Look, don't let her get away. If you can sort her out now, do that. If you can force her to crash the car, great. If you can't do either of those, then at least keep her in sight until we can come and take over. Right?"

"Right."

Lance rang off without another word. Getting down to business on his side, Graeme knew. Now he had to get down to business here. He flattened his foot on the accelerator. Causing her to crash would be tricky in this traffic, and she was driving fast.

Did she know he was behind her or not? Graeme really wasn't sure. His confusion deepened when she crossed over Rivonia Road and signalled to turn right at the next set of lights.

She was going into the Nelson Mandela Square underground car park.

What the hell? Was she really going to the winter sale? Either way, it should be easy enough to grab her in the garage, before she went into the mall itself. Graeme wrenched the wheel sideways and pulled up at the entrance boom as she accelerated away.

He mashed his thumb into the button for the parking ticket and waited for what felt like a year for the machine to feed the card into his hand. Of all the ridiculous things. Being held up by having to wait for a damned ticket.

And it wasn't going to be easy grabbing her either. What the hell were these car wash ladies doing? Clad in overalls and smocks, buckets and cloths and squeegees in their hands, they were all over parking level one like a rash, smiling at him and waving him into one of the available bays.

Each one a potential witness.

Resisting the urge to lean on his horn and send them scattering, he followed the girl's receding taillights. She wasn't parking on this level. She was heading further down. He followed, tyres squealing on the concrete as he took the car through some tight corners.

Level two was much emptier. Far fewer vehicles and not a car washer in sight. So, she was going to stop here. That was much better, even though he'd still have to be very fast.

And then his jaw actually dropped open in astonishment as she continued down the next ramp. Down again, to the third level. P3, with its yellow signage, which appeared strangely bright and light in these gloomy depths where there was hardly another car to be seen.

She was panicking for sure, unaware that by doing so she was making his job so much easier.

And there she was—stopping right next to the exit door that led through to the Sandton Towers lifts.

She yanked the car door open and ran.

He parked at a crazy angle, straddling two bays, flung himself out of the car, tore his keys from the ignition and bolted for the exit door. There in the lobby were the two lifts, the up button still brightly lit.

She hadn't waited for the lifts. Must have taken the stairs, then, he decided.

In three strides he'd reached the door to the stairway and pulled it open. The unglamorous back corridors of Nelson Mandela Square lay behind it. Stairs in raw concrete, dull and basic, smells and noises filtering down from the kitchens of the restaurants above.

He powered up the stairs. One flight, two flights, and then he was at ground level, sprinting along the long, narrow passage that led to the square proper.

Where the hell was she?

Definitely not in the corridor. He skidded to a stop as he passed the ladies' toilets. That would be a clever trick, hiding in there. He didn't know where else she'd have had time to go.

He pushed the door open and shouldered his way inside, ignoring the startled glance from the black woman washing her hands, who then grabbed her handbag and left in a hurry. He pushed all the cubicle doors. All were empty except for one. The scream that came from behind it when he hammered on it with his fists sounded like a young woman—a teenager. Even so, he went into the adjacent cubicle, stood on the rim of the toilet, and peered over the partition.

Yup. A screaming blonde teen. Not the woman he was looking for.

Jogging out of the toilet and putting some distance between himself and the cries of the terrified teenager, he went out into the square itself. The sun-drenched space, surprisingly warm for a winter's morning, was already bustling with people. People lining up for ice-cream at Baglios, breakfasting at Trumps, admiring the fountains in the centre and taking photo after photo of the massive six-metre high bronze statue of Nelson Mandela.

People of every race, colour and creed. Blacks, Asians, Europeans. Girls of every shape and size. But not the one he was looking for. The babbling of ten different languages assailed his ears.

Where, in all this chaos, could she have gone?

Graeme's heart sank as he realised she could have gone anywhere.

He searched the square for a few minutes, going through the motions just so he could say he had tried. And then he trailed back down the corridor and took the lift to P3. He'd been an idiot. He hadn't even locked Lance's car, he'd been in such a hurry, although he knew the chances of it being stolen here were very small.

When he entered level P3, his car was there . . . but hers was not.

She'd outwitted him. Used the Sandton City trip as a ruse, and now she'd gone. She could be anywhere in Jo'burg and he had failed in the simplest of tasks; to dispose of a single, helpless woman.

Graeme realised he was sweating under his leather jacket. He didn't dare take it off though, because he was carrying one of Lance's guns and the rule was when you were carrying, you wore a jacket at all times. He might have exaggerated about his marksmanship talents—certainly, compared to Lance's skill, he was an amateur who'd only done shooting for a hobby. He might also have lied about having shot and killed someone, when Lance had asked. He hadn't. He had aimed a gun in anger but he'd never fired it, although he knew Lance had done so. And more than once. It was, after all, his livelihood.

And now he wouldn't have the chance. His opportunity to become a full-time member of their team was gone.

Graeme ran a hand through his short, thinning hair and got back into the car, settling himself down with a heavy, defeated sigh before starting it up and driving out of Sandton City and straight into the slow-moving traffic that went all the way down to the corner of West and 5th, where the lights were not working.

Inching along in the queue, Graeme realised he was going to have to phone Lance and let him know that he had failed. What reason he was going to give, he had no idea. There was no excuse for his incompetence.

He took his cell phone out of his pocket and was about to dial the number when a woman's voice, coming from behind his driver's seat, said sharply to him, "If you want to live, put the phone down and keep your hands on the wheel."

29

Graeme let out a frightened yelp. He couldn't help it. What the hell? She was there, in his car, hiding behind the driver's seat, and she was threatening him.

Not for long. In this traffic . . . if he put the handbrake on and undid his seatbelt . . . he could have his gun aimed at her before she even had a chance to open the car door and run again.

"I know what you're thinking of doing," she pre-empted him in the same icy voice. "Let me explain to you why it's a bad idea."

The next moment a deafening explosion shattered his world and the vehicle was filled with the distinctive cordite-like stench that accompanied every gunshot.

He shouted again and this time the sound was of pure terror. Holy God, she had a weapon. That changed everything. How come she was armed? Lance had stated categorically he hadn't seen her carrying.

He glanced down and almost pissed himself when he saw where the bullet had gone. Just right of his ribcage, stuffing erupted from a hole where it had punched through the back of the seat and then re-entered so close to his knee that . . . if he'd moved an inch before she fired . . . well, it would have shattered his kneecap instead of embedding itself harmlessly in the car's undercarriage.

He broke into a sweat as he held onto the steering wheel, grasping it as tightly as a frightened tourist who had strayed into the bad side of town might have held onto his wallet.

"Don't shoot me," he pleaded, his voice thin and squeaky.

"I ran downstairs instead of up when I left the car park," she told him. "I went to P4 and waited there while you went into the square. Then I moved my car. I didn't drive it far. It's parked on level one now. The ladies are busy washing it."

"I see," he said. The conversation was surreal. And then his body went rigid as he felt her hand scrabbling under his leather jacket. Efficiently, she removed the firearm Lance had given him from its holster.

Now she had two weapons and he had none.

Graeme found himself blinking stinging rivulets of sweat out of his eyes.

"I'm telling you all this to explain my situation. My vehicle is being attended to, so I need a ride. You're going to take me where I want to go."

"Where's that?"

"To your friends. The two guys that have got Harris."

"But I . . ."

"They hired you, right?"

"What . . . ?"

"One or both of them was hired by somebody to do a job and they brought you on board too. Am I correct?"

"Yes."

Traffic was thinning now. He arrived at the intersection. Looked left and right, as if obeying that basic road safety rule would go any way towards saving his skin when there was a maniac sharpshooter bitch with two loaded firearms just a seat's width away from him.

"Who hired them?"

Oh, crap, a question he couldn't answer. He felt his bowels loosen.

"I swear to God I don't know. I'd tell you if I did; I'm not suicidal, okay? All I know is Lance is paying me five grand to help out."

"What were you supposed to do to me?"

"I was supposed to . . ." How could he tell the truth; yet how could he lie when she'd already found his firearm? "They told me I should shoot you if I had the chance. Otherwise, follow you and tell them where you were. That was what I was planning to do," he finished hurriedly.

"Have you ever killed a woman before?"

"I've never killed anyone. There was this one guy . . . I used to be a bouncer, okay? He was drunk and disorderly and we threw him out, but things got out of hand and he suffered a brain injury and never came right. We went down for it together, Lance and I, both did five years in Modderbee. But to be honest, he was the one that booted the guy in the head."

"You think you could have done it? Pulled the trigger? For five grand?"

"I don't know." He was breathless now. Shaking all over.

"My advice is don't. It changes you inside. Once you'd pulled that trigger, you'd never have been able to go back."

"I . . . I see."

"Now, phone your friends. Tell them exactly what I tell you to say, and sound normal. No funny business, no code words. I'll know from your voice and the next bullet will be in the back. But first, a question. The elderly man you guys shot at in Randburg. You do know he was killed?"

"I   I know Lance fired his weapon at him. And I know he's a crack shot. He does target practice every week at the range."

"Does he now? And the black man?"

"He's good. Experienced, but not at the same level."

Shit, he was spilling his guts to her. The woman fell silent, as if digesting his words.

"That changes my impression of your setup. It doesn't change what I'm going to do to you if I suspect any funny business is going on when you speak to Lance. If this gun has the same ammo as his, it means there's some fancy hollow-points loaded. When I shoot you, the bullet will shatter your spine, leaving you paralysed from that point down. Then it will tumble through your gut like a miniature chainsaw so you'll be able to see your intestines spread out all over the steering wheel."

"I won't . . . oh, Jesus. We don't have any code words."

"Didn't think you'd need any?"

"No."

"Tell them you've got me in the car. Tell them you caught me in the garage and knocked me out and you're bringing me through because you can't do it. Tell them you want one of them to pull the trigger."

"Right."

"Phone now. And I want the call on speakerphone so I can hear both sides."

With slippery hands, Graeme scrolled through the phone log to make the call he'd so nearly started a couple of minutes ago, before his whole world had changed.

"You get her?" Lance's voice. Excited, expectant.

"Caught her running in the parking garage."

"And? Where's the bitch's body?"

Lance, no! Lady, don't shoot me, please don't shoot me . . .

"She was knocked out when I tackled her. Her head hit the floor really hard." Graeme swallowed, praying he sounded normal. In the circumstances, though, he guessed it wouldn't matter if he sounded a little excited. Lance would surely expect it. "After that I kicked her in the guts a couple of times and loaded her up in the car. I can't . . . I'm too nervous to shoot. I'd rather bring her to you."

"This is not what I paid you for."

"You haven't paid me yet."

"Well, bring her here and let's sort it out." Lance sounded disgusted.

"Where's here?"

"At the guy's place. We caught him here and we kept him here. Number . . . um . . . sixty-seven Vantage Street in Northcliff."

"I'll be there in about twenty minutes."

"The gate's open. Drive straight in."

Lance hung up and Graeme waited, breathless, for the girl to comment on their conversation. His entire midsection felt as if it was on fire. Thanks to his fevered imagination, every nerve ending was anticipating the devastation of the tumbling bullet.

Jade didn't say anything until he was turning right off Jan Smuts Avenue and into Gleneagles Road, by which time Graeme was a bag of nerves. When she touched his right thigh he jumped so badly he nearly hit his head on the roof of the car. But all she was doing was removing his wallet.

"Graeme de Villiers. You still live at 23A Garden Clusters in Brackendowns, Alberton?"

"Y—yes."

An expensive walled complex with bond repayments that were just about crippling him. Ironic that he'd paid so much for security when he knew he would never feel truly safe there again.

"With your family? These blonde kids yours?"

His little angels. Now fear sank its talons deep into him.

"Please . . ." he whispered.

"Don't worry. Just getting a clearer picture of how things are for you, Graeme. Now, when we get to where we're going, you will park in the driveway until I get out of the vehicle. Then you will drive away. Immediately. Understand?"

"I understand."

"Whose car is this?"

"Lance's."

"You might as well keep it then." The dismissive way in which she said the words made his blood run cold.

"Why haven't they killed Harris yet?" she asked. "Seeing as how they're not shy about pulling the trigger. Why isn't he dead?"

"They . . . wanted to . . ."

"To ask him where I was?"

"No, no. They wanted to question him. He has to tell them where the girl is. The journalist; the one who lives in the Randburg house."

"They haven't got her yet?" She sounded over-casual and Graeme wondered whether this was new information to her, or something she'd known all along.

"Not yet. They think she's in hiding. That's all I know." Was it a test? All he could do was tell her the truth, as far as he was able to.

He drove on. Through Greenside, across Barry Hertzog, winding his way alongside the Emmarentia parkland until he reached Beyers Naude Avenue and turned right. Another five minutes and he was in Northcliff, obeying the GPS diligently as it directed him up increasingly hilly and zigzagging roads.

He knew he should be relieved that they were almost there, but instead he felt like vomiting. Up until now he'd been useful to her. Once they had reached their destination he knew all too well that his usefulness would have come to an end. In fact, he would become a liability.

He wondered what his guts would look like splattered all over the steering wheel and the thought made black spots start looming at the edges of his vision.

With an effort, he forced himself to breathe.

"This is the house," he said. He eased the car up the steep and winding driveway towards the house, which was a split-level mansion, set well back from the road in a large, treed garden.

Graeme parked next to the white truck, which now had different plates.

He heard a whine as she buzzed the window down. And then he saw Sipho, the black guy, walking out of the front door. Sipho was holding his gun unholstered. He looked pissed off, as if he couldn't be bothered with a subordinate that hadn't had the guts to do a proper job.

For a tiny moment, Graeme was unutterably relieved that he would never be working with these two men again.

Then came another massive bang from the seat behind him. The sound burst out of the car and bounced back off the tall walls of the house. A bullet hole appeared in the centre of Sipho's forehead. He stumbled forward and fell, flopping limply down three of the stairs before coming to rest on the neat face brick paving of the driveway.

Just like that. She had killed him just like that.

His hands fell from the wheel and he stared blindly ahead. Waiting for what he knew was going to come.

"Thanks, Graeme," the girl said. He heard the door behind him snick open. "Don't get involved in a setup like this again. It's not worth it. And now you'd better go to hospital and get that leg seen to."

"But there's nothing wrong with my . . ."

At which point there was a third explosion. Graeme screamed with all his might as her bullet punched its way through the meat of his right calf.

The car door slammed and then she was gone.

30

Jade sprinted for cover, dodging past the body of the young black man she'd just killed. She heard the grinding of gears as Graeme drove out, manoeuvring the car with some difficulty thanks to his injured leg.

In her right hand she held the gun she'd taken from the old man's house. She'd fired it five times now. Once yesterday when she'd tested it. Once through the seat of Graeme's car. Once into the forehead of the black man, once into Graeme's calf. Then she'd fired one further shot, which she regarded as a form of insurance. That left a single round in the chamber before she had to start using the other, untested gun with the souped-up bullets.

She was trembling now, with nervous energy and with fear. All she wanted to do was get out of here. Get away. Hide. Forget about the way that the black guy had crumpled to the ground. One minute alive, breathing, his mind filled with thoughts and feelings, plans and dreams, even if those plans and dreams had included putting a bullet into the unconscious woman he'd imagined was in the car. Even if he'd been a well-trained and cold-minded ex-army operator about to commit a cold-blooded act.

The next minute, dead. His life simply and brutally stopped.

She hadn't known his name, and she was glad about that. It was easier to kill somebody if you knew nothing about them.

Now, though, serious danger lay ahead. Lance was still alive and he was the skilled one; the sharpshooter. He hadn't come running out when he'd heard the shots. Perhaps he hadn't suspected anything was up. On the other hand, Lance might well have ordered that no shots be fired in this suburban neighbourhood, where police and security could arrive in a matter of minutes. He might have planned for them to drive somewhere else before "disposing" of her.

Multiple gunshots in this upmarket suburban area meant they had only minutes before security forces arrived. Jade was certain of that. So, if she could just stay alive long enough . . .

Lance had killed the pensioner deliberately and without compunction. For the hell of it; for the joy of it; because he could. That meant she needed to put him down fast and efficiently. Which meant that asking questions would either be difficult or impossible.

Always assuming that her hands would stop shaking for long enough to allow her to aim her stolen weapon.

In front of the white truck she saw Harris's car. The driver's door was still open from when they'd dragged him out. Out of the car and inside the house . . . and then where?

Jade edged her way to the open front door, listened, and stepped quietly inside. The house was light and bright and airy and absolutely quiet. No sound anywhere apart from the regular ticking of a large grandfather clock on the far wall. She pressed herself against the wall next to it and waited, trying to calm her breathing and slow down her thoughts. She was experienced in most of the areas her work got her involved in, but she didn't have enough mileage in situations like this. Ex-Special Ops soldier or mercenary, anyone who'd received such prolonged and specific training would have a huge advantage over her.

And then she heard Lance's voice, coming from upstairs. Cold, sharp, professional.

"Sipho? That you? Why the hell did you shoot her on the premises?"

Jade listened to the seconds ticking away on the clock's varnished wooden face, knowing that with each one Lance's suspicions would be multiplying furiously.

As she expected, he didn't repeat the question.

Like any professional, he'd immediately realised that the

situation had turned bad. Now he'd be doing exactly the same as her. Analysing, formulating a plan, collecting information to gain the initiative. To stay alive and destroy the opponent.

But something about his words troubled her.

"Sipho? That you?"

Jade had taken pains to be utterly silent when she'd entered the house. She was wearing rubber-soled shoes and her footfalls had been soundless as she'd padded across the hallway floor.

How, then, had Lance known to ask that question at that exact time?

Jade looked up.

The small implacable eye of a wall mounted security camera stared blankly back at her.

She barely dared to breathe as she realised the truth of her predicament. Lance had the advantage, all right. He must have seen movement on the video screen and assumed it was his accomplice returning. By now, he knew that it was her because he could see her clearly on the monitor.

And then, Jade heard an agonised shout from upstairs, followed by a muffled moan.

Her jaw clenched as she realised what his strategy involved.

Harris was still alive—but what had Lance done to him, and what was he going to do?

How many damn cameras were there in this house? She inched around the clock towards the staircase. The flooring and the stairs were covered with laminate, which was good news for her because she was lighter in weight and wearing shoes that allowed her to move more quietly than the man waiting for her on the first floor.

She would hear him if he was coming downstairs, but that hadn't happened, which must mean he was in the same room as Harris with his gun drawn and aimed.

She glanced up but could see no video cameras in the stairwell. This part of the house, at least, was not under surveillance.

Jade sneaked up the stairs, keeping as close to the sides of the treads as she could, knowing that any creaks or movements were more likely to occur in the centre.

The moans were more audible now and seemed to be coming from the second room. Her hand was welded to the grip of the gun she'd stolen. She was too wired to even blink. Any movement and she would shoot.

Far away she heard sirens. The flying squad were on their way.

And then another sound, coming from outside.

The sound of the truck starting up and the gearbox being ground into reverse.

Jade sprinted straight to the bedroom and skidded to a stop in the doorway, gun at the ready, but there was nobody there except Harris. And he was in a bad way.

He'd been tied up to a beam near the room's glass sliding door, which was open and led out to a garden on the upper level. The contraption his tormentors had used was deceptively simple. A car's tow rope had been slung over the beam. One end had been knotted to form a noose around his neck. The other bound his wrists together. The rope was short enough that his feet dangled helplessly above the floor.

A brutal and effective concept. When his arms couldn't bear his weight any more, he would strangle himself. Swinging, struggling and sweating, while his captors watched and waited for him to break.

He saw her and groaned again. His face was crimson and looked swollen from the tight bite of the noose. His eyes were popping in terror.

Through the window, she saw the white truck exit backwards through the gate, weaving unevenly through the gateposts, and then make a frantic three-point turn.

Jade had to chase down Lance. She also had to do something about Harris. But she had no knife and the knots in the rope were firmly tied. If she abandoned him, he would choke to death before she could return.

Looking around for a possible solution, she saw a thickly padded armchair in the corner of the room. She pushed it across the floor towards Harris and helped him as he scrabbled to get his legs onto its seat. His limbs were quaking with exhaustion. If he toppled off again, he might not be able to pull himself back up.

She couldn't wait.

In any case, she didn't expect to be gone for too long.

"I'll be back just now," she said. "Try not to fall."

Jade shot out through the French door and followed the same route through the garden that Lance must have taken a couple of minutes earlier. She dashed over to Harris's car and flung herself inside, praying that the keys were still in the ignition. She started the car and roared out of the property and down the hill in the direction that Lance had gone.

The polite chime of the warning alarm reminding her to fasten her seatbelt was totally incongruous, given the circumstances.

Jade didn't have far to drive. As she had anticipated, the short distance was punctuated by curved smears of rubber on the road and white score marks where the vehicle's wheel rim had scraped along the tarmac.

Jade had shot the fifth bullet—her insurance shot—into the front tyre on the passenger side of the white truck. Lance must have realised what had happened soon after he'd started driving, but desperation had kept him going. Perhaps he'd believed that even with a partially crippled car he could still get away. She'd expected that once he'd realised this was impossible, he'd abandon the truck and flee on foot, giving her a chance to close in and shoot him.

She had not expected this, though.

The truck had slalomed at high speed for less than a kilometre down the steep and winding road before finally coming to grief on one of the hairpin bends.

There, it had left the road, flattening the crash barrier, and sailed out over the edge of the steep and rocky hillside. From that point it had bounced and smashed its way down the slope, marking its passage with broken glass, pieces of engine and the exhaust and various items it had contained. It had come to rest about fifty metres down the slope, and in the process appeared to have rolled right over Lance, who had been flung out through the distorted gap where once the windscreen had been. Steam hissed out from under the twisted bonnet.

The crash must have made a thunderous noise, but by the time Jade got out of Harris's car, all she could hear was the sound of wind whipping through the foliage.

Quickly, she wiped down the two guns and hurled them as far as she could, down the cliffside, in the direction of the wrecked car. She'd have liked to have kept one, but in the circumstances, both needed to be accounted for. After all, how else were the police going to solve the puzzle of who was responsible for the shootings?

Two other drivers stopped and climbed out of their cars after turning on their hazard lights. Their expressions were anxious.

"How'd it happen?" one of them asked Jade.

"I think he was fleeing a crime scene," she said. "There was shooting just now, further up the hill."

Shocked, yet hypnotised by the horror of the sight, they stared over the edge of the cliff, taking in the sight of the devastation before, in unison, taking out their cell phones.

Jade turned away from the scene. For the time being, the threat was over. The hired gunmen were dead. But the situation had not resolved itself the way she would have liked, because she still had no idea who had hired them or why.

Had Sonet's ex-husband tipped them off? Although she hadn't told him she was going to investigate his old farm to see if what he'd said about the disappearing tribe was true, it was on her way back and it would have been easy enough for him to put them on alert.

Jade thought back to the hour or so she'd spent poking around the abandoned farm the day before. The only person she'd seen there had been the man on horseback, and she'd assumed the encounter had been a chance meeting with an innocent local resident. But perhaps he had not been what he seemed.

One thing was sure—those men wouldn't have been driving around in that sparsely populated part of the world without a good reason. They must have been briefed to keep a lookout for her, or for somebody like her, and she needed to find out who had made sure that happened.

As Jade drove away two police cars came into view, accelerating towards the accident scene, the wail of the sirens pulsing through her eardrums. She eased Harris's car over to the left to let them pass.

31

Jade took Harris to Weltevreden Park Clinic, where the doctor told her he had either broken or dislocated two of his fingers, and had probably fractured a rib during the struggle with his captors. He asked Jade if she could wait while X-rays were taken, and she said she would. To pass the time, she decided to flip through some of Zelda's notebooks. At best, something the journalist had jotted down might provide a useful clue. At worst, she'd get to know more about the woman who had disappeared over a week ago.

As she sat down on the plastic chair outside the cubicle where Harris was being given painkilling injections before going to the radiology department, her cell phone rang.

"Miss de Jong?" A woman's voice on the other end.

Jade preferred Ms, but she let it pass. "Speaking."

"It's Sister Baloyi here from the Theunisvlei Clinic."

"Oh, yes?" Drained though she was, Jade nevertheless felt a spark of excitement that someone was finally responding to her request.

"I just wanted to let you know that we did manage to find a phone number for the wife of the patient you were asking about, Mr. Khumalo. I've passed your details on to her."

"You have? She hasn't been in contact yet."

"I spoke to her earlier this morning. I'm sure she'll call you soon."

Jade frowned in concern. "But what if she doesn't have airtime? Can't you give me her number just in case?"

"I'm afraid not." The woman sounded sincerely regretful.

"I'm sure she'll call you. She's a reliable woman. She was there every day with Mr. Khumalo in the oncology ward, right up until the day he passed away."

The oncology ward.

"So Khumalo had cancer?"

"Unfortunately, yes, he passed away from stomach and intestinal cancer." The nursing sister seemed to realise she'd said too much and continued in a brisker tone, "If Mrs. Khumalo hasn't got in touch with you by next week, phone me again."

"Thank you," Jade said.

She disconnected, stared down at her phone and, without success, willed it to ring. Then she turned her attention back to the topmost notebook and found herself reading notations for an article Zelda had written entitled "The War of Land Reform."

Reading Zelda's abbreviated notes was a struggle at first, but became easier after a while as she tuned into her thought patterns. Squinting at the prescription-like scribbles, Jade slowly read her way through the skeleton of the story.

According to Zelda's interview with the director for the Institute of Poverty, Land Reform and Agrarian Studies, the occupation by white settlers of land previously used by indigenous black societies had played a key role in creating a racially polarised and unequal society from as far back as the 17th century.

In 1913, the first Land Act legalised land dispossession on a large scale. The situation became far worse in the mid-1900s when the apartheid government relocated millions of black people living in urban and rural areas in an attempt to create separate, racially defined zones and to confine them to specially demarcated "homelands." In this way the communities lost a great deal of their productive farmland as well as the ability to farm on a small scale in order to allow their rural households to survive.

In contrast, the white-owned farms, with their massive subsidies and government support, became extremely productive.

It was no surprise, confirmed the director, that these acts created immense bitterness among the dispossessed black people, together with a strong desire to have their land restored to its rightful original owners—or at any rate, their successors. In addition, he explained that the redistribution of farmland through land reform would also go a long way towards alleviating the wrenching poverty in the country's rural areas, where about forty per cent of the population lived and where the highest levels of unemployment were found.

The director concluded his interview by telling Zelda that land reform needed to take place faster, in a well-planned and strategic manner, including both large-scale commercial farms and smaller-scale subsistence farms. He argued that if land reform took place too slowly, it would provide fuel for "populist" politicians to call for forcible appropriation. If implemented, this policy risked creating the same inflammatory and destructive situation that had all but annihilated Zimbabwe's agricultural sector.

It all made sense to Jade, but then she read the next interview, which Zelda had conducted with a Doctor Van Eck. Here Zelda had been careful to quote Van Eck verbatim, "The racist and Marxist regime that the ANC has implemented is causing a state of famine in our land, while at the same time leading to genocide being committed against the farmers who have worked so hard to make it productive." Absolute power, Van Eck stated, came not from the barrel of a gun, nor from the might of the armies of the state, but through the control of a country's ability to produce its food supplies.

While Jade didn't agree with Van Eck's philosophy—in fact, she couldn't help wondering if he was a member of the Boere Krisis Kommando—she had to admit he'd also made an interesting and sobering point. Absolute power could indeed be gained through control of a nation's agricultural resources. They were a major, and hotly contested, political weapon.

It all depended, she supposed, on who was attempting to wield it.

Her thoughts were interrupted by the return of Harris's doctor, who told her that the X-rays had shown a fractured finger and had confirmed his tenth rib was broken. He also said they wanted to admit him in order to further assess the trauma to his larynx and trachea.

Jade gave the doctor Harris's car keys for safekeeping before walking out of the hospital and catching a taxi to Sandton.

Back in Sandton City, she was pleased to see that her car was still safely parked in the Nelson Mandela Square car park and that it was sparkling clean. The ladies had even blacked its wheels. Fifty rands well spent, she thought, taking out her phone and calling Victor Theron to give him a quick update.

When he answered she thought he sounded just as on edge as the last time they'd spoken.

"I'm making progress on your case," she said.

"Well, thank God for that," he said snappily. "Because my situation's just gone from bad to disastrous."

"I can meet up if you've got some time. If you're not too busy with the markets."

"The markets are hectic. I can give you ten minutes, but I can't leave my apartment now. You can come up here, if you don't mind. Sixteenth floor of the Michelangelo Towers. Number 1610."

Jade arrived at the entrance to the towers five minutes later and, after he phoned Theron's apartment, the security guard behind the wide, gleaming desk pressed a button to open the glass door that led to the elevators.

A lift swished her up sixteen floors in a matter of seconds, and soon afterwards she was ringing the bell of apartment 1610.

Theron pulled open the door almost immediately.

"Come in, come in," he said. Stress was emanating from him in waves. His hair was tousled and unkempt and his fidgety fingers were playing furious concertos.

Walking inside, Jade found herself in an apartment that looked more like a presidential suite than a home. Immaculate finishes. Lavishly decorated. Not one but two flat-screen televisions mounted on pristine walls. Clearly, professional contractors and interior designers had been responsible for creating this top-end living space.

"Er . . . coffee?" he asked.

Jade glanced over to the compact but well-equipped kitchen.

"I'll make it," she said. "Tell me what's been happening."

"No," Theron said. "First, I want to know what progress you've made."

He'd perched himself on the edge of a black leather couch, staring at the topmost television screen, which was tuned to CNBC. Jade turned the kettle on and took two cups out of the cupboard above it.

She'd thought that Theron would be a bare-fridge kind of person but when she opened it to look for the milk she saw to her surprise a well-stocked and organised array of groceries, as well as a stack of neatly packaged, tasty-looking meals in plastic containers with clear lids.

"You have a beautiful apartment," she said. It was the kind of place she could never even dream of owning. Perhaps she, too, should have worshipped at the altar of the money god, as Theron had chosen to do.

Theron gave an impatient sigh. "You can't imagine the hassles I've had with building management. And the decorators should have been fired, they were so useless."

The rich. Never satisfied. Jade didn't believe she'd ever met a wealthy person who was.

While she waited for the kettle to boil, she gave him a brief rundown on what had happened so far. He listened in sullen silence, without comments or questions, but before she'd finished her story he interrupted her.

"The police told me they've made a breakthrough," he said.

"What have they found?"

"One of the detectives came round yesterday to say that they got an expert in to analyse the parachute. Apparently it had been deliberately cut."

"Cut?" Jade turned to stare at him in concern.

"A number of slashes had been made in the canopy by a sharp instrument, most likely a short, non-serrated knife. Like it matters. The point is that the chute was sabotaged before she jumped, which is why it failed to open. And I'm the one who packed it. I'm the one who handled it. I'm beginning to wish I'd lied. Why didn't I tell the police that she packed her own chute? Or got a friend to pack it for her? All those questions they asked . . . the detectives nearly drove me mad."

"What did they ask you?"

"The same damn questions they asked in the first interview. Over and over again." He took the steaming mug she handed him and cupped his hands around it. "And I gave them the same answers. What more can I do but keep telling the truth?"

"Have the detectives been up to the scene yet?"

"Yes, they have. They said it was contaminated, though. That there were way too many different footprints for them to identify mine or hers."

Jade frowned. "The footprints were clear enough when I went up there. And I thought the building superintendent had restricted access to that area."

Theron shrugged. "He changed his mind, apparently. Said the builders needed to work on some waterproofing and on the drainage systems. That they couldn't put it off any longer without possibly compromising the structure and delaying the completion date. So, a whole team went up there and that was that."

"That's a pity."

"The detective said he thought so too. Even so, with this news about the parachute, it's like I was going out of my way to tag myself as a murder suspect."

"So it's a murder case now?"

"It is. Not culpable homicide any more, not after the police discovered the canopy was slashed."

"Did you know Sonet worked in Sandton Views?" Jade asked him.

Theron blinked rapidly. "She actually worked there? In the building?"

"Yes."

"I'd no idea about that."

"Didn't she speak to you about her work at all?"

"Not much. I know she was employed by a charity, and that she travelled out of town quite often." He tapped his index fingers together. "So, she worked in the building. That explains how she had the access card and keys. I wonder why she didn't tell me, though."

"One of the farms receiving assistance from the charity used to belong to her husband. It was awarded to an indigenous community a few years ago after a successful land claim," she said.

Theron's eyes widened in astonishment.

"You think her husband could have set this up?" he asked.

"I don't know. He's a very bitter man. I also saw some pamphlets in his house from a group called the Boere Krisis Kommando, which seems to be a vigilante organisation."

"So could he have hired the men who followed you?"

"It's a possibility. Unfortunately, both the gunmen are now dead so they can't be questioned."

"Sounds like a promising theory, all the same. But how will the police be able to prove it?" Theron put down his coffee cup and played another few arpeggios on a keyboard nobody could see.

"There's a process to be followed but it'll take time. The police will follow up on the calls that were made and received on the men's cell phones, and also look at the deposits into their bank accounts. That way, hopefully, they'll find out who did the hiring and why."

None of which I can do, Jade thought, frustrated. If only she'd managed to get her hands on Lance's cell phone before he'd misjudged the bend and sent his car skidding over the cliff.

"And how much time will that take?"

Jade supposed that any wait at all would seem an eternity to a man who was used to making split-second decisions involving millions of other people's dollars. "Probably a few months, but it could be longer." she said.

"Even a month is too damn long," Theron grumbled, as she had expected he would.

"Another significant fact is that the Siyabonga community who moved onto the farm has now disappeared."

"How do you mean? They've left? All of them?"

"Nobody knows. I think Sonet's sister Zelda may have been trying to find out what happened to them. Whether they were driven off the land or forced to leave."

"If they've all disappeared that won't be easy to prove."

"There is apparently a Mrs. Khumalo who is still contactable, although she moved away after her husband died. I'm doing my best to locate her to see whether she knows what really happened."

"I hope you find her. I just can't let this drag on, Jade. And I can't afford to be under suspicion. My clients trust me implicitly . . . I've never let them down . . . but the last thing I want is having my name made public at a trial, whether it's under suspicion of murder or manslaughter or whatever."

"I understand, Victor," Jade said. "I'll do my best for you."

"Thanks," Theron said. He took a deep breath and Jade saw him make a conscious effort to relax. "I'm sorry I'm so stressed out today. Tomorrow night, futures close-out will be over and the markets will be quieter. I'd really like to take you to dinner, as a thank you for your efforts so far. Can we call it a date?"

He sounded as if he meant it, and when he showed Jade to the door he gave her another cheque which represented the second installment of her fee, for any unforeseen expenses.

It was a sizeable chunk of money.

Given the fact her vehicle had been tampered with and she'd twice been pursued by hitmen, in addition to surviving two shooting incidents, Jade felt she deserved it.

She wished she knew, though, why something about her recent conversation with Victor Theron was nagging at her mind.

32

Jade was relieved to get back to her cottage. It was peaceful and quiet. The alarm on the electric fence had not been triggered in her absence and the lock on the front door was intact.

And Bonnie was waiting outside the kitchen door, tail a-quiver.

"You're the only one who routinely manages to breach my security," Jade admonished her. "Home! I don't have time to go out for a run now. And no, I'm not giving you a biscuit. You can't have a treat every time you come here, or you'll get fat."

She unlocked the door and Bonnie pushed through her legs to trot confidently into the quiet, cool kitchen and sit down beside the cupboard where the dog biscuits were kept. The dog was practically smiling at Jade.

"All right, then. Just one."

While the Jack Russell crunched up her biscuit, Jade made herself some coffee before sitting down at the kitchen table and turning her attention back to Zelda's notebooks.

As she read them, making a mental note of Zelda's occasional personal and anecdotal jottings, Jade slowly built up a picture of Zelda Meintjies. A frightened, hungry child growing up in a household where food was not always available and when it was, was often restricted as a means of control. Cowering from her father's mental and physical abuse. Seeking solace in the love and support of her siblings and the companionship of the skinny horses that lived on their remote smallholding.

A child who, from an early age, had begun to understand the true value of land, of food. And had started to question the use and abuse of power.

From the angle of the pieces she wrote, Zelda's stance towards farming and land ownership appeared to be both libertarian and naturalist. Surprisingly, Jade found her opposed to large-scale commercial farming. She had thought that, with her background, Zelda would be supportive of efficient production methods, but she wasn't, apparently preferring the lower productivity and greater diversity offered by smaller enterprises. Less surprisingly, she was vehemently opposed to environmentally unfriendly farming practices and the use of pesticides and fertilisers that contaminated the food chain.

It emerged that she had also written several pieces exposing the methods followed by North American bio-tech corporations who patented their genetically modified hybrid seeds, forcing farmers to rebuy from them every season and using bullying tactics such as lawsuits to crush any opposition.

By doing this Zelda explained that they had, in effect, robbed farmers of their most fundamental and long-standing right— the right to save and replant seeds from year to year.

In a series of articles with the working title "Prostituting and Poisoning South Africa's Farmland" Zelda had attacked the US-based corporation whose name was now familiar to Jade: Global Seeds. She had come up with information and facts that were so detailed Jade couldn't help wondering whether she had a source within the company itself.

"Now this is interesting," Jade told Bonnie, paging through the most recent notebook, whose entire content seemed to be devoted to this topic. "Zelda quotes somebody called Danie Smit here. I don't know who he is—a researcher, perhaps? Anyway, Smit says that Argentina introduced a pesticide-resistant soya product developed by Global Seeds. By subsidising the pesticide and encouraging widespread planting of this crop, 95 per cent of the soya market in that country became GM. Of course, this type of planting was most beneficial to commercial farms, who were better geared up to apply massive doses of blanket pesticide to the growing crops, so at the same time they were getting rich, thousands of independent smallholder farmers were forced off their land and bankrupted.

"So, it seems from what Smit tells Zelda here, that pesticide-resistant plants aren't by any means a success story. The development of super-weeds, which can also withstand the toxic pesticides, often follows. Giant pigweed plants can grow so rapidly they take over fields and choke water supplies. They reach such a height and breadth they can actually stop a combine harvester in its tracks. Of course, this has led to farmers needing to use increasingly toxic weedkillers in ever-larger doses."

She scratched the dog's head absently as she turned the page.

"And here, Bonnie, Zelda warns that these herbicides may not be as safe as they were originally considered to be. Her warning is backed up by the higher incidences of cancers in children exposed to these herbicides, and also in the illnesses suffered by the workers who apply them and the families who live close to the fields that are sprayed. This is especially prevalent in third world countries where proper safety equipment is not always used."

Bonnie cocked an ear in Jade's direction. She had such an intelligent look in her eye that Jade was half expecting her to offer a constructive comment in response. "Zelda's done some really thorough research here. Did you know that according to statistics supplied by a source at Global Seeds, South Africa is the major grower of genetically modified crops in Africa? And that our patent laws do more to protect the interests of the likes of Global Seeds than they do those of the farmers?

"Farmers here have already been signing technology agreements with Global Seeds that strip away their rights to save seed. Even illiterate smallholders have been signing these, most probably without knowing what they've actually agreed to."

Bonnie trotted over, her claws clicking on the tiled floor, and sat beside Jade's chair.

Jade took a sip of coffee, realising to her surprise that it was already cold.

"She concludes by stating that the decision to use GM-patented seeds will pose a serious threat to the smaller and poorer farmers in this country if it is continued. Well, I can understand that."

She was almost at the end of the notebook, and had decided that she supported Zelda's stance on this. The policies implemented by Global Seeds sounded both destructive and dangerous. As the journalist had emphasised again and again, it was not about feeding the world, but all about power and control. The people who control the food supply have the greatest power.

Jade read on in silence. Turning to the last page of the feint-lined notebook, she raised her eyebrows in surprise.

Written at the top of the page was the name she'd become familiar with. Danie Smit. And below it, no notes at all. Just a detailed drawing of an Arabian horse, in full gallop, nostrils flaring and tail streaming behind it like a banner.

The horse's ears were flat back, though, and its eyes were wide and white-rimmed.

It looked to Jade, from the drawing, as if it was scything its way through a field of ripening corn.

Turning to her laptop, she Googled the name Danie Smit. She hadn't expected to have much luck with such a common name and she didn't. There were hundreds of Danie Smits in Johannesburg, thousands in South Africa, and a fair sprinkling in other parts of the world.

What was interesting, though, was to read a short, recently uploaded newspaper report stating that, a week ago, the body of a man identified as Mr. Danie Smit had been found in his Mercedes Benz C-class, which had been parked in the underground garage of the Fourways Mall, with a hose running from the exhaust pipe into the car's interior. Police were treating this death, caused by carbon monoxide poisoning, as a suicide even though the man had left no note.

33

David had said he'd tell her when he next went to the gym. But he hadn't sounded like he meant it. Jade doubted that he had. Whether he'd admit it or not, she knew he didn't want to put her in any danger.

She phoned David's right-hand man, Captain Thembi, who was in the office that afternoon, and asked if he'd do her a favour and let her know when David left for the gym.

"I can phone you when he leaves," Thembi agreed. "But how do I know whether he'll be going to the gym or going home?"

"Call me anyway," Jade said. "And watch his face. If he's going to the gym he'll probably be looking miserable."

Thembi laughed. "These days the superintendent looks miserable when he's going home, too."

Does he now? Jade couldn't help the small surge of delight she felt at hearing these words. Unfounded, of course, since no matter how unhappy David was, he wasn't about to make any changes to his marital situation. Not with a new baby imminent.

She took Bonnie back home and then made herself some toast, which she thickly layered with a blend of mashed avocado, lemon juice and Tabasco sauce. The lemon and Tabasco were in roughly fifty–fifty quantities. A pinch of salt completed her culinary masterpiece.

She was about to bite into this delicious lunch when her phone rang. Thinking it would be Thembi, she snatched it up.

It wasn't. At first she could barely make out the husky voice of the man she was speaking to, and had to glance at the number ID to confirm the identity of her caller.

"Harris," she said. "How are you feeling? Have they fixed your fingers yet?"

"My hand is sore but they've strapped it up now. They can't do anything for the rib apart from painkillers, they said. I just have to wait till it heals." He really did sound hoarse thanks to his damaged windpipe. "Jade, I wanted to thank you for saving my life."

"Er . . . that's okay. No worries."

"I thought you should know . . ." He paused and cleared his throat with some difficulty. "I wanted you to know . . . just over a week ago, Zelda asked me to post a package for her. Speed Services."

"Is that so?" Suddenly all thoughts of food were forgotten. "Where did she want it posted?"

"A postbox address in Tankwa Town. For collection at the post office there."

"She sent something to her brother?"

"Yes. The package was addressed to Koenraad Meintjies."

"Was it large? Small? Did it state what the contents were?"

"It didn't, but it was a small parcel."

"How small? Compared to, say, a paperback."

"Smaller than a book. About the size of a cell phone, I think."

"Did she give a contact number for the brother? If you still have the waybill . . ."

"There was no contact number. The only one she put on . . . was her own number. I've been trying it every so often. It's always been turned off."

"Thank you for telling me this."

"I'm sorry I didn't discuss it before now. She . . . Jade, she was working on a sensitive story. She was working on it with somebody else helping her. I know that, but I don't know who."

"Did she ever mention the name Danie Smit?"

"No. She never mentioned any names. She asked me to post the parcel for her after our AA meeting. I sent it off the next day. She seemed . . . upset." Harris's rasping voice faltered. "Said she wasn't sure who she could trust any more and she needed this to be somewhere safe. And then I didn't hear from her again and she missed the next meeting."

Perhaps, Jade thought, Zelda had sounded upset because she'd just heard about Danie Smit's death.

She thanked Harris again and wished him a speedy recovery.

Then she ate her toast, even though the flavour seemed to have evaporated during the conversation she'd just had, and she was too distracted to enjoy the distinctive burn of the Tabasco.

Her meal finished, she drove all the way into the city centre, parking in Newtown outside the Market Theatre. She'd wait for Captain Thembi's call here, closer to Johannesburg Central police station. If she waited in Kyalami then by the time she'd managed to struggle through the traffic-clogged main roads, David would have finished his workout and gone home.

Thembi phoned as it was getting dark and told her that David was on his way out.

It took Jade ten minutes to reach the gym. She parked a few blocks away, pulled a grey hoodie over her head, and put on a pair of lightly tinted shades. She doubted whether David's stalker would recognise her, if he knew she existed at all.

Opposite the entrance to the gym was a tumbledown apartment block with a lobby thronged with residents and visitors. Enough of a crowd to allow her to blend in—at this time of day, at least. Jade stood near the door and pretended to be using her phone. She watched the entrance to the gym from out of the corner of her eye. Not once did she glance directly across at it. Then she went into the lobby and sat down on one of the benches listening to the babble of people around her. Apparently absorbed in sending SMS messages on her phone, she was keeping an eagle eye on the doorway across the road.

Nobody entered or left the building. This evening, at least, the anonymous note-writer was otherwise occupied.

David walked out of the door an hour later. His hair was tousled and he did indeed look miserable.

Jade sent him a text. "Been watching door. Nobody went in or out. Meet me in Newtown?"

Her phone buzzed in response almost immediately and her heart leaped.

Then, looking down at the screen, she saw the message wasn't from David. It was from a number she didn't recognise.

And it was obscure. The words "Pls don't sms or call me" followed by a meaningless string of numbers.

Jade stared at the text for a full minute before picking up her phone.

34

Over the hours, the landscape changed as Ntombi followed the N2 ever further southwest. Where were they headed and why? Her passenger clearly wasn't about to tell her, and she wasn't about to ask. He had pushed his seat back and appeared to be asleep, although she wasn't sure that was the case. Perhaps, under those face-hugging shades, he was watching her.

Surrounded by the flat, endless maize fields of the Free State, Bloemfontein came into view before them, sprawling below an empty sky, a dust-blanketed place of reds and greys and khakis that offered subdued relief from the endless golden-brown.

To her dismay, they drove straight through Bloemfontein. Ntombi's buttocks were numb from sitting in the same position for so long, and her hands felt as if they were welded to the wheel. Where were they going? Was he planning on going all the way to Cape Town, because already there were road signs and distance markers for the city. Slowly, imperceptibly, the car was eating up the kilometres, ticking the numbers down ten by ten, and as the hours went by distance signs for towns that had been hundreds of kilometres away grew closer until she thought of them as familiar, arrived, and then vanished as if they had never existed.

An hour after they had passed the Gariep Dam, when they were heading towards Colesberg, the man sat up and took the GPS unit off the dashboard. He pressed some keys before directing her to turn off the main highway and head in the direction of Kimberley.

Ntombi had never been to Kimberley, although she'd dreamed

of taking Small Khumalo there one day. It was a place steeped in history; the most famous diamond-mining town in South Africa, where stones like the Star of South Africa had been unearthed. She'd imagined Khumalo's wonder as they explored the museums together, walked the historic streets, and arrived at the famous Big Hole to peer, fascinated, down its steeply excavated sides and into its massive depths where today only stagnant, grey green water could be seen.

Thirty-eight, forty-two. Thirty-eight, forty-two.

The phone number that the nursing sister from the hospital had given her was lodged in her mind. It was puzzling, frightening, and yet, try as she might, Ntombi couldn't help but feel a surge of hope.

If she contacted this woman, she might get her only chance to find out what had really happened to her husband, and to her community.

Or perhaps—the thought sent chills through her body—it was a test to prove her loyalty towards her employer. Perhaps this was one of his people, and if she called her, then her employer would know she had disobeyed one of the conditions of her employment and she had made an unapproved phone call.

But he would find out anyway. If this woman was genuine, she might not wait for Ntombi to call her. She might get her number from the hospital and phone Ntombi herself. Right now, in this car, with this man listening, such a call could have disastrous consequences.

Panic flowed through her as she remembered Portia's words from earlier that morning. The wealthy woman was so determined she was an all-but unstoppable force. And now all her attention was focused on Ntombi's situation. If she insisted on trying to get labour lawyers involved then Ntombi and Khumalo were as good as dead. That much she knew.

And Portia would insist. She would simply not understand the seriousness of the situation. She lived in a different world; a far safer one, where her wealth and position insulated her from ever becoming a victim. She would never understand what it felt like to be vulnerable; without any protection; reliant on an employer who had made it very clear that anything except absolute loyalty would receive the harshest punishment.

Either way, then, Ntombi was doomed.

Mid-afternoon, much to her relief, because her bladder was just about bursting, her boss's vile client told her to pull over at the next petrol station.

This petrol station was very different from the Engen and Sasol garages they had passed on the main highway. Here, the station's floor was unevenly tarred. There were only a couple of pumps under a corrugated tin roof, and Ntombi knew that she would have to ask the way to the ladies' toilet, since she could see no signs for one at all, nor any brightly lit advertisements for food franchises like Wimpy and Steers.

When she set her feet on the dusty ground, Ntombi realised that they had left winter behind. The sun blasted down, its rays bouncing off the roof and heating the tarmac so it felt warm through her shoes.

The stop lasted fifteen minutes and followed the same programme as the morning's one. She stocked up on another batch of food, although this time her choices were limited to the small selection of flabby pies sweltering under a glass dome inside the tiny shop. The sandwich she had choked down earlier had been cold and tasteless. It still felt as if it was lying in her stomach like a rock. She couldn't bring herself to eat anything else.

In the toilet, which was located behind a struggling thorn tree at the back of the service station, Ntombi wondered whether she should risk calling the number that she now knew off by heart. She decided against it, which was just as well, because when she stepped outside again into the furnace of the afternoon, the man in the suit was waiting for her. He took her phone and scrolled through it, checking the recent call lists, before giving it back.

The message was clear. Her communications were being closely monitored. She was no longer to be trusted; if indeed she ever had been.

The landscape around her reflected her despair. Over the past few hours it had become drier and bleaker. The farmlands had given way to grey, rocky plains that stretched to a shimmering horizon; punctuated only by the occasional series of steep-sided, flat-topped hills on whose slopes nothing appeared to grow.

Every so often there were pockets and patches of soil where grasses and small bushes had taken hold. Otherwise, Ntombi saw only the occasional thorn bush clawing its way out of the steely ground.

The sun blazed mercilessly from an indigo sky.

A board so sun-bleached that its letters were barely legible informed them that they were in the Central Karoo. As Ntombi drove past she saw the sign was peppered with holes, their edges ragged and rusty.

The killer was checking the GPS carefully. He directed her off the main road and down a narrow minor road. Huge chunks of tarmac had broken off the sides and what remained was strewn with potholes. Eventually the tarmac stopped altogether, giving way to a seemingly endless, straight sand road.

Only the power lines running alongside it and the occasional straggling barbed-wire fence gave any indication that there might be civilisation near here.

It was 5:30 P.M. and the sun was setting in a blaze of reddish-gold when he ordered her to pull over and stop.

She eased the car to a halt on the bumpy roadside, although she thought pulling over was a waste of time, since they'd passed not a single vehicle since joining it an hour ago. She put the car into Park and turned off the engine. As the hissing of the air-con stopped, the silence screamed around them.

They waited, with Ntombi growing ever more apprehensive as night came. No lights were visible; not even on the horizon. Their absence was all-encompassing and disorienting. Glancing out of the deeply tinted window, she realised that the only illumination came from the sky, where a cold blanket of stars was spread above the darkened earth.

To try and ground herself, as a distraction from her surroundings, Ntombi started reciting recipes in her head. It was the same way she'd managed to pass those last, awful hours by Khumalo's deathbed, holding his hand and listening to his cries as he fought the pain and slowly succumbed to the disease. It was a strange way to calm herself, yet she found comfort in it. Now she went through the simple but tasty recipe for *dombolo*, or dumplings, which Nelson Mandela's personal chef, Xoliswa Ndoyiya, had made for the former president on many occasions and which was one of his favourites, enjoyed with oxtail or lamb stew.

Five cups of cake flour. A teaspoon of salt, a teaspoon of sugar. Ten grams of instant dry yeast. Two and a half cups of lukewarm water and two tablespoons butter. Sift the flour and salt together, combine with the sugar and yeast. Add the water gradually, mixing to form a soft dough. Knead until smooth and elastic, then cover the bowl and set aside in a warm place for an hour. Melt the butter in a pot. Roll the dough into balls the size of your palm . . .

"Get going," her passenger demanded, his hard, foreign accent yanking her back to reality. The comforting rhythm of the recipe flew out of her mind as she started up the engine. A few hundred metres later they reached a junction with a narrower and more uneven road. Ntombi did as she was told and turned left and carried on driving slowly and carefully. In this low-slung car it would be all too easy for a stray rock or a concealed dip in the road to cause damage that could lead to a breakdown.

And then, as they crested yet another shallow rise, she caught her breath as she finally saw lights ahead. Small but distinct. This wasn't a town or even a hamlet. As they drew closer she saw they were looking at the lighted windows of an isolated farmhouse.

She eased the car up the winding driveway and parked, as directed, a fair way from the house.

"Wait here," the man ordered. He leaned over and pulled the keys from the ignition, making it impossible for her to do otherwise.

He climbed out and, after reaching into the back of the car and taking out his gym bag, walked purposefully towards the house.

The door opened, spilling out more light, and she saw the silhouette of a tall man in the doorway.

Ntombi opened the door a crack. She thought she might be too far away to hear what they were saying, but the cooling air was clear and still and his voice carried further than she'd expected.

"Where is she?" the farmer asked.

"In the car."

Ntombi clutched the door handle, terrified, but then shock gave way to dread as she realised they were not, in fact, talking about her.

The killer was lying. There was nobody in the car but herself. She wanted to scream this fact aloud, shout the truth into the crackle-dryness of the night air.

"Give me the goods and you can have Zelda. You can bring them to the car and fetch her back with you."

"You don't get the goods until I've seen my sister, alive and well." The man's words were uncompromising but his voice sounded shaky and scared and Ntombi guessed this was because he was trying to negotiate while knowing he was at a huge disadvantage.

She wondered if Zelda was the unconscious woman that she had been forced to drive to a new location the day before. Most likely she was, but she was not here now. Ntombi didn't even know whether she was still alive.

"All right. You can see Zelda first."

Two sets of shoes scrunched over the sandy driveway as the men walked back towards the BMW. Ntombi cowered down in her seat, pulling the door closed again as quietly as she could and praying that she would not be harmed.

They walked directly to the back of the car and then Ntombi heard a jingle as the killer tossed the keys to the farmer.

"Here you are. She's inside the boot."

As the farmer bent to open the lid, the other man acted, lightning fast. He must have opened his gym bag on the way to the house because Ntombi had to swallow down a scream as she heard the dull, sickening thud of metal on bone, followed by a much heavier thump as the other man folded to the ground.

In an instant, the killer was on him. She heard muffled moans, and twisted round in her seat to watch in horror as he knelt on the farmer's chest and trussed his hands with a length of wire. Then he dragged the farmer, who was shouting and swearing and struggling like a landed fish, back up the sandy driveway to the house.

The farmhouse door closed and for a brief moment everything went quiet. And then the screams began.

High-pitched and animal-like, they shattered the stillness of the night and Ntombi clenched her teeth as tears spilled from her eyes. More than once she opened the car door and placed her feet on the sandy ground, bracing herself to flee. Running into the night would allow her to escape this horror, as short-lived as that escape might be.

Yet each time, paralysed by fear of the consequences, her body refused to obey. And with her door closed, the screams were at least a little fainter.

Gradually they died away, becoming fainter still when she curled up against the seat and jammed her fingers into her ears, pressing so hard her eardrums began to burn.

The wrench of the back passenger door opening jolted Ntombi from an uneasy sleep. She couldn't believe that she had managed to close her eyes and escape this place for a while, but now reality was back again.

The man heaved the gym bag onto the back seat and tossed her the car keys. He slammed the door and strode away again, heading back to the farmhouse.

The night was eerily silent. All she could hear was the rapid sound of her own breathing. But her sensitive nose picked up the taint of fresh blood close by.

Cloying and metallic, the raw-liver smell was emanating from the black bag that the man had so carelessly thrown inside. Ntombi fumbled for the window buzzer and stuck her head out into the night, taking in great gasps of the dry air. She noticed that there was now a light wind, blowing from the direction of the farmhouse, and it brought with it the smell of old blood and decaying flesh. She closed the window hastily and resolved not to breathe through her nose.

And then the man appeared in the doorway again and this time she could see that he was carrying something large and heavy on his back.

Not the farmer, she prayed. Please, oh please God, let him not be strapped into the back seat of the car. The thought of travelling those endless miles home with a bleeding victim or, worse still, a corpse, made Ntombi want to retch.

But as the man drew closer she saw that it was not a body he had slung over his shoulder. It was a large sack whose shape, size and appearance was all too familiar and all too terrible.

"Get out and come over here," he ordered her, his breath coming in gasps as he braced himself against the dead weight he carried.

"Open the boot."

She complied, and he heaved the object down into the empty space. It landed with a thud, sending up a puff of dust and causing the big vehicle to bounce on its springs.

She stared down at it wide-eyed, and for a moment felt the world spinning around her. Finally understanding what her employer had done. Finally aware of what her role in all of this was. Not just to play the role of a wealthy man's wife and help this killer get through roadblocks more easily. Oh, no. That was not the only reason they had forced her to accompany him.

No, oh no. Not this.

From his pocket he produced a small, sharp knife. At first she thought the blade was tainted with rust but then she realised what must have caused the discolouration.

He parted the tight weave of the sack carefully with the knife, exposing some of the contents which were clearly visible in the bright spotlight that shone from the lid of the open boot.

"Well?" he snapped at her. "Are these what you told your boss about?"

Koenraad Meintjies had known pain before, but never like this.

At his father's hands he'd suffered many times, often while protecting his younger sisters. The brutal punishment that man had dealt out had drawn blood many times. Broken bones more than once. Snapped fingers, cracked ribs, loosened teeth. All in the name of the Lord, whose vengeance he was supposedly channelling as he wielded his heavy buckled belt, the wooden staff he used to pound the floor during sermons, or his bare, meaty fists.

Koenraad had soon become accustomed to hearing his father's voice rising and falling ever more breathlessly in a series of chants as he worked himself into an ecstasy of rage. Just like when he gave his sermons, only at home the violence that constantly simmered inside him boiled over into brutal deeds.

"And then I saw the horses in the vision . . ." The shaft of the wooden pole would be used to give him a glancing blow on the head . . . "And out of their mouths issued fire and smoke and brimstone . . ." Another merciless blow, followed by more breathless exhortations. ". . . And the rest of the men who were not killed by these plagues yet repented not . . . Neither repented they of their murders, nor of their sorceries, nor of their fornications, nor of their thefts . . ."

When a younger boy, he had done his best to duck, dodge, roll with the blows, until he grew too tired or one of them found a vulnerable target.

Now, bloodied and butchered, all he could do was slump against the tight wire bonds that held him to the wooden chair and listen to his own cries, soft and strange, a faint mewling. As helpless and weak as a newborn kitten.

His eyes had been taken one by one. All he could see now was darkness; his last sight had been the implacable face of his tormentor.

Eventually he had given up the information he was withholding. He had told the man the location of the goods he had come to collect. But then the punishment had not stopped, and he had broken. Cried and begged and yammered and howled. He would have done anything to put an end to the pain.

They had tortured prisoners when he was in the army. Those who had been left too badly broken had been given the merciful gift of death after they had confessed what they knew. But now the man who had inflicted this pain was gone and the house was quiet and he was left with only the screaming spectres of his agony.

Zelda.

He had been betrayed, and now, after he had been unable to protect Sonet from her fate, he had failed Zelda too.

Let her not die the same way, he prayed. Let him spare her or, if not, let her end be quick at least. But please not this . . . not this. I cannot stand it. Please God, let it end.

And as if in answer to his prayers, he suddenly saw a clear image, although with his ruined eyes he had no idea how.

Two grey Arabian mares had lived in the veld near their farmhouse, roaming the dry ground and picking at the sparse grasses. They were skinny and rough-coated, but they were wild and proud, and over the years Zelda had tamed the broodmare and her daughter so that they had no fear of humans and would come when she called, arching their necks as they approached and stretching their soft muzzles forward in curious greeting.

Zelda had named them too. The mare was Shazeer and her daughter Serenade.

And now, there were Shazeer and Serenade, just as he remembered them, galloping towards him with a drumming of hooves. He gasped as he saw their beauty, nostrils flared, pale coats shimmering, manes and tails streaming out behind them like water as they ran. Their legs flashed forward in perfect rhythm, every stride strong and sure and true.

This time they did not stop to greet him but galloped past, ears pricked and heads high, and he was swept up with them and carried along, his pain forgotten, laughing in sheer joy at the exhilaration of speed; at the freedom he had suddenly found.

In the farmhouse kitchen where the overhead light still burned, the wooden chair tipped slowly sideways and then toppled to the ground, taking Koenraad's lifeless body with it.

35

Ntombi had not driven very far from the farmhouse when she was once again ordered to stop the car.

Immersed in her own frantic thoughts, she barely noticed her passenger had spoken, and he had to repeat his request again, this time in a sharper voice.

"Pull over."

When she stopped, he lifted the gym bag and its bloody contents out of the back seat and strode away into the night.

Ntombi buried her face in her hands.

How could she not have seen this coming? All the questions her employer had asked . . . the interest he had shown in her predicament . . . and then the arrival of this man and the start of her nightmare.

He had been following up all along on what she'd originally asked him to. But he hadn't been doing it for her. Like the farmer, she too had been betrayed. He had used the information against her and now the consequences would be more terrible than she could ever have imagined.

"How many people will die?" she breathed.

Then, with a jolt, she remembered the phone number she had been given that morning.

This might be her only chance. How to do it? And how much time did she have?

She fumbled around in her bag for her cell phone and keyed in the number with shaking fingers. She wasn't going to risk a call. She could not. But on this basic model, although there was a record of calls made and received, there was no record of SMS messages sent. It would be her only way.

"Pls do not reply to this or phone me," she typed. What next? The location of the farmhouse. She had very little idea where it was, but the man had left the GPS on the seat. She turned it towards her and keyed in the co-ordinates she saw there now.

Now what?

How could she condense into just a few words, sent to a stranger, the catastrophic consequences of what would happen now?

And then she realised she wasn't going to have the chance, because she could hear the sandy crunch of footsteps. Before she could have second thoughts or let her fear stop her, she stabbed "Send" and dropped her phone back in her bag as if it were red hot.

He wrenched open the passenger door and sat down heavily. He no longer had the bag with him. He must have disposed of it somewhere out there in the darkness.

She waited, heart thudding, expecting at any moment to hear the trill of her cell phone or the beep of an incoming message responding to what she had sent. But everything remained quiet.

"Drive back to Johannesburg," he ordered her impatiently.

Sick with fear that the woman she had so recklessly contacted would call or message her back, despite her request to the contrary, Ntombi wordlessly complied.

36

"Pls don't sms or call me." Jade considered what the words might mean as she listened to the phone ring and ring and ring.

Eventually her call was answered.

"Jadey." David sounded tired and stressed and as if his sense of humour had been rerouted to a foreign country where it was battling to get through Customs.

"You didn't respond to my message."

"Sorry. Only saw it now. I'm driving past Newtown as we speak. I'll meet you at Sophiatown restaurant."

Even over the phone Jade could hear the squeal of brakes and blaring of hooters that typically accompanied David's split-second driving decisions.

Ten minutes later she was back in Newtown and walking between the flaming oil drums that lit the outside seating area and into the restaurant. Black and white decor, oversized images of jazz musicians on the walls, plain wooden tables. David had two glasses of red wine already waiting. Jade sat down opposite him.

"I'm sorry. I watched the gym but nobody went in."

"No notes for me today," he said.

"It would've helped if you'd told me you were going."

They clinked glasses. The house wine tasted rough and sour. A reflection of her mood? Perhaps.

"I thought you had enough on your plate. In any case, you seem to have your own methods of finding out."

Was that a smile trying to breach the grim battlements of his face? Jade wasn't sure.

"This time, yes. But unfortunately, surveillance being what it is, one stake-out doesn't usually pinpoint a suspect. Next time give me some warning."

"I will," he said, but again she had no idea whether he meant it.

"I've got something curious to show you," she said as she took her cell phone out of her pocket.

Look at this," she said, handing him the instrument.

David read the message.

"Odd. Know who it's from?"

"No idea."

"Tried calling it?"

"No."

"Why?"

"Because the sender asked me not to."

"And you think they might have a good reason?"

"Good enough for me not to want to risk compromising them."

"Still, if the sender doesn't want you to respond, then what's the point of sending the damn message in the first place?"

"That's what I'm trying to work out."

"The message itself is clear enough. What the hell is that jumble of numbers after it, though? Three-two-two-three-four-zero-comma-two-zero-three-nine-four-two. Hmmm. Not a phone number."

"It's information, of a sort. It must be. Date, time, place . . ."

"Two sets of numbers. The comma separates them."

They fell silent for a moment, listening to the background strains of the plaintive saxophone.

"You got any guesses who it's from?"

"I've got one guess."

"You want to tell me?"

"Not yet. I need some information on the investigation, though."

David sighed.

"I spoke to the detective in charge today. Captain Nxumalo, who's working under Moloi."

"Has he sent a team out to interview Sonet's ex-husband yet?"

"Yes. He went there personally today, with one of his constables."

"What did Van Schalkwyk say?"

"He's been taken into custody pending further questioning."

Jade sat up straighter. "Really? Did that decision have anything to do with his leaflets about the Boere Krisis Kommando?"

"No. It was because when Nxumalo asked Van Schalkwyk if he'd ever participated in vigilante action or was a member of any vigilante groups, he lost it. Started getting violent and tried to punch him. So, with some difficulty, Nxumalo and his constable subdued him and he's now in a holding cell at Bronkhorstspruit police station, awaiting further questioning."

"Will you let me know what happens?"

"If I can, Jadey. And don't make faces like that. This isn't red tape. I know what you're going to say. This is just following due process. And you do know that I'm going to be obliged to tell Nxumalo about this message you've received. It may be pivotal to the investigation."

"I understand," Jade said. "But I can't let you give the team this phone number, David. I can't risk passing on the number of someone who expressly asked me not to call them back. Not even to the police. What if someone in Nxumalo's team dials it? You know how these things happen."

"It can only be helpful to Nxumalo, and he'll treat it confidentially if I ask him to. He's a good guy. He's only been recently promoted to captain and he's inherited a total screw-up of a backlog thanks to the previous captain's incompetence."

"Sounds a lot like your situation when you were promoted to superintendent."

"Very similar. You helped me out. Do me a favour for a friend and help him too."

"I'll give it some thought."

"Well, think quickly. My wine's nearly finished. And in the meantime it would be helpful if you could summarise for me everything you know so far about this case." David's face was serious.

Jade counted off the points on her fingers as she spoke.

"On the fifteenth of this month, Victor Theron and his base-jumping partner Sonet Meintjies entered the Sandton View skyscraper illegally and climbed onto the roof in order to jump off it. According to Victor, he jumped first and Sonet fell to her death a few minutes later. Right?"

"Is there usually a delay of a few minutes between one person jumping and the next?"

"No, there isn't. Victor said he'd begun to worry within a minute of being on the ground. He was wondering if she'd lost her nerve or had some sort of a problem. He was on the point of phoning her when she fell."

"And then?"

"Dead on impact. The investigators subsequently discovered that her chute had been sabotaged. The canopy was cut through. And it was Victor who'd packed it for her."

"That didn't have to happen when it was packed. Could have happened up there at the top of the building, especially if there was a delay up there. Someone with a knife . . . Grab, slice and shove."

"If you had a knife, why not just stab her and leave her up there?"

"Perhaps there was a struggle," David said. "Perhaps they meant to stab her but didn't manage."

"Oh, come on, David. If someone's up there with a knife and they had time to cut her parachute, they had enough time and resolve to kill her. Either they wanted to make it look like an accident, or . . ." Jade paused for a moment, thinking. Across the room a fashionably dressed black woman, in conversation with her business-suited partner, threw back her head and laughed loudly. The sound was unforced, spontaneous, merry. It was infectious, too. Other people around her turned and smiled. Not Jade and David, though. The sound was deflected by the darkness of their conversation and had no impact on them.

"Or?"

"Falling to your death with a damaged chute is a lot more dramatic; more frightening than a simple stabbing. That's what I've realised was troubling me during my last meeting with

Victor Theron. Her death was shocking. Attention-grabbing. So what's it drawing attention away from?"

"What are you thinking?"

"I'm wondering if her death was a warning or a message to somebody else. A threat of some kind: 'Look what we can do. We can get to her at the top of Sandton Views, on a base jumping mission nobody knew about, and we can ensure she dies in terror, falling a full sixty-four storeys.' That's a long way. Plenty of time to scream."

David exhaled sharply as if he didn't want to dwell on that scenario.

"And who would the threat have been aimed at?"

"Well, her sister Zelda disappeared at around the same time."

"Right."

"Sonet worked for Williams Management, a charity specialising in setting up sustainable farming ventures in impoverished communities."

"Go on."

"The Siyabonga community, who set up a farm in Theunisvlei, seemed to be doing well. Then they all disappeared. Practically overnight. Every last one of them. Nobody seems to know what happened. The fields are empty. Arid. In fact, they look as if they've been sown with salt. Their houses have been razed, as has the mill down by the river that they were using to grind the maize."

"Bizarre," David shook his head.

"Zelda is a journalist. I think Sonet asked her to poke around and see if she could find out what happened to them."

"A journalist? What sort? Features?"

"She's alternative. Off the beaten track. Rather extreme in her views—a bit of a paranoid conspiracy theorist."

"You're not a paranoid conspiracy theorist if they're really out to get you," David observed.

"Well, this is true." Jade found to her surprise that she had drained the last of her wine. It seemed the red hadn't been as undrinkable as she'd originally thought. "Anyway, Zelda wrote, or writes, on food mainly. She's militant on organic, non-GM, non-irradiated foodstuffs. Big on the power struggle surrounding food and farmland. She has a nice sideline going on the health risks of pesticides and herbicides and genetically modified organisms—well, anyway, after reading one or two of her articles I'm not sure what to put in my trolley the next time I go shopping."

"Is that all she writes on? I can't see how that's relevant."

"Well, that's not all. She has also written on land reform."

"Land reform? Now there's a thorny subject." David leaned forward, his face intent.

"It just so happens that Theunisvlei, the land the community was farming, used to belong to Sonet's ex-husband. It was given back to the Siyabonga tribe after a successful land claim."

"You've interviewed the husband?"

"Yes. He was the one who told me about it. He's very bitter." David considered her words before speaking again.

"You think he might have had a hand in destroying the community's farming operation? And that's why he became violent when Nxumalo questioned him?"

Jade shrugged, her hands palm up.

"If the theory held water, then every piece of the puzzle would fall into place. The angry husband who wanted revenge on the tribe who had taken 'his' land and at the same time get back at his ex-wife for helping them set up their operation. I guess a farmer would know what to do to make sure a harvest failed. Somehow he managed to damage the farming operation to such an extent that the community upped and left."

"And you say it doesn't work because?"

"Well, the piece of land they took over is huge. Thousands of acres. Only a small part of it had been cultivated, a big field near the river. The rest of the land looked fine. Why didn't they start again on a new piece? Or complain to Williams Management and ask for help and protection? Why would an entire community leave the beautiful farm that was their heritage and their tribal right, and disappear?"

"Perhaps they were encouraged to leave."

"Or perhaps they were made to disappear."

"You're talking genocide here?" David sounded alarmed.

"It's a possibility."

Jade thought again of the wind whistling through the deserted barn. Of the single rock she had found with the dark, rusty residue of what might have been blood.

"Would have been a hell of an operation," David said. "One man with a grudge couldn't have done it alone. And there must have been survivors. There always are. How many people were in that community? A couple hundred?"

"Yes, judging by what remained of their housing."

David shook his head again.

"Impossible."

"It is. The place is creepy. It had sad and desolate air about it. I know it sounds ridiculous, but I wished that the land itself could speak; that it could tell us what happened to the people who farmed it. I thought . . ."

"Go on?"

"Sorry. I just thought of something while I was telling you about the land."

"What's that, Jadey?"

"Distance. Place. Those numbers in the text message . . . they could be GPS coordinates."

David thought it over.

"Let's see the message again."

He re-read it and took out his own phone.

"If those numbers are coordinates, they're definitely nowhere near Jo'burg. Much further south. I've got an app that can pinpoint them, if I can make it work, that is."

David pulled a face in response to Jade's raised eyebrows,

"An app," he repeated. "Listen to me. I sound like Kevin. Why did I decide to get a bloody iPhone and turn into such a geek?"

"Well, it's certainly proving useful tonight."

"Don't speak too soon," David warned.

But his phone proved co-operative and within a couple of minutes it had come up with the goods. "It's mapped the coordinates," he told Jade, in tones of equal triumph and disbelief.

"Pass it over and let's see."

David slid the phone across the table.

"It's not working," Jade said. "This is just a blank screen. There's nothing here."

"That's because there is nothing there."

"What do you mean?"

"Zoom out. Yes, with your finger, like that. You can see now, right? Those co-ordinates are somewhere near the Tankwa Karoo national park. The vastest, emptiest, most barren area in the whole of the country. So, the numbers must mean something else. We'd better start thinking again."

"No," Jade said.

"Why?"

"Does your phone have an app for booking last-minute flights?"

David blinked. "Um . . . yes, it does. It's known as the facility to make a phone call."

"Very funny. I need to go there right now. I'll explain why later. If there's still a flight this evening then I'll take it. If not, I'll drive."

"You can't just fly into the middle of the bloody Tankwa Karoo. You'll have to fly to the nearest major town, which is probably George, and then hire a car. And it's nearly seven P.M. already. This could be tricky to sort out. Let me phone Kulula and see if there's a flight still available this evening. There's no way you're driving there and back on your own. It's a fourteen-, fifteen-hour journey."

Come with me, then, Jade wanted to say, but she didn't.

Still talking on the phone, David signalled the waiter for the bill. Pre-empting him, Jade slid a hundred-rand note under the ashtray.

"You're in luck," David told her, covering the phone with his hand as he spoke rapidly. "They have later flights scheduled tonight and tomorrow because of the long weekend. Tonight's leaves in an hour, which is touch and go in terms of timing, but I think it's doable. They've got a couple of seats still available on it. You want one?"

Jade took a deep breath. Handed over her credit card.

"Book them both," she said.

37

Strapped firmly in the passenger seat of David's unmarked Toyota Yaris, Jade clung to the handle above the passenger door as David zigzagged the car through the almost-empty backstreets of Johannesburg city, taking the shortest route to the airport highway.

She was still astonished he'd decided to go with her. He'd mumbled something about his workload, but the protest had been more for form's sake than anything else. After all, his family was away for the weekend. He'd told her that the last time they'd met up. And although Jade knew things would change once Naisha had had the baby, for now she fancied herself in an unspoken contest with the woman, to see how much of David's time she could monopolise.

Their marriage was on the rocks, Jade told herself. Another child wouldn't change the situation for the better. She thought David was an idiot for staying in the relationship. An honourable, old-fashioned idiot for standing by his estranged wife after a single night spent with her during their period of separation had resulted in an unplanned pregnancy.

Unplanned, Jade thought cynically, on David's side at least.

"Right. Ten more minutes and we're there." Engine revving furiously, the unmarked veered onto the highway and shot across the lanes at what felt like a forty-five degree angle.

Jade closed her eyes, but finding it was even more terrifying that way, she opened them again in a hurry. No matter how much of a lunatic David was behind the wheel, she found herself compelled to keep an eye out for obstacles.

"Taxi on the left," she warned, as the unwary driver began to drift into the fast lane. A blast from David's hooter saw him hurriedly correct course as they whipped past.

"So are you going to tell me why we're going on this crazy escapade with no luggage?" David asked.

"No. Concentrate on your driving. I'll tell you when we're at the airport. I've got to get on the phone now and book us a hired car."

"Pity we weren't nearer Sandton earlier. We could have hopped on the Gautrain and got there faster."

"Faster? I doubt it. There in one piece? Yes, much more likely." David laughed.

They reached the airport, parked in the first available bay in the underground car park, and sprinted to domestic departures. They ran up the escalator ramps and arrived at check-in seconds before the flight closed.

"Just in time," observed the attendant at check-in, as if she was slightly disappointed at not being able to tell them the flight was closed. "That'll be the two of you travelling to George? May I see your IDs please?"

The race against the clock was not yet over. Another feverish rush to the secure check-in area where David signed in his service pistol for transportation in the gun safe. Then a frantic shuffle through security and a full-on sprint down to the boarding gates, where the last of the stragglers were handing over their boarding cards. The ground hostess was on the intercom, announcing the final boarding call for passengers de Jong and Patel.

Jade collapsed into her seat feeling as if she'd taken part in some sort of urban half-marathon. Beside her, David's breathing reminded her of a pair of blacksmith's bellows.

She hadn't packed so much as a change of clothes. Between them, they didn't even have a toothbrush.

It might all be a waste of time, but surely not every lead would prove to be a disappointment. Eventually one, no matter how unpromising it looked, would have to get her somewhere.

They were in the air when their conversation resumed.

"You asked why we're flying down to George," she said.

"Yes. It did occur to me."

"Well, let me finish explaining the background to the case. Then you'll understand."

"Okay. Fire away."

"Zelda and Sonet were abused as children, apparently. There were three siblings—the two girls and a brother, Koenraad. Harris told me that the brother is off the grid, but I think tracing him is critical for the case, and perhaps for his own safety as well, given what's happened to his sisters. They're a very close family, Harris said."

"Aha."

"Their father was a preacher. Had a cult following. Used to rant and rave about the Book of Revelations and about the Second Coming and how sinners would be destroyed in hellfire. It made me think—it sounds crazy, I know, but looking at that abandoned farm . . ."

"What?"

"It made me think of the four horsemen. Of the white horse, galloping across that landscape, leaving death and destruction behind."

"Death rode a pale horse, not a white one," David corrected her. "There's a difference."

"There is? How do you know that?" Jade asked, surprised.

"Ages ago I dated a woman who was studying theology."

Jade bit back a surprised comment. She'd always thought of David as having had just two lovers in his life—herself and Naisha. She'd never wanted to believe he'd had more, even though logic told her otherwise. It was just surprising. Disconcerting. For a moment she felt oddly jealous that another woman had shared his time and had told him her stories. Pillow talk about the Book of Revelations . . . she could only hope the relationship had been short, and that they hadn't started dating when she was reading the Book of Genesis.

"So tell me about the horsemen," she said.

"The imagery is vivid, which is why it's stuck in my mind. In the scriptures, the white horse appears first. His rider has a bow and a crown, and he is the conqueror. Then the fiery red horse comes out. I suppose you'd say that one was war, because the rider was given power to take peace away from the earth and to make men kill each other. He carries a sword, obviously."

"Who's next?"

"Next is the black one, and the rider carries a pair of scales, but I can't for the life of me remember what his role is. He says something about measures of crops for a penny. Wheat and barley, and he also talks about oil and wine."

"Sounds like the origin of the futures markets," Jade commented, remembering Theron's drawn and intense expression when he'd spoken about his work.

"Anyway, finally, the pale rider and his pale horse appear. The rider is named Death, and Hell follows close behind him. They have the power to kill by sword, famine and plague, and by the wild beasts of the earth."

Jade found herself hugging her arms as if to ward off a chilly draught while she considered his words.

"Its rider was named Death, and Hell followed close behind. They were given power to kill by sword, famine and plague."

Jade wondered what it would've been like to grow up under the iron rule of an abusive preacher who, through his interpretation of those disturbing verses, had gained both power and control over his followers.

"So now Sonet's dead and Zelda's disappeared. She seems to have been helped with her research by a man called Danie Smit. I don't know anything more about him, but I do know that a Danie Smit was found dead in his car in Fourways Mall last week. Suspected suicide through carbon monoxide poisoning."

"Now there's a coincidence."

"Anyway, a parcel was posted off to the Tankwa Karoo Post Office a week ago on Zelda's behalf, addressed to her brother. Which is why this set of co-ordinates is worth investigating."

David nodded slowly.

"Well, let's go see what we can find out," he said.

38

At George airport, Jade and David were met by a red-uniformed Avis representative holding a card on which their names were laser-printed. While David signed the paperwork and went to retrieve his firearm, Jade headed over to the only kiosk which was still open and bought a couple of T-shirts from the limited selection available. One for her in medium, one for David in extra large, just in case they needed a change of clothes. The kiosk's stock didn't stretch to toothbrushes so she had to settle for a packet of sugar-free gum.

After taking possession of the air-conditioned VW Polo, they drove out of the airport and headed to one of the nearby three-star guesthouses that Jade had contacted just before take-off.

They were travelling in style, courtesy of Victor Theron's sizeable payment. He'd be glad that at last she was incurring some significant expenses on his behalf. He'd been getting edgy, Jade thought, probably believing that if she wasn't spending much of his money, she couldn't possibly be doing an effective job.

But then again, as she'd discovered, it didn't take much to make Theron edgy. Perhaps that was what intrigued her most about him. He wasn't a typical base-jumper, that was for sure. She'd known extreme sports fanatics in the past and most of them had been so laid back that they might as well have been horizontal.

She and David had booked separate rooms and Jade paid their bill in advance, as the night porter checked them in, explaining that they had a very early start the next day. The plushly decorated en-suite she'd been assigned felt as lonely as an isolation cell, and she couldn't help remembering the early days of her friendship with David, when he had first moved to Johannesburg and joined the investigation team headed up by her father. On their infrequent trips away together, she and David had occasionally shared a room, and a bed, sleeping companionably back to back and fully clothed.

Of course, turning back the clock now was impossible.

Jade set her alarm for four-thirty A.M. and fell asleep listening to the sounds of the ocean, which she could hear, but not see.

She didn't get a chance to see it in the morning either, although the crashing rhythm of the waves resonated through her as soon as she woke.

Peering through the curtains she saw it was still pitch black outside. She dressed quickly, putting back on the clothes she'd taken off the night before, and headed downstairs. David appeared ten minutes later.

"Sleep well?" she asked. He gave an annoyed headshake in response.

"Damn waves kept on breaking on the rocks. I can't sleep if I'm too close to nature. I kept on listening out for normal, everyday noises. Gunshots, sirens, screaming."

The air outside felt heavy, dense and laden with salt after the thin, dry winter air of Johannesburg. The wind was gusting, driving rain and spray into their faces as they braved the short dash to the car.

"Would've liked to have had breakfast," David remarked as they drove onto the road. "They do the works here. I saw the menu outside the dining room. Eggs, bacon, boerewors, chips, mushrooms, melted cheese and grilled tomatoes on a pancake."

"We can stop for breakfast later," Jade said.

David put the windscreen wipers on high.

"Damn rain," he observed.

"Enjoy it while it lasts," Jade said. "I don't think there's going to be much of it where we're headed."

She felt a sudden queasiness in her stomach. Part excitement, part nerves. There was always a chance, she supposed, that the

SMS was a trap. That somebody was baiting her with a cryptic clue, waiting to finish the task the hired thugs had failed to accomplish.

There was more of a chance that it was genuine, because of the one loose end that she hadn't yet explained fully to David.

Khumalo's wife. The woman she'd been trying to contact. The woman the hospital receptionist had told her they'd managed to track down just a few hours before the message came through.

And, as far as she knew, the only traceable person once part of the Siyabonga community.

This woman must have some of the answers.

If her husband had been hospitalised with cancer at the time, perhaps she had been in the ward with him. Perhaps that was how she'd escaped whatever fate had befallen the rest of the village.

Perhaps she'd travelled, or been transported, to the farm-house in the Karoo to keep her safe.

Although why, then, if she was so safe, had she expressly requested that Jade not contact her?

That fact was only one of several that worried Jade, making her doubt that her proposed solution to the puzzle was as simple and straightforward as she was hoping it would be.

It was still dark when they joined the highway and drove out of George, over the Outeniqua mountain pass, heading away from the lush sub-tropical coast and into the rain shadow.

An arid expanse of land. From the glimpses Jade could see in the headlights, it was flat and stark and becoming increasingly dry as the kilometres ticked by.

It was barely approaching dawn when David pulled over, hazard lights flashing, and came to a standstill on what was now just a single strip of tarmac.

"We've got a problem here," he said.

"What's that?"

"We're starting to move away from these co-ordinates. We were getting closer until a few kilometres back. There must have been a turnoff we've missed somewhere; unless it's up ahead."

"No other road was signposted," Jade said. "Perhaps we need to turn onto one of those sand tracks."

"Yup," David said, sounding gloomy.

"So let's backtrack, slower this time," Jade tried not to emphasise the word "slower" too much, "and take a closer look. If it isn't back there then it has to be up ahead."

The side road was three kilometres back, and Jade only spotted it because of a bank of sand that had been washed alongside the main road when, months and months ago, it must have rained.

David eased the car over the ridge. Jade watched the GPS closely. The degrees and the minutes were identical to those on the strange text message. It was only the seconds, now, that were slowly changing as they navigated the uneven terrain.

On the eastern horizon, Jade noticed the start of a faint pink glow. A minute later the landscape in front of her had lightened to a sombre vista of various shades of grey. The horizon was occasionally punctuated by a rugged, flat-topped hill.

There was absolutely no sign of what she'd been hoping the co-ordinates would lead them to—an old-fashioned, gabled Karoo farmhouse.

"David, stop the car here," she said, sounding worried.

"Sure." he responded. Giving her a questioning look he carefully—for once—brought the car to a halt and they both stepped out into the morning's temporary chill and stood in a silence that was vast, enduring and absolute.

"I thought it might be better to walk the last stretch," Jade explained. She spoke in a low voice, even though there was nobody else around to hear. "If we carry on driving, we might miss something."

What, she didn't know. Signs of a struggle? A message in a bottle? What was she hoping to find out in this uninhabited and peaceful looking place?

Even the air smelled of nothing. Dry, pure and clean.

She took the GPS out of the car and carried it with her.

The road they walked on was little more than bedrock and stones, but every so often there were swathes of sand. It was in one of these that Jade saw the imprints of another vehicle's tyres.

"Someone's driven through here recently," she observed. But of course they must have. After all, that someone would have had to embark on an extremely long and lonely walk from the main road to have reached these co-ordinates on foot.

David stumbled over a protruding rock and slipped on some gravel as he tried to right himself. He ended up sprawled on his side on what passed for soil. Getting up and dusting himself off, he cursed under his breath. "That damn stone would take out the sump of most cars," he grumbled. "When was this road last graded? During the Anglo-Boer war?"

Jade resisted the temptation to ask if he was all right, knowing she could only expect a grumpy response. Instead she studied the GPS, and now with some concern, as it was signalling that they were almost at their destination.

Then the co-ordinates flicked over to match the numbers on Jade's cell phone. And, at the same time, David remarked, "Looks like they pulled over up there."

A little further ahead, heavy tyre tracks curved off the road, such as it was, and through a tract of sand. Slowly walking closer, Jade noticed a set of footprints, most likely a man's if the size was anything to go by.

"Someone got out here. And got back in from the looks of it." David bent down to scrutinise the prints, stepping carefully so that his own feet remained on a stony surface.

"Got out from the left side. The passenger side."

"Or the driver's side if it's a left-hand drive vehicle."

"But why get out here? To do what?"

David gazed at the landscape, turning slowly, taking in the endless horizon, the sparse, stunted foliage, the shape of their car visible half a kilometre away. The only other sign of civilization was the tall, red- and white-painted cell phone tower now visible much further down the road.

"To take a piss?" he suggested. "Jade, I just don't know. But somebody thought it was important enough to send you the co-ordinates. Perhaps we should take a look round. Comb the area. Just in case . . ."

He didn't complete the sentence but Jade understood his fear: Just in case a body had been dumped somewhere.

"You look on the right-hand side of the road, Jadey. He might have crossed over. I'll take the left."

There he went again. Protecting her. Volunteering to search the side where they both knew it was far more likely that something might be waiting to be found.

She didn't know whether to feel touched or annoyed.

To her right there was another deep stretch of sand but she couldn't see any footprints in it. Still, a search was a search.

She walked for fifty paces alongside the road, scanning the ground carefully, seeing nothing but rocks and sand and the occasional desiccated clump of grass.

Then she turned round, stepped four paces off the road, and walked back a hundred paces, looking carefully to the left and the right. When she'd reached a hundred she took another four paces away from the road and walked the line again.

Her grid-like search took her even further from the road and deeper into the beginnings of the desert. Opposite her, she saw David following the same methodical pattern.

About twenty minutes later, Jade heard him shout.

39

Jade abandoned her search efforts and jogged in the direction of David's voice. He was almost out of sight now; standing on the other side of a stony ridge in the ground. Here lay a deep channel, presumably a result of centuries-old water erosion, back when the Karoo had had a different climate.

At the bottom of the channel lay a black gym bag.

It was a new-looking item, and it must have been dumped recently because it was free of dust and sun-damage.

Jade found herself unable to tear her gaze away from it.

This was what they were looking for; what they had been informed about.

Surely it had to be.

David climbed down into the trough, causing rivulets of sand to cascade down its sides, and unzipped the bag. Jade craned her neck to see inside but his body was blocking the view. Then he zipped it up and heaved it out. From the way he was holding it, it looked heavy.

Back up next to Jade, he placed it on the ground and glanced at her, his face grim.

"Not good," he said.

"Why? What's in there?"

"Wire. Pliers. Blades. Other stuff . . . Jade, it's bloodstained, and the blood's not old. I can still smell it. You probably can, too."

Jade bent down closer to the bag and inhaled. David was right. The scent was unmistakable and unpleasantly familiar.

"But there's no body," she said flatly.

"Nope. And this is the only piece of ground for miles that isn't flat. If a body's been dumped, this is surely where it would be. Whoever these tools were used on is somewhere else."

"In the car that stopped here?"

"Perhaps."

They stared disconsolately at the unforgiving landscape.

"Well, better get going, I guess," David said. "We can take a drive a bit further down the road if you like, just to be sure. Then I'll have to check this bag in with airport security. Get it sealed in plastic and fly it back to headquarters."

"Wait a minute," Jade said. "There's something else I want to do. It won't take long."

Ten minutes later, they were parked further up the road, a few metres away from the cell phone tower. At close range it didn't look so narrow, but it did look much taller. The four-legged tower was set into a deep concrete base. The struts that formed its legs were reinforced by a lattice of strips of metal welded at forty-five degrees angles. The structure was painted in broad stripes of now-peeling white and red paint and it was fenced off, but only by a few flimsy strands of wire.

"What on earth do you think you're going to find in there?" David asked as Jade pushed the wire strands apart and climbed through.

Standing on the concrete, Jade touched one of the legs. The metal felt icy cold, chilled from the desert night. Perhaps by the afternoon it would be too hot to touch.

Looking up, she could barely see the top of the tower. From this angle it appeared impossibly tall, its tip piercing the endless expanse of sky. Just the thought of how it would look and feel from up there made her dizzy.

Lifting her right foot up high, she placed it onto the lowest bar of the support. Reached above her and pulled herself up, the narrow edge of the strut digging into her palm. Now she was on the tower itself, her feet placed rather awkwardly in the "v" formed by the lowest diagonal strut, her hands gripping the "x" of the one above.

"Jade, what are you . . . ?"

She didn't answer. David would work the answer to his own question out in a minute, if he hadn't already done so.

She grasped the next beam and swung herself higher, again wedging her foot into the "V-shaped corner of the strut.

"Jade, we don't have time for this. We need to go," David called out.

"Sonet's husband told me something that stuck in my mind," she shouted back down to him.

"What was that? How to kill yourself by falling off a cell phone tower?"

"You're sort of right." She stretched, grasped, pulled herself up again. It was easy, she told herself. As long as you didn't look down, she added, catching her breath when she caught a glimpse of David. She was only three or four metres above him, but it already looked like a sizeable gap. And she hadn't even got a tenth of the way up.

"He said that Sonet used to travel to the Karoo in order to do base jumping," she called down to him. "He said there was a site near her brother's house that she used to jump from. I'm wondering if this might be it. And if I climb it, whether I'll be able to see the house."

David took a few seconds to respond.

Having digested Jade's words, he shouted back. "Okay, dammit, that makes sense. But Jade, bloody hell, why do you make me do these things?"

"I'm not making you do anything!"

But her protests went unheard as David grasped the rail and, causing vibrations in the structure that she could clearly feel from her higher vantage point, swung himself up and planted his feet heavily on the bottom beam.

It'll be all right if you don't look down . . .

Easy advice to give, Jade found, but difficult to take, especially when she could feel the structure shuddering under his heavier weight.

As she climbed, so did the sun, spilling its morning brilliance onto the panoramic view she was doing her best to ignore. It was strong enough to provide light, but not heat, not at this early hour. It seemed that nothing could remove the chill from the metal struts.

Grasp, pull, climb, stabilise, clutch at the clammy metal with hands that she realised to her alarm were becoming sweatier and ever more slippery. Technically, the tower's angled inwards because the structure narrowed towards its apex. Practically, though, and no matter how much she attempted to convince her brain and body otherwise, the inward gradient was so slight as to be meaningless.

The hard truth was that she was clinging to the side of what was to all intents and purposes a vertical wall of metal struts, and keeping herself from falling only by the strength in her fingers and arms.

She kept looking straight ahead, through the angled metal bars to the hazy point in the far distance where land met sky. She was too frightened to look down and unwilling to look up. She didn't want to know how much was left to climb. She'd already passed the point where she could hope to survive a fall. If she slipped there would be a few seconds of terror and then that would be it. Game over.

Below her she heard David slip, lose his footing and swear. His body thumped against the structure and she heard a violent bang as he fought to retain his hold.

"Are you okay?" she called shakily.

She risked a glance below and her stomach dropped away from her in a sickening rush, plummeting down the crisscrossed metal to the ground so very far below. The car looked tiny now, like a toy. She couldn't even see the gym bag David had put down beside it.

To her relief, David had managed to regain a secure footing.

"I'm fine," he said in a small, breathy voice that didn't seem to belong to him at all. That was okay. She hadn't sounded much like herself either.

As she forced herself to climb higher the breeze grew stronger, tugging at her hair and clothing, rattling at loose sections within the structure that she couldn't see and didn't want to think about. She was convinced that the tower was swaying gently in the wind. The struts seemed to be getting more and more slippery and as her hands grew tired, every grip brought a fresh bolt of pain.

She climbed past a couple of abandoned bird's nests wedged into the corner of the struts. The woven grasses were now unravelling, ancient, brown and dry. Jade wondered what type of birds had once made their home there—hawks, perhaps, or other birds of prey.

Then she was too high for the nests and climbing still higher. Her legs and arms were quivering now, as the effort caused her aching muscles and throbbing hands to progress from physical pain, which she could control to an extent, to weakness, which she could not.

Jade realised that if she lost her footing, she probably wouldn't have the strength to hang on and save herself.

She forced herself to look up and see how much further there was to climb.

To her immense surprise, it was less than two metres away. Above her loomed the radio receptors, grey and bulky, and in their centre a small platform, a little over one metre square.

A thoughtful engineer had even provided a railing around the outside.

Jade soon had a tight grasp on the railing, but she was reluctant to put too much weight simply because it was narrow. Awkwardly, she manoeuvred herself onto the platform and sat there, staring blankly ahead, breathing hard as she felt the sweat pour from her body.

Within a minute David had appeared and they sat, shoulder to shoulder, getting their breath back.

"Well, I can cross that off the 'to do' list," he said eventually in a voice that sounded slightly more normal. "Not that climbing to the top of a bloody antennae was ever on it to start with. You realise we've still got to go back down, Jadey? No parachutes for us up here."

"Pity. I was hoping we could just stay on this platform for the rest of our lives," she responded.

Feeling braver, she took hold of the railing and eased herself to her feet. Balanced herself on trembling legs and surveyed the astonishing view. The Karoo stretched to the horizon, its lunar landscape mostly flat but with occasional steep, rocky sections. Yellows and ochres eventually merged to form a distant sea of brown.

And far, far below them, the car. If she had a pebble up here she could throw it over the side, aiming for its matchbox-sized roof, and that pebble would take one . . . two . . . three . . . four . . . five . . . seconds to—

"Stop it," she said aloud, gulping.

"Stop what?" David asked, sounding surprised.

"Oh, nothing." Clutching the railing she knew, right then, that base-jumping was not for her. There was absolutely no way that she could step over this narrow railing, grasp the rip cord of her chute and launch herself outwards into the thin, cold air.

And then suddenly she saw it.

Nestled in the shelter of a steep hill, the weathered roof blended perfectly into the landscape. The only reason she'd noticed it was thanks to the glint of the sun reflecting off a convex whitish structure that was almost hidden by the house itself.

"There!"

She pointed excitedly and David got up to see what had caught her eye. They both moved over to the south side and stared at the only dwelling that was visible from their eyrie.

"What's behind it?" David squinted into the distance. "That shiny stuff—what is it?"

"I've got no idea. Roofing of some kind, perhaps?"

"Look. From here you can see where the roads go. If we drive back the way we came, then look for a right-hand turnoff . . . I can't see beyond that gully . . . but that track seems to carry on past there. Shouldn't take us too long to drive."

"Easy enough," Jade agreed. Neither of them mentioned the distance that lay between them and the car.

"We should have brought some water," David said.

"It would have been a good idea."

Their arms touched again and she could feel the warmth of his skin. She wanted to suggest starting the climb back down, but something prevented her from speaking. Perhaps David would take the lead, when he was ready.

And then, as simply and naturally as if it had already been discussed, as if it had always been the intended way of commemorating their risky climb, they turned towards each other. Jade locked her arms around David as she felt his own crush her tightly. Her lips found his and she kissed him hard; the electricity between them as powerful and instant as it had always been, like a light that had come suddenly back on after a break in power.

She pulled away, a minute later, breathing hard.

He dropped his hands to his sides. She looked for any sign of guilt or regret on his face but saw none.

"Better get going, hey?" he said.

"I'll go first," she offered.

"No, let me. I'm no good with descents. Better that if I slip, I don't fall on to you."

"All right," Jade said, surprised. She remembered from the hikes and climbs they had done together that David was better at the downhill bits. Despite his height, he was surprisingly agile. It was she who struggled with them, resenting the gradient, preferring always to climb up and up, pushing her body to its limits as she sought the elusive summit.

And then it hit her, yet again, that this was why David had insisted on going first. He wanted to be in a position where, if she got into trouble, he would be able to help.

Before she could say anything, he'd hooked a foot over the railing and lowered himself onto the metalwork.

She followed. The struts were warmer now and although the distance between her and the ground still yawned, she felt more settled now, her fear manageable. It was as if, were she to fall now after that precious kiss at the top of the tower, she would at least be going out on a high note.

40

Jade was halfway down when a question occurred to her. At first she thought it would be better to wait until she'd reached the bottom before voicing it, so that she could speak with a clear mind and without gasping for breath.

Then she decided differently.

A hard question was surely best delivered in adverse conditions.

"Tell me something, David," she called down.

"What?" His voice sounded strained, and the wind did its best to snatch it away from her.

"Why did you come with me?"

"How do you mean?"

"Why did you fly down here with me? You didn't have to, you know." She stopped climbing and hooked an arm through the bars, her gaze firmly fixed on the metal tower as she gasped for breath to speak. "You're not on this case. You didn't even complain about it going to be too expensive, and you usually have something to say about costs. So, tell me."

David didn't utter a word. All she could hear was him puffing and the squeak of his shoes as he eased himself ever lower, from beam to cross-beam.

The shadow of the cell phone tower stretched darkly along the bleached ground, a black bridge spanning the desert.

Jade unhooked her arm and carried on down the tower. He didn't have to reply. It was, after all, a difficult question. Perhaps there was no clear answer.

And then he spoke.

"Tell *me* something, Jade," he called up to her.

"What?" she responded, taken aback by the unexpected turn the conversation had taken.

"Why did you ask me to book two seats on the flight?

"Er . . . what do you mean?" Playing for time, she knew.

"You didn't have to. You didn't need me with you. Not for a two-hour flight and an hour and a half of driving. You're not one for incurring unnecessary costs on a case either. So why did you ask me to come along?"

She tried to gather her thoughts, to provide David with a logical and appropriate answer, but they developed wings and took off into the dry, golden air, leaving her open-mouthed and struggling to come up with a coherent explanation.

Neither spoke for the rest of the descent. When Jade stepped down off the lowest strut, David was waiting to help her. He took her right hand and she put her left on his shoulder. But instead of him guiding her onto the ground, she found herself being pulled into his arms. He held her tight and they kissed again. Her lips mashed against his face and his day-old stubble burned her skin. He fumbled under her clothing with an urgency born of desperation and waiting too long.

She grabbed hold of his pale grey-collared shirt and pulled it open, snapping a couple of the buttons off in her haste. She twined her legs around his, digging her nails into his shoulders. She pressed herself hard against him, gulping in his smell, devouring the taste of his skin. She heard him groan. His arms crushed her close, fingers digging into her thighs so tightly she knew she would be bruised. There was no time for gentleness. Not out there under the empty sky, where no walls or ceiling could conceal the truth of what they were doing, or hide their transgression.

Afterwards, exhausted, they lay naked on David's ruined shirt. Propping herself up on one elbow, she gently ran her fingers across his stomach and up over the puckered scar on his chest that was the last remaining evidence of a bullet he'd taken for her. She'd never before had the chance to touch it until now.

These were moments Jade wished could have lasted longer but she knew they could not. Once again, there was no time.

Reluctantly, they got up and dusted themselves down. The cotton shirt had provided some protection, but pale sand still clung to the front of her legs.

"Well, this is trashed," David said ruefully, shaking out his shirt which was mottled with sweat and very much the worse for wear. "I might as well throw it in the next bin, if we ever find one."

But he didn't. He folded the garment up carefully and put it on the back seat of the car. "You said you bought shirts at the airport? I think I need a replacement now."

He pulled on his boxers and trousers, pleased to see that his torso was more muscled and the slight paunch that he'd noticed had started to develop over the past year was all but gone. The obsessive exercise was producing results.

"I did. No idea what's on them, though" she said, taking out the plastic bag. "I need a fresh one as well." She peered down at the plastic-sealed packages. "This one's mine. Let's see what I got." She ripped it open. "Surfer Girl," it read. The lettering writhed its way in neon pink cursive across the blue fabric of the shirt. Not her style, but better than nothing.

"Hmm. Very nice. Chuck mine over, will you?"

Jade threw it across to David, and as he tore it open and unfolded the garment, her eyes widened and she clapped her hand over her mouth, trying unsuccessfully to muffle a snort of laughter.

"Oh, David, I'm sorry. I really am. But that was the only one they had in extra large so I grabbed it without . . ."

But David wasn't listening to her. With a panicked expression, he was staring down at the logo.

In proud black and red lettering on the white background, the shirt announced, I LOVE GEORGE.

"Jesus," he muttered, and then something that Jade didn't hear properly but sounded suspiciously like "coming out of the damn closet."

When Jade had got her laughter under control, she did her best to placate him. "Don't worry. Undercover is what it's all about, isn't it? I'm sure George is a fabulous fellow. You must introduce me sometime."

"And it's too tight," David grumbled, ignoring her last comment, as he shoehorned his torso into its close embrace.

"Well, it only adds to the effect, doesn't it?" She punched him on his arm. "Come on. Let's get going before you start singing 'YMCA.'"

4I

As Jade and David climbed into the car's warm interior and drove away from the cell phone tower, the light-hearted mood evaporated, and in its place Jade found worry creeping in. Thinking of the gym bag and its bloodied contents, now stowed away in the boot, she was starkly reminded of what was at stake.

It was as if neither of them dared speak; unwilling to risk shattering the last fragile remnants of what they had so recently shared.

Eventually, though, Jade had to speak in order to give him directions.

"Turn right here." She indicated the dirt turnoff that was hardly worthy of the term "road." A couple of faint, flattened tracks stretched away from them, winding through the sparsely covered terrain and around the rocky side of the donga.

"Right it is. Shouldn't be much further then," David responded. And just like that it was back to business again.

"There's a fence ahead. Just past the donga. Look." Jade pointed to some low triple-strand barbed wire. Hardly sufficient to keep human intruders out, this was no security barrier. It must be a simple method of keeping animals within adjacent farms' outer boundaries. Her guess was confirmed when they drove between two simple metal gateposts, although the gate, equally low and made of a metal frame with a simple plain wire mesh, was wide open. Any livestock could easily have strayed off the property.

"The boundary of his land. Koenraad Meintjies, or whoever the hell is crazy enough to live out here. A postbox with a name on it would be helpful," David offered with a wry smile.

"No such luck. We'll know soon enough, though. I can see the farmhouse in the distance."

"Drive up to a place like this, the owner will probably take potshots at you. I'm sure that's what passes for security out here. He's probably seen us coming already and when we get closer he'll run outside holding a gun."

But David's words lacked conviction.

They approached the house slowly, but despite their conservative speed, a trail of dust still kicked out from the wheels, announcing their arrival to anyone inside and whoever else might be watching.

The farmhouse was a whitewashed building made from thick blocks of sandstone, with a gabled front and a tin roof that had once been painted white. The paint jobs appeared to have been done a long time ago.

The front garden was demarcated by a neat row of small rocks arranged in a rough square and extending a short distance from the wide, covered porch. Not that there seemed to be very little difference between what grew within the garden and what grew outside.

"Guess it's difficult to get a good lawn going in this climate," David said in a deliberately casual tone, stopping a few metres from the line of stones. Strapping his holster around his waist, he clicked the safety catch off his pistol and slowly got out of the car, motioning her to stay inside. He was taking no chances with what kind of welcome might be waiting for them; not after what he'd found in the dumped bag.

The front door of the farmhouse stood ajar. That fact did nothing to dissolve the knot of unease that had tightened itself in Jade's stomach. She realised that she was dreading what they might find and clinging to the hope that this was not in fact Meintjies's place; that it belonged to another farmer, whose smiling wife would appear at the door, asking them in Afrikaans if they were lost. She would be wearing an apron and a freshly baked apple pie would be cooling on the kitchen counter top.

"Hello?" David called. He reached inside the car and pressed the horn. The blast of sound shattered the stillness, but nobody appeared at the door and Jade's last hopes of the friendly local dissolved.

She climbed out. It was hot now, although the slight breeze made the temperature bearable.

Jade sniffed the air. Was it her imagination or did it carry a sickly reek of decay?

David squared his shoulders. "Okay. Let's have a look, shall we?" he said.

They walked towards the farmhouse and through the open door.

A distinctive tang assaulted her nostrils as soon as Jade stepped inside. It was not the stench of rotting flesh she thought she'd picked up earlier. This was the coppery odour of blood recently spilled, congealed perhaps, but not yet dried.

Glancing to her right, she noticed to her surprise that a rifle with a wooden handle stood propped in the corner between the hall table and the wall. It was an old-looking, well-worn weapon. The type of firearm that a farmer might own in a territory where the biggest threat was the occasional nighttime predator.

"Stay back, Jadey," David cautioned. But she ignored his words and followed him through the doorway into the kitchen, where morning light streamed in through the yellow curtains and the smell was so much stronger. The shocking sight of the body bound to the toppled chair caused both of them to stop in their tracks.

Jade looked down at the floor, where more blood had spilled, and then hastily focused her gaze on one of the windows. She tried to breathe deeply and only through her mouth. She tried to blank out the ruin of the man's body; what had been done to him; the buzzing and feasting of the hundreds of flies and larvae.

Where an apple pie should have been steaming on the counter-top, there was only this in the room . . . and yet, there was something about it . . .

"I'd better take some photos," David said, his voice hollow.

She forced herself to look again, to analyse what she was seeing while fighting the urge to retch.

What had been done to Harris back in Jo'burg had been brutal. Callous. Cruelly creative and would certainly have resulted in his death had Jade not got there in time.

Meintjies's agonised demise was a different story entirely. His torture had been slow, methodical and intentionally painful.

Worse, there was a shocking artistry to it. It was as if whoever had done this had wielded his tools with evil joy and accomplished expertise. Slicing into flesh, mutilating organs efficiently and expertly, causing maximum agony while ensuring that his victim remained alive.

There was no way you could compare the two scenes.

"Right. I'm just about done here." David sounded drained from the effort of training his camera on the horror in front of him. "I don't think there's anything else in here, so let's not contaminate the scene any further. I think we should take a quick look around the house in case there's anything obvious, and then call forensics and get out of here."

"The scullery door's open," Jade said.

"You want to step out for a while?"

"I want to see what's back there. What's in those big plastic structures."

They left the kitchen and stepped outside. Jade was grateful for the cool air on her face, but also aware that it too was tainted, stronger this time, by something unidentifiably unpleasant. She could tell David had picked it up, too.

"I can't take much more of this," he snapped. "What the hell's been going on? This place smells like a slaughterhouse."

"No slaughterhouse in evidence. There's a barn beyond the greenhouse," she said. She guessed a farmer would need to grow fresh produce in a sheltered environment in order to be self-sufficient in this harsh climate. Not much would survive outside.

She was surprised, though, by how new, clean and shiny the plastic structures looked. As if they had been put up only a few months ago. Unlike the old windmill to the right, whose blades looked weathered and rusted by comparison. They turned slowly in the light breeze, letting out a harsh creak every so often.

"Well, the smell's not coming from in here." David sounded relieved as he pulled open the greenhouse door and stepped inside. "Nothing in here except . . ."

"Except nothing," Jade said, surprised.

It wasn't much cooler under the plastic covers, but it was more humid.

The ground was thick with damp, fertile-looking soil, and from the plastic pipes she could see, it appeared that a complex irrigation system was in place. But instead of the rows of vegetables and herbs she'd expected to find, all she saw was a series of short, brownish, truncated stalks that were withered and dying.

She gave David a questioning glance. He shrugged in reply.

They turned away from the entrance to the greenhouse and Jade followed David around the tall side of the massive structure. The plastic rippled in the breeze, making a hollow, flapping sound.

Behind it was a barn and a small paddock, the latter encircled by steel posts and more of the barbed wire fencing that surrounded the farm's perimeter. This too was empty, although Jade could see a steel water trough that looked almost full by the open gate.

"So, no plants. No livestock. One dead farmer. And what on earth's that building been closed up for?" David asked, pointing ahead to the barn.

The tall wooden doors to the solidly built barn were tightly closed, and a length of steel piping was wedged through the handles to ensure that they could not be pushed—or pulled—open. It was difficult to see with the sun in her eyes, but Jade thought the barn's high windows looked strangely blank, as if they might have been boarded up from the inside.

The smell of rot was definitely stronger here. It seemed to be emanating from the structure; seeping out from the chinks and gaps in its stone wall and tin roofing.

"Do we really want to know what's inside?" David muttered, in a tone that suggested he was expecting the worst. He strode over to the doors and studied the rusted piping and steel handles.

"Those won't hold fingerprints," he said, sounding almost

disappointed. He grabbed hold of the steel and wrestled it out of the narrow gap. It loosened reluctantly, with a screaming of metal.

With some difficulty, David forced the doors apart. As they opened, they brought the smell out with them, causing them both to gag as they stepped up and stared into the poorly-lit interior.

"Jesus Christ," he said, shock in his voice.

Jade stood beside him and stared at the charnel house in front of them.

It was almost dark inside the barn because the windows had indeed been boarded up. Even so, she could see the motionless forms, bloated and stinking, their coats saturated with now-dried blood.

"Sheep," she said softly. "It looks like an entire flock was slaughtered."

"Were they, Jadey?" David spoke in the same low voice. Just like her, he was taking small breaths in through his mouth to escape the almost tangible stench of putrid flesh.

"I—how else could they have died?"

"It's just that I don't see evidence of slaughter."

Trying not to breathe at all, Jade stepped forward to take a closer look at the lamb closest to the doors. It lay on a pile of straw close to a steel water trough, limbs stiffly extended. The trough was almost completely full of water, so they hadn't died from dehydration. Or starvation, either. In terms of meat on their bones, the animals had not been in poor condition.

"You're right. Their throats haven't been cut," she said. "But I can't see any other sign of how they might have died."

It was difficult to see what damage the animals had sustained, with the buzzing mantle of flies and maggots that covered the carcasses.

Settled, it seemed, in certain preferred areas. The flies were crawling around the mouths of the animals, as well as their bellies. Jade could see that some of the short wool around the dead sheep's muzzles was also discoloured by what appeared to be blood.

They must have died recently because they were still bloated and the rot had not yet fully consumed them. She supposed a few days from now, in this heat, they would be little more than writhing piles of maggots.

"Where there are flies, there's rot," her father had said once. Those words she had always remembered, even though at the time she'd been young enough to know he wasn't really talking about flies, but not old enough to know what it was he had actually meant.

Now here she was looking at the physical proof of his words.

"Perhaps they were sick," she said.

"Would've had to have been an epidemic. Maybe they were poisoned. In fact, is that blood around their nostrils?"

"I think so. I can't think of anything else it could be."

The heat was stifling in the enclosed space. The sun was beating down on the metal roof now, sending the flies into frenzies of activity.

"Could that be why this place was all closed up. So predators couldn't get to the carcasses."

"The flies seem okay."

David snorted. "When have you ever known a bloody fly to die from sitting on anything toxic?"

"True."

"Well, I guess we'll also have to ask the Crime Scene boys to take some of these bodies away for analysis. Now let's get out of here, Jadey. If they were poisoned, I don't want to stick around."

"Wait," Jade said. Thoughts were swirling in her mind; the evidence of what she had seen both in this gloomy barn and out in the deserted settlement of the Siyabonga tribe. The rusty bloodstain on the rock. The words that the nursing sister at the hospital had spoken to her.

A long shot . . . a scenario she didn't even want to visualise but which maybe, just perhaps, made sense.

"What?" David asked. He was already at the door.

"That gym bag."

"What about it?"

"Were there any unused knives inside?"

"There were a few, yes." Now he sounded unsure, as if he was regretting even having given her that answer. Quite probably she would end up regretting it too. But she had to try.

"Please could you bring me one," she said.

42

David hesitated for a moment as if deciding whether or not he should comply with Jade's bizarre request. Then, without speaking, he turned and strode off, heading not towards the hired car but towards the empty farmhouse.

A few minutes later he returned holding a long, shiny carving knife.

"I found this in the kitchen," he said, and from his sickened expression Jade knew how much it must have cost him to go back in there.

"Thank you."

"Better you use one of the farmer's knives. Those others—even if they weren't used, they might still have prints. But Jade, what on earth are you going to do?"

"I want to see if my hunch is correct."

She walked over to the lamb. Its stiffened legs jutted at awkward angles and its beady eye stared unseeingly up at her. Now she could clearly see the blood that flecked its muzzle.

"Surely you don't have any experience of this," she heard David say. His voice seemed to be coming from somewhere well behind her.

"I don't. I'm hoping that I won't need a lot, though."

Jade bent down, grasping the handle of the knife more firmly than usual. She didn't want to touch the dead creature with her hands, but putting a foot on it to hold it down seemed somehow disrespectful.

"Could you pass me one of those sacks?" she asked David. "There are a couple there in the corner."

The sacks had been used for carrying feed here. David shook out a dry corn cob before passing the topmost one to her.

Jade grasped the animal carefully, feeling the delicate bones of its rigid limbs through the weave of the sack. Even though she knew the lamb was already dead, she felt herself hesitate, as if unwilling to defile it any further. Which was ridiculous, given that she had, in the past and on more than one occasion, eaten and enjoyed free-range Karoo lamb.

She brought the knife down to its stomach and wiggled the stiletto-sharp tip of the blade through the dense wool. She shook her head, blowing away the endlessly buzzing flies. Then she pressed down, hard and decisively, into its distended belly and was rewarded by a rush of gas and foul-smelling, blackish, soupy liquid that spilled onto the straw in front of her.

"God, Jadey. What are you looking for?" David sounded as if he was going to be sick.

Her anatomy skills were limited. She hadn't known if she would be able to see what she hoped she would find. But to her astonishment, after making just a couple more cuts into the lamb's stomach and guts, the evidence was there. Even to her eye it was clearly and gruesomely obvious.

Blackened growths bulged from the flesh, feeding off the lamb's otherwise healthy viscera. Their roots were deeply embedded in its intestines, its stomach, its bowel. The creature had died from an aggressive strain of cancer.

Glancing down at the now-stained sack, Jade saw a logo she recognised. Three leaves forming a large green-coloured crest.

Below it, the legend: Global Seeds.

David shoved the barn doors closed and wedged the metal piping back into place, leaving the flies to their spoils. Then they walked back into the farmhouse via the front door to avoid having to go past the horror in the kitchen and Jade went to the bathroom. A typical second bathroom in an old farmhouse, with a stained toilet and an ancient, dried-out looking bar of soap in a crusty dish, and a plumbing system that choked and gurgled for a couple of minutes before any water was forthcoming.

When the tap finally ran hot she lathered her hands up. She soaped and scrubbed and soaped and scrubbed as if she couldn't rid herself of the contamination she had touched; as if the lamb's diseased flesh was ingrained in her being.

She washed her arms as well, and her face too, for good measure. There was no hand towel in the bathroom and the toilet roll on the holder had nearly run out, so she reached out to remove the spare roll from an old-fashioned pink and blue crocheted cover with a pompom on top that stood on top of the cistern.

When she picked it up it felt heavier than it should have done. She pulled off the crocheted cover, her heart suddenly racing.

Wedged into the middle of the roll was a small black device, shaped rather like a compact cell phone.

A digital Dictaphone.

This was what must have been in the package that Zelda had told her friend Harris to post so urgently.

"David?" she called, but there was no answer.

She weighed the instrument in her hand, suddenly doubtful.

If this was what Meintjies's tormentor had come looking for, why was there no evidence of a search? And why, having found nothing, had he not torched the place?

In any case, why would Meintjies have hidden the device inside his home when he had the whole of the Karoo in which to bury it without trace?

Obviously, this was not meant to be a permanent or effective hiding place. It was a temporary concealment point, nothing more. If this was what Meintjies's torturer had been looking for, Jade was certain that he would have found it.

But he hadn't. Or wasn't.

What, then, had Meintjies been tortured for?

She slid the device into her jeans pocket and left the room.

Walking back to the hallway she heard the door to the main bathroom slam. David had been doing the same as her. Scrubbing himself clean again—or trying to—after being exposed to the rot and the disease.

"The local police are on their way," he said. "I'm going to have to get the investigation team from Johannesburg to fly down here, but in the meantime the scene has to be protected. They said they'd be here as soon as possible, but that could take a while. Do you want to wait in the car?"

"Yes. And while we wait . . ."

But he handed her the key. "I'm going to take another walk around in the meantime," he said. "Make sure there are no other surprises waiting. I'll join you as soon as the police have arrived and I've briefed them." He squeezed her shoulder before turning away and striding back through the house.

Jade turned the car's engine on and the air conditioning up high when she climbed in. Once the interior was a comfortable temperature, she turned it down to a whisper so that its noise would not interfere with the sound from the recording machine.

Offering a silent prayer that there would be usable information on the device, Jade pressed the PLAY button.

43

A swishing, hissing background noise filled the car.

And then, surprisingly loud, Jade heard a woman's voice. Clear, confident, well-spoken.

"25th February, 10 A.M. Interview with Danie Smit, General Manager, Global Seeds."

Jade stabbed the PAUSE button and picked her jaw up from where it had dropped to the region of her chest.

Danie Smit. The man whose name had been written down in Zelda's notebook; the one who'd been found dead in his car in Fourways Mall.

She had assumed that Danie Smit had been the person Harris had told her about, the mystery man who had been working with Zelda on the story. But he hadn't been.

He had been her source at Global Seeds.

Jade resumed play, listening intently.

Some more shuffling noises. The sound of a chair moving and a man's throat being cleared. Perhaps they were in a restaurant. Although, given the confidentiality of what Jade guessed they were going to be discussing, perhaps it was somewhere more private. A hotel room, or even in the cluttered living room in Zelda's Randburg home.

The speaker—Zelda, Jade assumed—continued.

"Danie, thanks for making the time to talk to me again."

Again. So Smit was probably her regular source.

"No problem."

The man's voice was softer, but decidedly wary. Perhaps he wasn't entirely happy about having agreed to the meeting. Jade wondered how Zelda had persuaded him to disclose information on a steady basis. She felt ashamed of herself for immediately supposing that Zelda had been sleeping with Smit.

"I know you have a tight schedule, and I'm going to have to ask you to go over some background information for the record, so let's get started. Can you tell me about your company's relationship with Williams Management," Zelda said.

"Global Seeds was approached a couple of years ago by Sonet Meintjies from Williams Management. She explained that the charity was starting up a number of farming initiatives to help previously disadvantaged communities become self-sustainable. She wanted to know if we would be prepared to donate maize seeds to this project."

"What was your response?"

"At first we declined. To subsidise the number of farms she had in mind with the amount of seed she requested wasn't going to be remotely cost-effective. However, as you know, she is a persistent woman and during our fourth meeting, we came up with a possible solution."

"What did that involve?"

"Our committee put forward the proposal of using these farms as testing grounds for various new hybrid varieties of maize. This would allow us to monitor how well the seed coped in varied climatic areas, often under sub-optimal growing conditions, and sometimes without the use of the recommended herbicides and pesticides. We agreed that doing this would be a useful field test, thereby justifying the expense. I was in charge of this project and I visited the farms two or three times a season to assess, photograph, and report back."

"Now, Mr. Smit, could you please explain what Global 10-422AM is."

A pause, presumably while Smit collected his thoughts. Then he spoke again; his tone measured and precise.

"Global 10-422AM is a hybrid variety of corn, or maize as we more commonly refer to it in this country. It was first developed by Global Seeds at their research headquarters in Nebraska, USA, during the 2009–2010 season. The number "10" is a reference to the development date, the "A" indicates it is for human consumption and not for industrial use. "M" indicates it is one of the speciality hybrids developed during this season."

"What's special about this particular hybrid?"

"Like the others, it was developed with the intention of producing a very fast-growing variety, uniform in size, and with an inbred resistance to pests as well as to the effects of the most commonly used pesticides and herbicides marketed by Global Seeds. However, the "M" in its code name referred to a brand new sub-series of hybrids—the medical series. This hybrid was a pioneer. It represented groundbreaking research done by the company in this field."

Jade glanced over at the house and saw David in the distance, walking back from the greenhouses towards the kitchen door.

"Why was the decision taken to plant Global 10-422AM on the Theunisvlei farm?"

"Mainly due to costs. It was a very expensive hybrid to produce and, had it reached market, it would still have been expensive, largely due to its multiple benefits. The Siyabonga community was the smallest of the farms run by Williams Management, and it was its first year in operation. Because of the small scale of the planting area we felt it would be financially justifiable to donate half a ton of seed from the new hybrid in order to run field tests on it."

"Had any of this seed been through a field test or tested on animals before?"

"No. It had been grown, of course, in our laboratory green-houses, but this particular variety had not been tested comprehensively on animals, although its predecessors had." His voice sounded flat and toneless, as if he didn't want to talk about this, even though he had come to the interview prepared.

"Could you tell me more about the medical benefits this seed was going to offer consumers, Mr. Smit."

Another clink. Jade imagined Zelda putting down a glass of water, perhaps jotting the occasional note on her pad while keeping a watchful eye on the dictaphone's red flashing light.

Smit's tone suddenly changed, and for the first time she could pick up the high top-notes of stress and frustration. "Christ, babes, is this all actually necessary?"

Jade didn't need to think long about what the word "babes" might mean. Either a current or a past relationship, for sure. Her first guess had been right.

"What's the problem, Danie?" Zelda sounded surprised.

"It's just that . . . never mind. Don't worry."

"Well, are you ready to carry on?"

"Ja . . . let's carry on." A heavy sigh. "The research—you wanted to know about that, right?"

"Yes."

"It was done after various investigations into the unusual longevity of a certain rodent, the naked mole rat."

"Why the naked mole rat?"

"This animal not only lives ten times longer than a typical mouse, but it has an exceptionally high resistance to cancer. Scientists have, from previous research, identified that this is due to the mole rat's having eight cancer-resistant genes, including the protein P16, which is one of the major human tumour suppressor proteins."

"So you used this gene in the creation of the hybrid? An animal gene? How is that possible?"

"You know how it's possible. I've told you before."

"Please could you explain again—for the record," Zelda responded. Jade could hear a hint of dryness in her voice.

"Well, DNA itself, which is found inside every cell, is an extremely complex molecule. It contains literally billions of atoms which are coiled into the double helix formation that you are probably familiar with. About one to three per cent of this molecule consists of genes."

"Carry on."

"Now, DNA can and does mutate. Some of these mutations will be passed on to the next generation. Farmers and breeders have, for hundreds of years, bred plants with other plants and animals with other animals in the hope of combining, or amplifying, their more desirable traits. Sometimes it works, sometimes it doesn't."

"And this is what genetic engineering does?"

"No. Genetic engineering is as different from this as . . . as car travel is from time travel. Instead of helping Nature's processes along, biologists simply identify the gene they need from the DNA of one species, cut it out, and insert it directly into the DNA of another. This means that plants can, and do, have genes from animals, bacteria and even viruses spliced into them, creating new organisms that would never have come about through natural means."

There was a short silence. Jade wondered whether Zelda had been listening as intently as she was now.

"It sounds like a very scientific and exact process," Zelda observed.

"It is and it isn't. In fact, the actual process is very much a hit and miss affair. For example, one of the most commonly used and cheapest methods of gene insertion is to simply launch them into the host DNA by blasting a 22-calibre gene gun at a dish containing the cells. Scientists do this hoping that at least some of the genes will end up in the right place in at least some of the DNA."

"Is that so?" Zelda's tone was filled with irony and Jade had no doubt that this was not new information to her, but that she was enjoying having Danie state it for the record.

"To find out which cells got the new DNA, they attach antibiotic-resistant markers to the genes. Once they've fired the gene gun they then douse the host cells in antibiotics. Those cells that die didn't get the new DNA. The few in every thousand that survive, did get it."

"You're right. That doesn't sound very scientific. Or very safe."

"There are risks attached to every procedure. The major risk, though, is that gene transfer by this method,—in fact by any method—does not always produce reliable results."

"And why is that?"

"Very often, a phenomenon called gene silencing occurs. This is when the foreign gene or else existing genes in its vicinity get shut off during the transfer process and become disabled. They no longer work, i.e., they cannot produce their protein."

"Could you expand on that, please, and explain more about how Global 10-422AM was produced?"

"To obtain accelerated, vigorous growth in the plant, our technicians experimented with splicing certain special genes into the hybrid. Some of these genes were obtained from fast-growing cells. Others, from the naked mole rat, produced the P16 protein. In addition, we used a promoter which was obtained from the cauliflower mosaic virus. This promoter acted as an engine, allowing the newly implanted genes to express themselves."

"Is it common practice to insert virus genes into plant seeds?"

"Using viral DNA promoters is commonly done, yes."

"And do you have any further details on those fast-growing cells your company used?"

"Not at this stage, no," Smit snapped.

"Because the only fast-growing cells I can think of that could logically have produced those results would be cancer cells. It sounds to me like something a group of scientists who believed they were the next best thing to God might do. Use the DNA from cancer cells to promote faster growth, while assuming, in their hubris, that the presence of the P16 protein would actually cause the plant to suppress cancer in its users."

"This *was* a highly experimental project," Smit muttered.

Jade looked through the passenger window to where a plume of dust was visible on the horizon, signalling the approach of a faraway vehicle.

Hopefully this was just a passing resident, or else perhaps the local police arriving. Even so, Jade kept watching the dust cloud, its progress punctuated by the softly spoken words on the recorder.

"So nobody took it a step further and did any other testing, even though it was grown for human consumption." Again, the irony in Zelda's tone was impossible to miss. She was starting to like this woman more and more. "According to my research the standard safety test for a genetically modified plant includes seven main parts. Part three is assessing the risk of gene transfer occurring from the food to micro-organisms in the human gut. In retrospect, that would have been useful."

"Full testing had been done on mice with earlier prototypes and was on the agenda for Global 10-422AM."

"In the meantime, though, the crop was planted by the Siyabonga community."

"It was." Smit's voice sounded dry, as if he was not used to talking for protracted periods. He coughed twice and Jade heard the sound of swallowing as he drank some water.

"You monitored the crop?"

"As I said, I visited the site three times. Once during planting and once midway through the growing process, and finally just before harvest. This was all in the space of three months. The crop thrived and grew phenomenally fast, despite a lack of water. It was a dry summer and the irrigation system that was piped in from the river was faulty and worked erratically."

"What happened after harvest?"

"Babes, can we please stop the interview here?" Now Smit's voice sounded low and urgent.

"No. Of course not. I need the full story, Danie."

"It's just that . . . Look this whole situation is giving me a really bad feeling. Not just what happened, but the way everyone's been behaving since then. Trust me, I've never been shit-scared passing information on to you before, but I am now. If they find out . . ."

"How could they find out?" Now Zelda sounded troubled too. "Did you make sure you weren't followed here?"

Danie gave a short laugh. "I didn't have a chance. I was on the damn cell phone to my boss just about the whole way over here."

"Oh." Zelda paused. "Shit," she said.

"Exactly."

"Danie, you need to get out of there. I've told you before."

"I know. But resigning now would be the worst thing I could do."

"Mmm. Take a holiday, maybe, and don't come back? Sick leave?"

"I'll think about it."

"While you're thinking, could you tell me what happened next?"

Jade jumped as David's voice cut urgently across the hiss of the recorder.

"Jade, could you come over here a minute please?" he called. Glancing up, she saw him standing by the front door.

She pressed the STOP button, got out of the car and walked over to the farmhouse.

44

The temperature must have climbed by five degrees during the short time Jade had been in the car. The sun was shining directly onto the front of the house and in through the front doorway. Dust motes danced in the glare.

"What's up?" she asked. Her mind was still spinning with what she'd heard on the recording machine.

"Thought it would be safer if we both stay here while this car arrives," he said, pointing to the vehicle that Jade had seen earlier. Now it was close by, rattling its way down the endless sand road towards the house. "I'm pretty sure it's the local cops, but as I can't get hold of either of them on their cell phones, I can't be certain."

"Good idea to wait together, then," Jade agreed.

The car, a silver Isuzu truck, reached the farm gate. It powered its way down the driveway, small stones snapping out from under its wheels. When it turned and parked beside her vehicle they could see the SAPS logo on the driver's door.

Even so, David did not remove his hand from his holstered service pistol until two burly police officers climbed out, similar firearms on their substantial hips, and made their way towards the house at a pace that could only be described as a "mosey."

Introductions were formal and polite. She saw them both glance at his tight T-shirt but they remained very carefully expressionless and she doubted any comments would be made to his face.

When the three of them had gone inside, Jade went back to the car, turned the Dictaphone back on, and was instantly transported back to the quiet meeting room and the subdued conversation taking place within its walls.

"All right," Smit said. "Let me tell you what happened next. One morning I received an urgent call on my cell phone from one of the residents at Siyabonga. She said that something had happened on the farm after the harvest, and that the cattle had died and people were getting very ill."

Jade held the machine closer to her ear, hoping to be able to hear better.

"Could you speak up please, hon? My recording equipment is sensitive, but even it has its limitations."

"Sorry." In a louder voice, Smit continued. "I didn't think for a moment that this could be due to the hybrid itself, nobody did, but I went out to investigate and what I found was . . . shocking."

"What had happened?"

"From what we could make out, the entire community had developed a highly aggressive form of stomach and intestinal cancer. There had been a vast number of untreated fatalities. A couple of the residents had sought medical assistance at the hospital, but to no avail. When we arrived the place was basically a morgue. Bodies in all the houses. Most dead; a few still dying, although they were beyond help. It was one of the most sickening sights I've ever witnessed."

"Did you suspect the maize was to blame?"

"Well, of course the fact this had occurred after the harvest was significant, but we thought it was impossible."

"Why?"

"Well, probably the real reason is that we were in denial. First, that this could have occurred at all from consuming a crop that had been genetically engineered to promote cancer resistance. Second, that such a disease could have spread so fast, and could have affected everybody except one resident. Obviously, we were extremely anxious to prove that the hybrid had had no adverse effects. So, I took samples of the river water for testing in case it contained toxins, and I also took a sample from one of the leftover bags of seed. This we fed to livestock under controlled conditions at one of our testing stations."

"And what were those results?"

Outside, Jade saw David walk out of the back door and lead the men to the greenhouses and the barn beyond. It was some distance away, but she thought the two policemen were walking more slowly; their heads bowed; their complacency shattered by the sight of the farmer's mutilated body.

"The river water tested clear for contaminants," Smit said. "But the cattle who ate the maize all developed internal tumours. It happened incredibly fast; over just a couple of weeks. Every animal that had been fed the grain got stomach cancer and died."

"What caused it, Danie?"

"In retrospect, we believe what happened was due to a tragic series of coincidences. During the gene transfer, we believe that in this particular hybrid the P16 genes were in fact silenced, while the effects of the fast-growing genes were enhanced. In addition, the viral DNA promoter caused genetic instability within the seeds, as well as horizontal gene transfer within the hosts. The virus then acted as a growth promoter, encouraging the runaway growth of polyps within the stomach and colon of the people and animals who consumed the maize. These swiftly turned malignant."

"What did you do when you had discovered this?"

"Well, right at the start, when research into what had happened was still ongoing, I was called into an urgent top management meeting."

"What happened there?"

"Look, Zelda, you have to understand two things. First, this was a massive shock to all of us. We had never had anything like this happen before; we did not believe it could or ever would. It was a tragic series of coincidences . . . a fatal mistake. What we did was damage control, pure and simple, and you must forgive me for telling you this story because we acted in panic. A team from head office flew to South Africa immediately. Everyone involved in the project was called in urgently and forced to sign additional confidentiality agreements."

Jade paused the recording again. The damn car was becoming a furnace, but she didn't want to waste time driving round the property in search of a shady spot. Sweat was trickling down her back and calves and was beading on her arms. She turned the air-con up to full and let it run for a few minutes before turning it down again. Instantly, the heat battered at the window glass again.

"They say . . ." Smit sighed and Jade heard the sound of the glass touching a coaster and wished she could be drinking what he had ordered. Preferably something with lots of ice and lemon.

"They say corporate behaviour is psychopathic, and I have to agree. The decisions we made as a team were not decisions that I believe any one of us would have felt comfortable with making individually."

"What were those?"

"Our brief was two-fold. To prevent this contamination from spreading any further and to kill the story at all costs."

"So what did you do?"

"We buried the bodies immediately; humans and livestock alike. We didn't want the disease to spread, or the food chain to become contaminated, as we had no idea how persistent the effects were."

"How did you do that?"

"Our CEO Michael Muller sourced a couple of men, ex-Army, who specialised in, well, um, sorting out difficult situations. We supplied them with certain equipment, including a bull-dozer as well as bio-hazard suits, just in case the disease could be spread through other methods. They went to the site and disposed of the evidence, so to speak."

"The bodies were buried? All of them?"

"Yes, about twenty metres to the north of the barn. Very deep, but in a sealed grave, so that there could be no risk of contaminating the water table. There was nobody left alive by that stage."

Jade heard Zelda make a small noise. Regret, sympathy—she didn't know.

"Then they tore down the housing and removed the rubble, dismantled the mill, destroyed the remaining bags of seed and salted the fields so that nothing could grow."

"Why did they do that?" Zelda asked softly.

"Global 10-422AM is not a sterile hybrid. The maize produces seeds that are not only fertile and viable, but whose daughter plants grow exceptionally true to type. Of course, there is a reduction in yield when seeds are replanted, as there is with all hybrids, but we didn't want to risk a second crop germinating from even one stray seed. And, of course, we canned all further research on that hybrid."

"So you didn't tell Sonet the truth?"

"We did not enter into any communication with her. Mr. Engelbrecht from Williams Management attended the meeting and explained this was to go no further. He said that nobody at the charity should be told."

Jade paused the recording for a moment. So Engelbrecht had known what was going on at the farm, although Sonet had not. That was interesting. Certainly, it explained how the hired gunmen had followed her car from the farm to the hospital so soon after her interview with him. They must have been briefed to be on the lookout for her and told that, if she were to drive to the hospital, it meant she had guessed too much and should be disposed of.

Jade re-started the recording and Zelda's voice once again filled the car.

"But surely . . . and this is what I'm battling to understand . . . those residents must have been in contact with friends and families elsewhere. What did you think would happen long-term if they suddenly disappeared?"

There was a very long silence. In fact, Jade turned the recorder off and on again to make sure it was still running properly.

"Again, this was not a decision I would have made, and it was decided on at the end of a very long meeting. Overnight, in fact. I was exhausted. Eventually I agreed to it just to get out of that damned boardroom."

"So what was the decision?"

"The decision was to say nothing."

"To do *what*?"

"I know, I know. The executives agreed on the fact that Siyabonga had been a very small and isolated community, and also that these residents had been among the country's poorest people and were, as such, not well connected to anybody in a position of power."

"I don't believe that. How arrogant. How brutally cold-hearted . . ."

"I know. Trust me, I thought so too, but the decision-makers here were directors and board members, many of them from overseas. They made the judgement call that there would never be sufficiently high numbers of questions asked to form a critical mass. They decided that even if friends and family went to the authorities their enquiries would end up falling on stony ground, to use an agricultural metaphor."

"And if they had been wrong? What if a civil servant had investigated?"

"We were told funds would be made available that would . . . satisfy such an individual that there was no point in pursuing the matter."

The dictaphone hissed and Zelda's sharp, intelligent voice interrupted her thoughts.

"So Global Seeds had no idea that Ntombi Khumalo and her son had survived?"

"No. We assumed that the woman who had contacted us had died with the rest of her community. Right up until she got hold of Sonet and gave her the seeds. At which stage Sonet contacted you about doing the story, I presume."

"Ntombi Khumalo didn't contact Sonet herself. Her employer did—she went off to Johannesburg and found work after this happened. He's been in touch with us, and has been very helpful in getting facts and information for the story. I've never met Ntombi. I'd love to meet her one day. Hopefully I will, when I see him again."

"Well just be careful of this helpful employer, okay? At this stage, I don't trust anybody."

"I will." Zelda sounded taken aback, as if she hadn't considered this possibility.

Jade nodded slowly. She wondered why Ntombi Khumalo had remained silent on this matter. As the only survivor of the tragedy that had befallen her community, the woman must surely have wanted to tell her story.

Now she knew that Mrs. Khumalo had fled to Johannesburg, taking a sample of the seeds with her. After hearing her story, her employer had got in touch with Sonet and Zelda, who had then sent the seeds to Koenraad Meintjies's Karoo farmhouse for cultivation.

What Jade still did not know was why the evidence pointed to the fact that Mrs. Khumalo was now being forced to make a road trip with a brutal killer.

45

Waiting in the car for David to finish with the local police, Jade's mind filled with the implications of the story that Zelda had extracted from Danie Smit during the interview.

An experimental hybrid of corn that had proved to be a genetic aberration; one that thanks to its unique combination of virus DNA and fast-growing genes had caused malignant tumours to erupt in the digestive systems of its consumers.

"I suppose that if you keep messing with Nature without really knowing what the hell you're doing then once every so often, just like the slot machines, you're going to end up with the wrong set of numbers all in a row," she said aloud.

Instead of creating a new innovation in the agricultural market, the researchers had unwittingly created a monster; magnifying the deadly properties of the fast-growing cells and viral DNA that had been spliced into the plant and manufacturing a lethal weapon.

A short while later, the frightened Smit had indeed turned up dead and probably quite soon after that, Zelda had gone missing.

Jade understood why Koenraad Meintjies had cultivated the seeds. It had been done, surely, in order to provide incontrovertible proof to back up Zelda's story.

But why had he been so badly tortured?

And why hadn't he used his gun in self-defence? It had been there, waiting in the hallway. There was no way he could have been taken by surprise; not in those quiet surroundings. Nor had there been any sign of a struggle. So, perhaps he too had ended up trusting the wrong person.

The gunmen in Johannesburg had been on the hunt for Zelda Meintjies. They had tried, and failed, to find her. Perhaps that meant she had taken Smit's warning to heart and was even now in hiding.

Had Koenraad's torturer also been trying track her down? Was he still?

Although Jade still had unanswered questions, she couldn't wait to tell David what she had discovered on this device and then let him listen to the recording, watching his face as he felt the same excitement she had done as piece after missing piece slotted into the puzzle.

This had changed the profile of the case from a murder investigation to a crime of a much larger scale, one which might even cross into David's jurisdiction of Organised Crime.

David had finished briefing the two policemen and was pacing up and down outside the front door, speaking furiously on the phone. Presumably he was updating the Jo'burg team with the latest developments. She watched as he ended the call.

And then, as he shook hands with the two officers and then started striding towards the car, Jade realised she couldn't do it. She couldn't reveal anything to David about the conversation on the Dictaphone she had discovered. At least, not yet.

After all, it was Zelda's story, and the woman might well be still alive. If she was, she deserved the chance to break it herself.

As he drew level with the bonnet, she hesitated, torn by the implications of what both decisions would mean. She was tempted beyond logic to share with him the crucial information she had just discovered. Leaving it now would mean lying to David about its whereabouts forever, because she couldn't come to him a day or a week later and tell him what she'd found at the farm. For now, the interview between Zelda Meintjies and Danie Smit would have to remain a secret.

She grabbed the recording instrument from the central console and stuffed it into her pocket as David pulled open the driver's door.

They didn't speak much on the journey back to the airport. Each was silent, immersed in their own thoughts. Whenever Jade's thoughts drifted to the Dictaphone hidden in her pocket she felt a sense of impending doom, as if she'd singlehandedly sabotaged the investigation. Well, not even "as if." By her actions, she had. The recording represented a critical piece of evidence, and without it, for a while at least, the investigation was likely to veer in the wrong direction.

At George airport, Jade's suspicions were confirmed when she overhead David speaking on his cell phone as they were checking in.

"The animals were poisoned, or something," he said. "Get a vet to travel with you when you go out there tomorrow. We had a look at one of them and saw signs of cancer." He waited, listened. "No, I don't know. A dead end so far, with no bloody witnesses. No living ones, anyway. Yes, I'd say it might be related to the land claim somehow. Sabotage in some form. God knows where the residents of the Siyabonga community went. Hopefully, Van Schalkwyk, the parachutist's ex-husband, can shed some light on the situation."

He paced up and down just outside the cordoned-off area of the check-in zone while Jade waited for their boarding passes to be printed out. Once again, they had managed to arrive just minutes before the flight closed.

"Yes, intimidated into leaving, perhaps," David said in a loud voice, causing a group of Japanese tourists, their trolleys piled high with luggage, to stare at him curiously. "If any of them come forward at some stage you may get more detail. For now, though, there's a hit-man on the loose. Somebody murdered that farmer, and that man will now be on the run."

The tourists exchanged worried glances and the little group shuffled closer together.

"Follow up on the Boere Krisis Kommando." He waited, listening. "Yes, I know we'd pegged them as a hate speech group, but it may be they've changed tactics. Or have aligned themselves with one of the more militant organisations."

Jade took the boarding passes together with her and David's ID documents, and as she shuffled them together and slid them carefully into her pocket, her cell phone beeped.

For one moment she thought it was simply the airline sending confirmation of the flight bookings. But then she realised that was impossible. With David finishing off his phone call and the boarding gates on the verge of closing, there was no time to waste.

She took it out and had a look.

It was from the same phone number that had sent her the message earlier begging her not to call or SMS back. The number that she now suspected belonged to Ntombi Khumalo.

This time the SMS was only two words long.

"u there?"

46

"Right, Jadey," David said. "Let's move it."

Over the loudspeaker came the final boarding call for their flight.

"Just a sec," Jade said, frowning at the text message.

This time there was no request not to respond. Presumably, then, contacting the sender was okay.

Or was it?

She sent back a short reply: "Ntombi? Can I call u?"

"Jadey! Come on. We have to get through security."

In lieu of luggage, David carried only a plastic bag from Markhams, the gents' clothing store they'd stopped at on the way to the airport. He'd been rather furtive about it, but when they were returning the hired car, she had noticed that he'd taken the muddied, sweat-stained shirt he'd promised to throw away, folded it up carefully, and put it into the carrier bag.

Preserving the memories, perhaps?

Now, impatiently grabbing his keys and phone and looking around to locate the boarding gate, David hadn't noticed that Jade, following behind him, had put two items into her plastic tray and not one.

Her phone and the recorder.

She swiftly pocketed the recorder, but as she was about to do the same with the phone it beeped again.

She snatched it up.

"Pls do not call."

So messaging was all right; calling not. Why?

Either she was in a meeting and could only send and receive messages but not speak, which Jade thought unlikely, or . . . ?

Or somebody might overhear. Or see that a call had been made. Jade was convinced someone was monitoring Ntombi Khumalo's actions but that she'd managed to snatch some time on her own. If she was in a car with the man who had murdered Koenraad Meintjies, Jade could understand her caution.

"Where ru? I want 2 help," Jade sent back. She stuffed her phone into her pocket as they reached the boarding gate and, a minute later, Jade was crammed into a centre, David on one side and a large lady with a burgundy-coloured hairstyle and doused in heavy perfume on the other.

She took her phone out again, willing it to beep, for Ntombi to send a message back.

Over the loudspeaker came the tinny tones of the captain's welcome and the flight safety briefing. Stewardesses sashayed up and down the aisles, checking that everything was in order before takeoff. Jade snapped her seatbelt shut and slipped her phone under her leg and out of sight.

It beeped again just after the stewardess had passed and Jade snatched it up, earning a disapproving glare from the lady on her left.

"Leving Blmfln."

Christ, she'd been an idiot. Jade could have slapped herself on the forehead. She knew the woman was in a predicament and she hadn't yet asked the most obvious, the most important question of all.

She typed the message in, fingers going at lightning speed.

"Whats yr cars no. plate?"

She stabbed the SEND button and waited breathlessly for a response. David was looking at her curiously and the woman on her left was glancing up at the call button. Clearly she was about to summon an air hostess to force Jade to turn her phone off.

The seconds ticked by until Jade could wait no longer. Ntombi had not sent a message back. She turned off her phone and put it away.

Ntombi quickly deleted Jade's message. She'd been too long in the toilet already, and in any case, as exhausted as she was, she couldn't remember the BMW's numberplate. She'd have to look and message Jade de Jong back later.

She flushed the toilet and opened the cubicle door, stepped out into the brightly lit ladies' washroom still holding her phone.

And the killer was there.

Waiting just outside her cubicle.

He grabbed her; his steely fingers digging into her upper arm, and dragged her towards him as she let out a shriek of pure terror. Her bladder loosened and she thought if she hadn't just been to the toilet she would have wet herself.

"What were you doing? *What were you doing?*" he shouted. His face was contorted and now she could see only too clearly that there was madness in his eyes.

He yanked her out of the Ladies, her shoes slipping over the tiles and her ankle twisting painfully. She tried to struggle, to scream, but it was as if he had stolen her voice away. The next thing she knew he'd pulled her through another door and they were in a utility room. Small and windowless, it stank of disinfectant and cheap cleaning materials. He shoved her against the wall, clamping his hand around her throat, sending brooms and mops clattering to the floor.

"Let me see that," he growled, tugging her phone out of her hand. His grip was an iron band around her windpipe and the blood started to pound in her head. Staring directly at his snarling face, she noticed that his upper and lower incisors had been filed to razor-sharp points. Whether this had been done as part of a tribal ritual or a gang initiation she had no idea, but the sight of it froze her and she could only wait, fighting for each choking breath, as he scrolled his way through her phone's applications.

"I heard you pressing keys in there. Were you sending a message?"

"I . . ." It was no use denying it. All she could do was lie, and pray that it was close enough to his idea of the truth. "I was texting my son. I told him not to worry that I am not back yet; that he must go and wait at his friend Bongani's apartment."

Desperately afraid, every single muscle in Ntombi's body was shaking with fear. There was a singing in her ears and for a while she imagined that she would simply pass out in that stuffy, stinking space and be held there by him until the blood flow to her brain ceased and she died.

But suddenly he released her and she fell heavily to the ground, landing hard on her knees, bumping her shoulder against his granite-hard thigh.

She remained crouched over, staring into an empty plastic bucket, its bottom encrusted with a white residue, and waited for him to administer her fate.

To her relief, instead of the killer blow she'd been expecting, he simply said, "Get back to the car. We are running late. We need to be in Johannesburg before dark."

Even though her legs felt as though they were made of rubber, she managed to get to her feet, and, brushing ineffectually at the creases in her skirt, stumbled back to the car. The man walked behind her. This time he did not give her cell phone back.

When they were an hour out of Bloemfontein it rang. Ntombi jumped in her seat. She couldn't help it. She hadn't realised he'd turned the instrument's settings from silent back to ringing, and now the piercing Nokia ringtone filled the car. The sound hattered her eardrums, while her physical reaction to the sound offered him ample evidence of her own guilt. She started to tremble again and sweat doused her forehead and hands, causing the steering wheel to momentarily slip in her hands.

She had no idea who was calling. The man did not answer, nor did he show her the phone's screen. She waited for what felt like an eternity until the call rang through to voicemail and, a while later, she heard the beeping that signalled a message.

He made sure she was watching as he dialled her mailbox and then put the call onto speakerphone.

Let it not be . . . she prayed. Let it not be . . .

Relief surged through her as Portia's loud, jovial voice came clearly through the speaker.

"Ntombi, my sister, where are you? Where are you? Khumalo is too worried. I have told him you are fine, but please phone him soon as possible. We are leaving shortly for Durban and he wanted to say goodbye before we set off. Go well, have a safe trip home, and remember that when we are back from holiday, you and I are going to explain to a labour lawyer exactly what your employer has been asking you to do."

Her passenger said nothing. Just kept watching her, his gaze intense, his lips ever so slightly parted in a cruel smile, so that she could see the ivory points of those needle-sharp teeth.

Ntombi felt as if the air conditioning had sucked all the oxygen out of the car. Her thoughts flailed for coherence. How was she going to explain, under these circumstances and to this danger-ous man, that Portia was meddling in Ntombi's business without any idea of what was really going on. He would never ever believe her.

Then, as she opened her mouth in the futile quest to try and persuade him otherwise, the truth all but punched her in the solar plexus.

It wasn't Portia's mention of the lawyer that had caused the man's reaction. It was her mention of Small Khumalo. Ntombi had said that the boy was worried; that he did not know what had happened to his mother.

Now the killer knew that the last message she'd sent hadn't been to her son after all.

It also meant that he knew that she had lied.

47

Jade switched her phone back on as soon as the plane touched down, in direct defiance of the air hostess's polite but firm exhortations to please wait until the aircraft had come to a complete stop before activating any electronic devices.

There was no message waiting for her, though.

During the flight, she'd told David who she suspected was sending them.

"I wonder why Mrs. Khumalo, if it is her, would be travelling with that man," David had mused, keeping his voice low to avoid attracting the attention of the woman sitting next to Jade.

"Perhaps it makes for better cover," Jade said. "A couple, a wealthy looking black man and woman, probably politically connected, how often do the police pull them over? They're just about lowest on the suspicion scale."

"Yes, yes, I know that." David had sounded impatient. "What I don't understand is why—or how—on earth she's ended up with him."

Jade couldn't tell him that, thanks to the recorded interview she had listened to, she was starting to suspect the worst. Ntombi Khumalo knew what had happened to the Siyabonga tribe. She had somehow survived the disease that had wiped out every other resident of the farm—perhaps, as a chef in training, she had prepared her own dishes and not eaten the toxic maize. Ntombi had been incredibly lucky, but now her luck had run out. Jade had a cold feeling that somehow this poor woman was being used, that the knowledge she possessed had landed her in a dangerous situation.

As the two of them walked into the arrivals terminal she found her thoughts straying. Not to the events of the past twenty-four hours, nor to her evening meeting with Victor Theron that lay ahead. Instead, she found herself thinking of the vastness of Africa. A continent so large that North America, China, India and the whole of Eastern Europe could fit inside, with room to spare.

A continent where in some areas the earth was so barren that nothing grew, but in others the sub-tropical climate bestowed its fertile blessings upon the people, keeping starvation at bay for even the poorest inhabitants thanks to the abundance of natural foods that thrived in the humid, steely skied surroundings.

A continent where almost every leader had his price.

Where a field of seeds could surely be cultivated in secret with no questions asked.

And then . . . ?

"Where are you off to now, Jadey?" David interrupted her thoughts as they climbed into his car, heading back to the Market Theatre car park.

"Back home. I have a late meeting with my client, Victor Theron."

"Evening meeting?" Jade picked up a note of jealousy in David's voice.

"He wants to take me to dinner to say thank you," she said.

It was nothing short of a miracle, she thought, that they managed to arrive back at the Market Theatre in one piece, because after hearing that news, David drove as if Hell himself was on his tail.

"And you? What are you up to?" she asked as she opened the car door.

"Work," he muttered. "I'll go to gym first. I need a shower. See you around."

As soon as she'd slammed the car door David sped off angrily.

It was the thought of having to sit in the rush-hour traffic that made Jade decide to follow him. It was now close to five P.M. If she killed an hour staking out the gym she'd be able to drive home a lot faster and still have more than enough time to get ready for her seven thirty meeting with Victor.

Decision made, then.

She got into her own car and set off along the same route that David had so recently taken, although driving at approximately half the speed.

This afternoon the apartment block opposite the gym was quieter. Fewer people were coming and going, probably because it wasn't quite the end of the working day.

Sandwiched in between two empty bays, David's car was parked at a careless angle, its bonnet jutting out into the street. She suspected he'd bashed the bottom of its bumper against the kerb on his way in.

Temper, temper.

She drove past slowly, not wanting to park too close by, deciding to stop around the corner and walk back. And even then, she felt she was going to be far too visible this time.

The security guard inside the apartment lobby was leaning on the desk and chatting to an elderly man in green overalls. Across the street, a slim Indian woman in a denim skirt and sports shoes—a student, perhaps—was striding purposefully towards the traffic lights, her arms swinging as she walked, a folded piece of paper held carefully in her fingertips.

A piece of . . .

"Wait a minute!" Jade said out loud.

She stamped on the brakes and twisted round to see, to her astonishment, the student pause by David's badly parked car and casually slip the small, white square under the windscreen wiper before casually continuing on her way.

Jade felt as shocked, as if she'd been slapped. Who on earth was this innocent-looking youngster? More importantly, who was she working for?

Only one way to find out.

Jade scooted the car into a yellow-demarcated loading zone, parking at an equally crazy angle. She was out, tugging the keys from the ignition and closing the car door so fast that her jacket got caught in it. She spun back, wrenched the door open, freed it and, slamming it once more, set off in pursuit.

She didn't know whether it was the repeated sound of the car door closing or simply instinct that made the dark-haired young woman look round.

For one astounded second she watched Jade sprinting towards her. And then she was running too; her slender limbs pistoning in her haste to get away. She fled round the corner and disappeared from Jade's sight.

Seconds later, Jade was also skidding round it, her breath burning in her lungs, praying that she wasn't about to be ambushed.

All she saw was the student's fast-retreating back. Damn it, she must be a runner, because she was proving to be cheetah-fast. No matter how desperately Jade flung herself forward the other woman's lead was increasing. Twenty metres, then thirty. Jade's foot crunched down onto a loose kerbstone and she stumbled, losing her rhythm. Her quarry was heading towards the busy Commissioner Street crossing and the red man on the pedestrian sign was already flashing. She was going to make it across before the light changed and Jade was going to be stuck on the approach, separated from her quarry for a few crucial minutes by a thick, fast-moving stream of traffic.

And then the pretty Indian student glanced over her shoulder, gasping for air, her face wide-eyed and open-mouthed when she saw Jade was still in pursuit. She seemed to stumble and the next moment fell flat on the worn paving, her head thumping down onto the brickwork with a solid thud that, even half a block away and over the noise of traffic, Jade thought she could hear.

Another few strides and she was onto her. Dropping to her knees, Jade slammed the heels of her hands into the woman's shoulders, ready for a struggle.

But there was none.

The young woman's breath was coming in agonised sobs and she was moaning. "Ow, ow, so sore. My head . . . my head."

Her hair had worked loose from its clip and it streamed out over the dirty paving. Close to her feet Jade saw a blackish smear with a distinctive aroma. When she'd turned to see how far behind Jade was, she had failed to notice the discarded banana skin that had effectively taken her down. Old and rotten; as slick as black ice and almost as invisible.

A couple of passing pedestrians gave the fallen woman a concerned glance, but seeing Jade already at the scene they walked on, assuming that she was there to help.

She blinked tears away and Jade moved her hands enough to allow her to turn onto her side. She was younger than Jade had first thought. Perhaps even still a teenager.

"Are you all right?" she asked. Never in a million years would she have expected these would be the first words she'd say to the person leaving anonymous notes for David. But then, the skinny Indian student she was looking down at now didn't fit that person's profile either.

"I think I'm okay." She lifted a hand—with a neon orange manicure—and touched the back of her head tentatively, wincing as she did so. "I'm going to have a lump there. Do you think I am concussed?"

"I have no idea," Jade found herself saying. And then, finally getting the conversation on track, "Who told you to leave those notes for Superintendent Patel?"

Pushing herself up into a sitting position and letting out another moan, the girl then looked straight at Jade.

"How do you mean?"

"Who are you doing this for?"

She blinked. "Am I going to get into trouble for it?"

"It depends," Jade said. "If you give me the name of the person you're working for, the one who's sending the notes, then probably not."

The girl stared at Jade with an expression so incredulous, it suggested she might just possibly be the most stupid person on the planet.

"I'm not doing it for anybody," she said. "Why on earth would I do that? It was all my idea, all along."

48

A few minutes later Jade was sitting opposite the student—who had introduced herself as Bhavna—in an almost-empty Wimpy on the other side of Commissioner Street. The two waitresses had looked just about ready to cash up for the day, but Jade had persuaded them to make Bhavna a cup of tea, and bring a bottle of water for herself.

Right then, however, she could have done with something stronger.

Bhavna stirred some sugar into her tea, blew on it, sipped at it. Traces of acne scarred an otherwise pretty face. She was rake-thin and her white sports top had a logo on the breast pocket for Wits University Athletic Club.

"I did it as a prank," she explained. "I never meant to cause trouble, but I wanted to get the message across."

"Bhavna, why on earth would you want to play a prank on a police detective? And what message did you want to convey? Is a friend or a relative of yours involved in a case he is handling?"

"You really don't understand, do you?" Bhavna said, and yet again Jade had the impression she was trying not to roll her eyes as she spoke.

Teenagers. Why anyone would ever want one was beyond Jade.

"No, I obviously haven't got a clue. So, handicapped as I am by not knowing everything there is to know, are you going to tell me?"

Looking slightly shamefaced, Bhavna responded. "Well, I didn't do it to cause trouble with the police detective. I did it to get back at his wife, that bitch Naisha."

Jade had the disconcerting feeling that her world was spinning suddenly out of control. She drew in a long slow breath and did her best to maintain a neutral expression.

"How do you mean?"

"You promise I won't get into trouble?"

"Bhavna, I can't promise you anything until I know exactly what the situation is."

"Well, she suspended my mom from work. Who just happened to be her best friend."

"When did this happen?"

"I don't know. A month ago, maybe."

"And your mom worked in the same department as Naisha at Home Affairs?"

"Not exactly. She headed up the Commissioner Street branch. They used to work together until Naisha moved to Pretoria."

"So then why did Naisha end up suspending her?"

Bhavna shrugged, her bony shoulders turning it into an expressive gesture. "There was corruption in the department. She had to blame someone, didn't she, or it would end up looking like it was all her fault, even though nothing was proved."

As she seemed to have found her conversational stride, Jade nodded encouragingly and waited for Bhavna to carry on.

"But anyway it was still a totally unfair thing to do. My mom practically had, like, a breakdown. She really struggled after that. Everyone in the department hated her. She cried every night until the day she finally resigned and then they made her clear her desk and leave that afternoon. She's got another job now, with my uncle's company, and so now I thought, well, I'll show Naisha that I know about her."

"Why leave the notes with her husband, then?"

"Because that was the whole point. I knew he'd tell her about the notes, so she would know, and it would make her feel bad inside. And scared that he'd find out."

"To be honest with you, Bhavna, I don't think he did tell her about them. You see, he thought they were related to one of the cases he was working on."

"Oh." Bhavna stared down at her teacup, disappointed.

The one remaining waitress was casting impatient looks in their direction, in the manner of a woman who had a taxi to catch. Jade asked for the bill and put two twenty-rand notes under the salt cellar.

But something that Bhavna had said didn't make sense. Jade decided to probe a little.

"You said if Naisha knew about the notes, she would be worried David would find out."

"Yes."

"Find out what? Your notes were very cryptic."

"Not to her, they wouldn't be." Bhavna treated her to a Mona Lisa smile. "You see, she would know immediately what they meant."

"Well, would you mind explaining to me?"

"They meant that the baby she's about to have probably isn't her husband's," Bhavna said, as casually as if she'd been telling Jade what she'd had for lunch.

Jade couldn't help it. She felt her mouth fall open.

"What do you mean?"

"Because she told my mom. Like I said, they were very close friends. They talked about stuff like that. And she made my mom help her even though she didn't want to, and didn't approve."

"And you know all this how?"

"Our house is small, and when those two talk, they get loud. When I realised it sounded interesting, I started listening."

"Could you tell me exactly what happened?"

"Well, she came round to visit my mom a while back. Nearly nine months ago now. She said she'd just slept with her husband again and she thought there was a chance she could be pregnant. They talked about it for a while, and by the end Naisha was actually hoping she was. She said this would be her chance to get back together with him."

"Go on," Jade said. She was surprised by how calm she sounded.

"Well then she phoned a bit later and I was interested to hear what happened so I picked up the other extension and, well . . .

I kind of listened in. She said to my mom she didn't think she could be pregnant, that it had been too early. Then she said she needed to find a donor. She said this would be her only chance. She wanted her husband back and she wanted another baby."

"What did your mother say?"

"My mom was against it. She said it would be wrong to do that. She didn't approve. But in the end she gave Naisha the number of a place she knew."

"What place was that?"

Another shrug. "Don't know. Some fertility clinic place. I know Naisha went there, because she phoned afterwards to thank my mom. But I don't think they were such good friends after that any more. Like I said, my mom disapproved." She pushed her cup away and stared across the table at Jade. "So, do you think I'm going to get into trouble?"

"I wouldn't leave any more notes if I were you." Did this precise, restrained voice belong to her? It seemed impossible, Jade thought.

"Well, it was fun doing it for a while but it was starting to become tedious. And varsity's getting busy from next week. In any case that gym is creepy. I get scared going there. And my mom's feeling better now and that's the main thing."

They stood up and walked over to the exit. Through the grimy glass, Jade could see the rush-hour traffic was thicker now. Cars practically gridlocked. Taxi drivers making their own rules, blowing an incessant tantivy on their hooters as they wove their battered Hiaces in and out of the slow-moving rows.

It was all the same as it had been ten minutes ago, but Jade stared out as if she'd never seen it before. It was the same but she was not. What Bhavna had told her had changed her world.

"Well, nice meeting you, er . . ." Bhavna hesitated, obviously realising too late that she hadn't asked Jade her name. Jade didn't fill her in. She just said goodbye and walked outside into the evening noise, watching the student as she hitched her bag over her shoulder and headed off in the direction of the university.

49

Jade retraced her steps along the now-darkening streets. A hundred different emotions clouded her thoughts, but as she walked, one became stronger, standing out until it eclipsed all others.

She felt sick with betrayal.

It was not David who had betrayed her. It was Naisha.

Up until recently, Jade had always considered her unspoken war with David's wife to be a fair fight. After all, David had had free choice as to whom he decided to spend his time with, and as she knew only too well there were pros and cons to both decisions. His relationship with Naisha was loveless, but she was the mother of his son, Kevin. His relationship with Jade was filled with passion, but she could be a cold-hearted killer who was capable, through her actions, of defying everything that he stood for as a policeman.

Then Naisha had fallen pregnant after David had spent just one misguided night with her. That meant the decision had been made for David. He could no more turn his back on this situation than he could stop breathing.

Jade had accepted this as the workings of fate. Why had she not questioned it at the time?

Now it was all too clear that Naisha had betrayed them both. She had broken the rules. She had visited a fertility clinic soon after she'd slept with David and, through artificial insemination, had made sure that their one night together had resulted in a pregnancy.

Now the notes made sense.

"Did you know you have a double? Who's the proud father-to-be then?"

It must have been a challenge, Jade thought bitterly, to find a donor who matched David's description. His height and his mixed-race heritage had always set him apart.

According to Bhavna's explanation, there was a small possibility that Naisha's child was actually David's. There was a much greater chance, though, that Naisha, with a cunning born of desperation, had given fate a helping hand.

She had wanted two things: another child and David back. Clearly, the two did not have to be directly related. Through this single, startlingly devious act, she had managed to achieve both.

Traitor.

Jade let out a deep sigh, realising that her nails were digging deeply and painfully into her palms. With an effort she unclenched her hands. Her fingers felt stiff and sore.

She turned the corner and there, ahead of her, was David's car. The note that Bhavna had left was still pinned under the windscreen wiper. She decided to remove it. Keep it, perhaps, until she'd had a chance to think more logically about the situation and what she should do.

But before she'd crossed the street, David strode out of the gym, kit bag slung over his shoulder. He stopped dead when he saw the note and then approached the car cautiously, eyeing the folded letter as if it might prove to be actually explosive.

By the time Jade had crossed the street, it was too late. He'd opened it and was frowning as he read it. His expression dissolved as he looked up and saw her standing on the other side of the car.

"Got another one here, Jadey, as you can see," he said. "This one's a direct bloody threat. It says: "Who's going to be a daddy soon, then? You . . . or maybe not?"" He met her eyes and she saw his face as if for the first time. Not the tough, cynical David she knew and loved but a careworn and vulnerable man who feared his family was at risk.

"I don't know what to do," he said. "I really didn't want to involve Naisha in this but it looks as if I'm going to have to install extra security precautions, in which case I'm going to have to tell her."

"Why don't you do that?" Jade found herself saying. Despite her best efforts at control she spat the words out and David glanced at her, frowning.

"You think I should?"

"I'd tell her everything. Tell her about all the notes. Even tell her what's in them. You never know, David, somebody could be trying to get at her through you. A disgruntled ex-employee, perhaps."

"Now you mention it, there was someone she fired a couple of months back. Perhaps I'll do that, then." He glanced at his watch. "Jade, do you have time to . . . ?"

"I'm busy now," she snapped, knowing her abrupt response would be hurtful and that she was powerless to explain it.

Leaving David standing by his car, still holding the note and now staring at her in concern, she turned and jogged back across the road. She wrenched her car door open and twisted the key in the ignition with so much force she thought for a moment she'd broken it.

She didn't look back at David. Found she couldn't. Imagining the demurely dressed Naisha standing in the path of her car, she mashed her foot down on the accelerator and sent the vehicle screaming forward.

"*There!*"

Smack!

"*Take that, you lying bitch!*"

When David told Naisha about the notes, perhaps his wife would crumble and confess what she had done. If so, then David would be free to make his own decisions.

But if Naisha held her nerve and kept her secrets . . . Well, then, a decision would still have to be made.

And Jade would be only too willing to make it for her.

50

It was fully dark when Ntombi arrived back in Johannesburg. Once again, she was exhausted. So exhausted that her arms were trembling and her face felt tight and stiff from fighting off the slackness that preceded sleep.

Terror had kept her awake through the endless, flat afternoon hours on the N1 from Bloemfontein. But the killer had done and said nothing more; he'd simply reclined in his seat and gone to sleep. A light sleep, such as a predator might indulge in. The slowing of the car when she reached a toll gate woke him immediately.

Now she was drained; empty; dead. Driving automatically, her reactions gluey and hopelessly slow. In this state, she knew she could not hope to avoid an accident, should that situation occur. Desperately, she tried to recite recipes to herself; this time not to calm her thoughts but to keep herself awake.

The Baharat combination of spices which she'd discovered in Silvena Rowe's Nine-Spice Lamb dish and used many times in dishes since then. "Three teaspoons mustard seeds. Three tablespoons coriander seeds. Three teaspoons fennel seeds. Two cinnamon sticks. Three teaspoons ground nutmeg, three tablespoons cumin seeds, six tablespoons dried thyme and oregano, black peppercorns . . ."

But the image of the recipe blurred and softened and the words she had memorised so faithfully slipped from her mind.

And then, just as she thought they were home; that this savage journey would soon be over, the man directed her to turn right, towards the suburb beyond Randburg, and her nerves started jangling all over again. This route was taking them in the direction of the house where she had been made to drop off the supposedly sleeping woman.

Was she still imprisoned there? If so, what was he planning to do with her now? And what did this mean for Ntombi?

She glanced at the street sign as they turned into the road. "Robin Avenue." Her eyes strained into the darkness searching for a house number.

None to be seen. But it was the third house from the corner. That was easy to remember. The third house on Robin from the corner of Rabie Street. The one with the tall, wood-panelled gate. From his pocket the man produced a remote control and the gate slid smoothly open.

Ntombi braked hard as she saw a shabbily dressed man standing in the road as they turned in, but on closer inspection she realised he was only a pedestrian, politely waiting for them before he continued on his way.

The man pressed the button again and the gate closed behind them.

"Stay here," he said, as if she had a choice, as he opened the passenger door.

Climbing out, he walked purposefully towards the front door before disappearing into the darkened house.

Leaving Ntombi with no means of escape . . . and no phone.

Scenarios, each more desperate and ludicrous than the last, spun through her head. She could hide in the garden—but she knew he would find her.

She could reverse the car into the gate, try to knock it down—but the gate was tall and solid and the driveway was a steep uphill slope. She knew that was also a battle she would not win.

She could simply close her eyes and let herself rest, after all that had happened. One last, short, blissful sleep before her evil passenger—and her waking nightmare—returned.

Ntombi rested her cheek against the cold glass of the window. Bizarrely, despite the terror of her situation, she was so tired that she knew sleep would come easily. Another moment or two, and she could be dreaming . . . dreaming of Khumalo her husband, and her little boy whom she knew deep down she would never see again.

The pedestrian!

The thought sliced through her exhaustion like a razor. She sat bolt upright, eyes wide, already fumbling to undo her seatbelt with her tired and shaking hands.

It was her only chance. She had to do it, and do it now. The killer could return any minute. How long had it taken him last time to subdue and drug the woman? She could not remember, but it had not been too long.

Ntombi ran up the steep driveway to the gate and slid her fingers through the wooden panels, peering through the slits to see if she could spot him. She thought she could hear the scrunch of his footsteps. But how to get his attention? She didn't dare to rattle the gate. That would make too much noise and the man inside would hear. But perhaps she could speak to him . . .

"Hello?" she called softly. "Are you there? Hello! I need help."

Silence.

Ntombi's hopes crashed. He hadn't heard her.

But then she realised the silence meant that he had stopped walking. Perhaps he had heard.

"Please, could you come here quickly," she asked again.

Now the footsteps came back in her direction. And then she saw him. A tall, young man in a worn blue overall, his clothes flecked with cement stains. A construction worker.

"What is it, sister?" he asked. He was looking at her in puzzlement, as if wondering what a well-dressed woman driving a luxury car could possibly need from him.

She needed to be fast.

"Do you have a phone? I desperately need to make a call."

She saw him hesitate. "I have one, but not much airtime."

"Please. I will pay you." She rummaged in her pocket and came out with a crumpled ten-rand note and a handful of change. "It's not much but it's all I have. I need to be quick, though. Please help me."

He pushed the phone through the gap in the gate. She threw the money at him and in her haste the coins fell to the ground and she heard them clicking and jangling into the darkness. The construction worker bent down to hunt for them and Ntombi jabbed at the scratched and softened keyboard of his phone, dialling the number of the only person that could possibly help her, pressing the keys as fast as she could.

Thirty-eight, forty-two . . .

Please answer, she prayed, waiting for the call to connect and the person at the other end to pick up.

Please answer . . .

51

Back home, after a much-needed shower, Jade took her time getting ready for her evening dinner date. Unusually for her, she took extra care with her appearance. She considered the options in her rather limited wardrobe before deciding on one of the few dresses that she owned—a clingy black garment with a scoop neck, lace sleeves, and a lace-trimmed skirt whose hem didn't quite reach her knees.

After some further thought she added a pair of sheer stockings and chic, black leather ankle-length boots. Around her neck she fastened a string of hematite beads and she clipped a matching bracelet around her left wrist.

She took care with her makeup, too. Black eyeliner, smoky-grey eyeshadow, mascara, a coat of shimmering taupe lip gloss. She so seldom wore makeup that her face felt coated with it; her pores clogged and sealed with the powder and foundation and blusher. Finally, she added a spritz of the Issey Miyake that David had given her two years ago and which was still almost full. Its sweet, floral scent filled the air.

She had no pocket to carry her wallet and phone so she put them into a black velvet clutch.

Glancing at the clock on her kitchen wall, she realised that her preparations had taken longer than she'd expected.

Pulling her cell phone out of her bag again, she dialled Victor Theron's number.

He answered after eight rings, just as she was beginning to think she would have to leave a message.

"Victor? I'm on my way now. I'm sorry I'm running a little late. I should be there in twenty minutes."

His reply sounded strangely subdued, although his voice was tight with tension.

"That's okay. That's fine, Jade. The markets have been up and down like yo-yos all day and I'm still closing out positions in the Dow Jones. If you wanted to make it in half an hour, that would be better."

"Would it be more convenient to meet you somewhere?"

"No, no. Come to the flat. It'll be . . . it'll be great to see you. To be honest, I wasn't planning on going out."

"You weren't?" Jade wondered if he could tell that she was smiling.

"No."

"But you've asked me for dinner?"

"Yes."

"I never figured you for a cook, Victor."

"No. No, you're right. I'm not much of a cook at all."

"So are we ordering in takeaways, then?" Heels clicking, Jade walked towards the hook on the wall and collected her car keys.

"No, no. I've got some wine here, and plenty of stuff in the fridge. Really good food, I mean. Restaurant quality dishes. You see, I have a domestic worker who cooks. She's actually got ambitions to become a top chef."

Ntombi shoved the phone back at the pedestrian.

"Take it, quick. Go now. Please, run!"

She sprinted back to the car and collapsed into the seat just as the front door swung open and the dark-suited man reappeared, carrying the same woman as before.

As he settled her into the back seat her body lolled to one side. Roughly, he shoved her into a semblance of an upright position. Then, grasping her shoulder to hold her in place, he pulled at the seatbelt and fastened it tightly around her.

He looked up and saw Ntombi watching and issued the same warning he had done before, his voice icy. "Remember, this is our friend. She has had too much to drink and we are taking her home. No other story, if we are stopped."

"I understand," Ntombi said.

The killer got into the front of the car and settled himself down. Once again, the smell of his unwashed body hit her and she had to struggle not to gag.

It was only after she'd fastened her own seatbelt that he pressed the buzzer to open the gate.

"Where are we going?" she asked.

"Where I tell you," he responded.

He dialled a number on his phone and in a moment she heard him speaking to her employer.

"I will have the goods with you in thirty minutes," he said. He waited, listened. "Yes, cash. Have it ready. No, I won't need a taxi to the airport. The Gautrain will still be running."

He pocketed the phone and told Ntombi to turn left.

Left.

Towards Sandton.

It was a ten-minute drive from where she was now to her employer's garage. Ten minutes. No longer, not at this time of the evening, when rush hour was already over.

But the man sitting beside her had told her employer thirty minutes, and Ntombi knew that there was only one possible reason for this. Only one job he had still left to do, after which a taxi or a train would whisk him away to the airport.

The man had done everything asked of him. Except for one last job.

She felt a terrible coldness fill her. She knew she should attempt to escape. Try to undo her belt, wrench the door open and simply run. But there wouldn't be enough time. The seat-belt would slow her down and he would grab her and then . . .

Ntombi didn't want to think about the screams she'd heard in the Karoo the previous night, piercing the silent, star-filled night sky.

Instead she thought of Khumalo in Umhlanga, being looked after by Portia. She was a responsible woman, and a wealthy one. Ntombi had no doubt that Portia would arrange for

Khumalo to be well cared for. Her child, at least, would be all right. More importantly, he was safe for now.

"Turn left here." The man's voice broke through her reverie and she obeyed automatically, turning off the main road and down a tree-lined side road where she saw notice boards advertising another construction site. This one, though, looked old and abandoned. The boards were faded; their wood splintered, leaning at tired angles on rusted metal poles.

This was the place, then. The end of the road, and in more ways than one.

The bite of the seatbelt, holding her prisoner inside the car.

Portia's words in her head. The woman's voice, loud and confident and kind.

"If you are ever hijacked, my sister, this is what you must do . . ."

Faintly, in the distance, Ntombi could hear the sound of approaching police sirens. Too late for her, though.

"Khumalo," she said aloud.

The killer's head whipped round, but she was too quick and too sure. She stamped with all her force on the accelerator and heard the car's engine scream as its sixteen perfectly tuned cylinders responded with a brutal thrust of power.

The car flew across the road, Ntombi's hands tight on the wheel, aiming the accelerating vehicle squarely at the centre of the biggest, thickest tree trunk she could see.

She had feared the moment of the crash almost as much as she feared her passenger's retribution, but for her, neither happened.

There was only her husband, for one blissful moment, his dear, familiar face smiling at her as he held out his hands in welcome.

52

Exactly thirty minutes after their phone conversation, Jade arrived at Victor Theron's apartment and rang the bell.

A full minute passed before the door opened.

Unlike herself, Victor hadn't smartened up. He was wearing an old Pringle sweater and a faded pair of Guess denims. His jaw was unshaven; gaunt and hollow, skull-like, as if a terrible anxiety had devoured the very essence of his being.

He stood in the doorway and looked at Jade as if he wasn't really seeing her at all. He made no comment on her appearance but simply just stepped aside and said, "Come in."

She entered his showpiece apartment for the second time. It was unchanged. Every piece of furniture immaculate and in place. No cluttered surfaces. It had more in common with a hotel suite than a home.

"Are you finished with the markets for today?" she asked. The words fell heavily into the awkward silence.

"Yes. Yes, I think so. Positions are closed out and everything." Jade noticed the electronic trading gadget he'd paid so much attention to in the past was lying, face down, as if forgotten, on the couch. Instead, Theron's hand strayed continually to the cell phone on his belt and he kept frowning down at it as if willing it to ring.

"Did you trade successfully?"

"No, not really. Not today."

"I'm sorry, Victor," she said.

"That's okay."

For a moment the tension in his face softened and he squeezed her shoulder. A rough caress. She could feel the wiry strength in his hands.

"Shall we go onto the balcony?" he asked. "We could have a glass of champagne out there. There's a great view. Sandton is quite a spectacle at night."

Jade walked ahead of him across the carpeted lounge and up to the glass sliding doors. She stood aside to allow Victor to open them and then he stood aside to let her go out first.

Jade stepped carefully off the carpet and onto the tiled floor. The balcony was small, enclosed by a simple waist-high metal rail with Perspex panelling below. Out of the artificially warm cocoon of the apartment, the air was bitingly cold. She shivered.

The lights of Sandton were spread out below her in a shimmering blanket. Victor was right. The view was spectacular. Stepping closer to the rail, Jade looked down, all the way down the dizzying sixteen-floor drop to the sidewalk below and the nearby road, where distant headlights wormed their way along.

"Are you cold?"

"A little."

Behind her she felt Theron's hands close around her shoulders and move down over her arms. His skin was surprisingly warm. Heat radiated from him and she could feel the tension in his grasp.

"Do you really have the guts to do this, Victor?" she asked him, and felt the breath huff out of him as if she'd elbowed him in the solar plexus. His fingers tightened around her biceps, their wiry grip making her think of an eagle's talons.

"Wh . . . what are you talking about?" he stammered.

"Your plans have gone wrong."

"My plans?"

"You weren't supposed to be alone when I arrived here, were you?" she told him. "Your hired gun was meant to be here too. After he'd dealt with Ntombi Khumalo and Zelda Meintjies, I guess his final assignment would have been to dispose of me."

Victor was silent. Totally rigid. She couldn't even hear him breathing.

"He was supposed to bring you the seeds," Jade said. "But the seeds aren't here, are they? And he hasn't called in."

She was quiet for a moment.

"Who were you going to sell them to?" she asked. She didn't expect a reply and Victor didn't offer one.

"My guess is that you made a deal with a terrorist organisation—some sort of extremist group. The asking price wouldn't even have been that important to you. After all, a weapon like this has such incredible potential to destroy, doesn't it? I think they were going to take those seeds up into central Africa somewhere and plant them. There's plenty of space there, after all. In a continent whose area could swallow up North America and India and China, and still have room left over, who'd ever notice or care about a few hectares of maize?"

Victor's grip clamped down harder. Jade didn't know if he was even aware of his telltale physical reaction to her words.

"They'd be able to create a sort of 9/11 all over again if that deadly crop got into the food chain in the States. Consumed directly it would cause mass fatalities, but that would only be necessary once. Then sow just a few of those seeds into a field and you'd be able to contaminate the entire harvest. Even the risk of their presence would render a crop unusable.

With farms and fields covering thousands of hectares, who could ever tell the lethal plants apart from the safe ones? Millions of acres of corn would be left to rot where it grew, in the black soils of the heartland. The US farming industry would collapse, followed by the economy. Famine, disease and death—it would be the apocalypse all right. And you, Victor, safely tucked away here in your precious Michelangelo Towers—you'd be okay. In fact, you'd be laughing all the way to the bank if you'd taken a short position on corn futures. While the bottom dropped out of the market, you'd make millions."

Finally, Victor Theron spoke.

"How did you work it out?" he asked quietly.

Jade took her time answering. She was silent for a while, thinking of the short phone conversation she'd had earlier with Ntombi Khumalo. Who had left her home after her husband had died, bereft and terrified, the only survivor of the plague that had swept through her community.

She had come to Johannesburg to look for work, and she had told her new employer the story of what had happened. Had shown him the sample of the seeds she had brought along with her, which she suspected had produced a toxic crop. Had asked him to help her find answers, to get the authorities involved, to find out why this had occurred; why the harvest that was supposed to feed her people had made them terminally ill.

Straight away, Victor Theron must have seen his chance. He had stumbled upon a potential goldmine. An irresistible opportunity for a man who, long ago, had sold his soul to Croesus. He had taken the information Ntombi had given him, contacted Sonet and Zelda, organised for the seeds to be cultivated in Koenraad Meintjies' greenhouse, and strung all of them along while making his own plans.

Global Seeds had hired a group of gunmen to eradicate all evidence of the diseased community.

Theron had hired somebody far worse to help him pursue his own ends once the harvest was ready to be reaped. That man had murdered Sonet, kidnapped Zelda, and demanded a ransom from her brother for her safe return.

The ransom had been the crop that Koenraad Meintjies had so innocently been growing.

Zelda's safe return had never been in the cards.

The base-jumping episode in Sandton Views had provided a useful excuse to get Sonet alone at a convenient time, and stage her dramatic death.

From the footprints Jade had seen in the dust on the top floor, it was clear that Sonet had never walked along those dusty floorboards. In the semi-darkness there would have been no way that Theron could have placed his feet in her footsteps so accurately that no trace of Sonet's prints remained. More likely she had been carried, hopefully unconscious, by the killer who then pushed her over the parapet to fall to her death.

Theron himself, Jade thought, had probably never ever base-jumped; still less packed Sonet's parachute. But, by making himself a suspect in the eyes of the police, he had given himself credibility in this regard, and nobody had doubted his story. He had confessed to a crime he never committed, and that confession had misled them all.

Until now.

"I looked into your past," Jade continued. "I found out that your wife was shot in an attempted robbery just a few days after the 9/11 market crash. You were caught on the wrong side of the markets back then, weren't you? You lost every penny, but you managed to keep from going under by putting out a hit on her and cashing in her life insurance policy. You paid out your panicking clients and you used the rest to start again. But you never quite got back to where you were, did you? Not until this opportunity came along."

Now Jade heard him exhale; a long, shuddering breath that tickled the hairs on the back of her neck. But still he didn't say a word.

"When the buyer signed the deal, you took Zelda hostage and then you had Sonet killed because, by doing that, you could control her brother. With Zelda's life at stake, he would do what he was told, up to and including handing over the corn he was growing in the greenhouse to back up his sister's story."

Now Theron spoke. "I see." His voice sounded hoarse.

"It's all gone wrong for you now," she said. "The reason I know is that I spoke to Ntombi Khumalo earlier on. She told me about the seeds that your hit man was bringing to you." Jade fell silent for a moment, allowing time for the words to sink in. "She didn't have time to say much—she was terrified—but she told me that neither the hit man nor the seeds would reach your flat. That she would do what she had to do to stop them. A brave lady and, it seems, one who kept her word."

Now Jade turned slightly so she could look up at Theron while she spoke. His hands remained on her shoulders but did not prevent her from moving in his grasp.

"I didn't know what would happen when I came to your flat tonight. I didn't know what I would find or who would be waiting for me here. Whether it would be you, or the killer you hired. So why did I come at all? Did you wonder?"

"Seeing as you're so smart, why don't you tell me?"

"I said when I met you that this case had come at a bad time in my life. I was not exaggerating. I've done some evil things. Crimes I know I can never atone for. And when I look at where my life is going, all I see is more evil ahead. I guess what makes us different is I have done everything myself. Not once have I paid somebody else to do my dirty work for me. But you have. In fact, you've never done it any other way."

Now her throat felt dry, too.

"You could push me over the balcony and say I jumped, or even fell. And the police might well believe your story. But like I said, you'd have to do it yourself. And I don't know if you have it in you. It's a gamble, I suppose. Like playing the markets."

Jade paused for breath.

"So, do you, Victor?"

53

The Randburg Chronicle, 19 June, page 2

Passenger dies in vehicle accident
By Junior Reporter Busiswe Lephele

An unidentified male passenger died on Thursday evening after being thrown through the windscreen of a BMW when the vehicle swerved out of control and hit a tree on Partridge Street and burst into flames. The man, who suffered severe head injuries, was declared dead at the scene.

Onlookers managed to free the driver, Mrs. Ntombi Kumalo, and the female passenger, Miss Sonet Meintjies, from the burning wreckage. Attending paramedics rushed the two to the Sandton Clinic. Both were suffering from concussion, bone fractures, minor burns and smoke inhalation. A spokesperson for the hospital reports that both women are out of ICU and recovering well.

By the time the fire brigade arrived, the car had burned out beyond recognition.

The Sandton Gazette, 21 May, page 5

Suspected suicide in Michelangelo Towers

Mr. Victor Theron, a resident of the Michelangelo Towers, Sandton, fell to his death from the balcony of his

16th floor apartment in what appears to be an act of suicide. Residents of this exclusive apartment block say they are shocked and distressed by the news. A visitor to Theron's apartment, Miss Janet de Jong, said: "Victor had become very stressed and depressed after the recent accidental death of his close friend Sonet Meintjies, who fell to her death while base-jumping after her parachute malfunctioned. As an independent financial trader, he had been having a difficult time with the markets as well, and had mentioned more than once to me in the past that he did not see a way out."

The chairlady for the Michelangelo Towers residents' association, Mrs. Portia Ndumo, speaking from her holiday home in Umhlanga, said, "We are shocked and grieved to hear about this tragic incident and will take steps to make sure such a disaster cannot happen again. At our next meeting, the Michelangelo Towers Body Corporate will be looking at the feasibility of installing higher safety railings and security glass as a standard feature on all the balconies."

EPILOGUE

Surely it couldn't be her again?

Setting down her soy latte carefully in its china saucer, Magdalena Eckhardt leaned forward, pressing her hands against the armrests of her well-upholstered chair, craning her neck to get a better look at the new arrival.

It was her. The same woman she'd seen in here a fortnight ago. She even looked as if she was wearing the very same outfit, too. Black shirt, black jeans, brown hair tied back in the ponytail, not a trace of makeup.

She'd had such a time discussing that woman with her book club friends. When Magdalena had described how the woman had looked at her with eyes that stared out from a tormented soul, every lady in the reading circle had told her they'd come out in goosebumps.

Collectively, they had pieced together the story of what had happened. Clearly the woman was bereaved—hence she had been wearing black. She had lost her husband, or partner, and now, after a period of mourning, she was starting to date again.

The man she'd been with last time had obviously been unsuitable. But this man—the one who at this very moment was sitting down in the chair opposite her—he looked like a far better prospect. An older gentleman wearing an immaculately cut suit and silk tie, with silver-streaked hair and a fabulous platinum Rolex watch. A wealthy man, for certain.

He would take care of her.

Look at the way they were leaning forward, closer to each other, as they spoke! The chemistry was there, no doubt about it. And the woman . . . she looked so much happier than she had the time before. More confident. Her head was held high and her eyes were sparkling. Yes, definitely—he was the one. There was no way she was going to interrupt them though. True love must take its course without her help. But her book club friends would be thrilled to hear this. Simply over the moon!

As Magdalena got up to leave, she caught the woman's eye just for a moment, and felt a warm glow of pure happiness as she gave Magdalena a conspiratorial smile.

Jade turned her attention back to the grey haired man sitting opposite her.

"Thank you so much for giving me an overview of the futures market in this country, Mr. Anderson," she said to the financial advisor from Trading South Africa.

"It's wonderful to have you on board as a client, Ms. de Jong. We received your deposit yesterday."

Jade was surprised the investor wasn't rubbing his hands together at the prospect of earning commission off such a large sum. She'd transferred every penny of the blood money she'd had in her account from the contract killing she'd done with Robbie. It was a sizeable amount.

"Good."

"You mentioned that you would like to begin trading in single stock futures today?"

"That is correct."

"Now I must explain to you how your funds will be allocated. Part of this deposit may be used to trade, but a portion will be held to cover your margins, should the market move against you."

"I understand that."

He produced a small electronic gadget identical to the one that she had seen Victor Theron use.

"If you'd like some advice on where to start, I'll be happy to offer it. At the moment we are fortunate to be in a rising market, which means that taking a long position will probably be advisable. The indexes for the past few days have been looking very positive. This is due to various reasons, including the strength of the rand, the drop in interest rates, and some other financial and also political factors. Markets, you see, are very much influenced by sentiment."

"I have heard that, yes," she said.

He continued speaking but she tuned him out.

She thought instead of the story that Zelda Meintjies had now completed, which would make front-page headlines in every major newspaper the next morning. After finishing her research, Zelda had contacted the police and handed over all evidence, including her recording device. As a result, David, heading up a team of detectives and forensics experts, was even now arriving at Theunisvlei, where the mass grave would soon be exhumed.

Meanwhile, in Jo'burg, Moloi and his team were busy making several arrests. By the evening, Jade knew that a number of senior managers from Global Seeds South Africa would be in police custody, as would Mr. Engelbrecht from Williams Management. The image of that arrogant man being bundled into a police van made Jade smile whenever she thought about it.

In the chaos that would follow when this news broke, one fact would be certain. Despite the positive trends in the market, the shares in Global Seeds were going to plummet.

"So, have you decided where you would like to start trading?" Mr. Anderson asked her.

Resting her elbows on the table, Jade nodded confidently.

"I'd suggest a balanced portfolio to spread the risk . . ." the financial advisor began, but Jade interrupted him.

"I would like to put all my available funds in one position," she told him.

He pressed some keys on his gadget.

"Which one would that be?" he asked.

Jade thought briefly of Ntombi Khumalo and Zelda Meintjies. Two women who, having lost loved ones and now alone in the world, both deserved a very generous compensation payment. Thanks to the leverage available in the futures market, Jade was confident that the profits from a single, well-timed trade would set them both up for life.

"I'd like to take a short position in Global Seeds," she said.